Who hasn't thought Pride and Prejudice could use more dragons?

Praise for Maria Grace

I've INHALED this series since the first book. The only thing I have found frustrating is the author hasn't been able to write them quickly enough for me! Hate having to wait to see what comes next... a well-written, well-researched, feel-good series ... this series is perfect. *~Kristen Lamb, WANA International*

I found it wicked brilliant!*~Jorie Love a Story*

I followed Ms. Grace down that rabbit hole as she truly held me captive. ~ *Roofbeam Reader*

Leaves me in awe and delighted to have found it. *~Ramblings of a Traveling Bookworm*

I was *still* surprised by how well this concept worked. Maria Grace makes the introduction of dragons into Regency life seem seamless, and in a very clever turn, actually uses them to explain a lot of the formalities and customs *of* Regency life. It's by turns clandestine and tense, and playfully silly, and I found myself weirdly invested.~ *The Book Rat*

MISS GEORGIANA
AND THE
DRAGON

BY
MARIA GRACE

Published by: White Soup Press

Miss Georgiana and the Dragon

Copyright © December 2022

Maria Grace

For information address author.MariaGrace@gmail.com

Author's Website: **RandomBitsofFascination.com**

DEDICATION

For my husband and sons.
You have always believed in me.

1

Chapter

April 28, 1815

So, THIS IS WHAT the fairytale princess felt like when carted off to the dragon's lair to await rescue by a handsome prince.

Except in her case there would be no handsome prince, only her ghastly brother, Fitzwilliam, who had cast her into the talons of the angry dragon. And the evil stepmother's part played by her sister-in-law, Elizabeth, who always took the dragons' side.

Georgiana pulled her plain grey spencer tighter around her waist, pressing deeper into the coach's stiff, cracked squabs that magnified each bump and rut in the road. Anything to be that much farther away from her horrid dragon-companion, Auntie, and the equally horrid Mrs. Fieldings, headmistress of the Blue Order's Academy for the Improvement of Young Ladies. The cloying, stuffy air within the meanly equipped carriage confirmed it was too small to house such large personalities.

The very thought that she needed improvement! How could Fitzwilliam possibly think such a thing? After all the masters and governesses she had studied under, the praise she had earned for her accomplishments on the pianoforte, and her near-perfect French? She was an accomplished young woman of nineteen, highly marriageable, who should have made her come out this year, not be in the care of a governess. How humiliating!

She held herself together with elbows pulled tightly into her ribs as she fought back the burning in her eyes. How could one ever recover from such humiliation?

Fitzwilliam would never have entertained the notion, save for the dragoness he had married. Despite his preoccupation with dragons, he had been the one person who had actually taken notice of her. Their life had been perfectly lovely—well, perhaps not lovely, but certainly less complicated—until Pemberley's egg was stolen and *she* came into their lives.

Had Pemberley hatched as she should have, all would have been well. Pemberley would be a proper little dragon, managing on her own as all the cold-blooded did from the time they broke shell. Not some spoiled little lizard who claimed attachment sickness and required constant attention and management.

Georgiana had tried to see to her care. Lord knows she had tried! She stared into the coach's faded ceiling lining and blinked rapidly. Dealing with the scale mites and tail itches and whatever else seemed to plague the infant dragon. Constantly at the drakeling's beck and call.

In the beginning, Pemberley had been rather enchanting, at least until it became impossible to fulfill all her demands. Soon, everything in her life began to revolve around the little dragon.

Everything.

All of Elizabeth's letters were about the little dragon. At first, Elizabeth's efforts to help Georgiana manage the dragon's care were endearing. It became clear, though, Pemberley was Elizabeth's only concern. Never once did she inquire about Georgiana's health or comfort or opinions, much less her preferences. Never. How could a proper lady be so inattentive to all proper forms of social discourse? Unless she was trying to send a specific message: Georgiana was nothing compared to the dragons.

Even so, Georgiana managed to read all the letters and notes *Her*—as Pemberley referred to Elizabeth—had sent and tried to put it all into practice, no matter how ridiculous the advice seemed. But it was never enough.

Never.

Nothing ever was where dragons were concerned. Why did no one else recognize that?

The mere thought seemed to earn her an icy stare across the coach from Auntie. Although the leggy blue-green drake with wire glasses perched on the end of her long nose rarely smiled, she usually reserved her glares for when one had actually said or done something she considered untoward. Apparently now, even thinking ill of dragons was considered untoward. What matter if it were the dragon at fault—which actually did happen occasionally, despite the fact no one seemed to believe it.

She closed her eyes and drew a deep breath. Yes, Auntie and Mrs. Fieldings were right, there were advantages to being "Miss Darcy," to the connections and privileges afforded her because of her family name and fortune. And she was grateful for them. Truly, she was.

But no one considered the extraordinary trials that went with her life, too.

All that mattered at the Pemberley estate were the horrible, scaly dragons. People, including—maybe especially—the daughter of the estate were wholly irrelevant beside them. As neither heir to the Keepership, nor male, nor possessing any great affinity to the cold-blooded, her accomplishments were meaningless; her efforts were meaningless; she was meaningless. Georgiana only earned notice when, somehow, she had made the dragons unhappy.

Like when she had innocently wandered into horrible Old Pemberley's lair, and he had all but breathed fire and eaten her! She not been more than nine or ten years old and had every right to wander her father's estate. It was not as if she even knew the property *housed* a dragon lair—no one had told her! Somehow, she was to have known that by virtue of being a Darcy! Yet, one and all, they treated her as though she were the trespasser and a criminal!

Georgiana swallowed hard, though it burned her tight throat. Not even Mama had stood up for her then—although Mama was so sick at the time, she could hardly have been expected to.

But Papa, Fitzwilliam, even Mrs. Reynolds, could have. Should have. If Georgiana had been remotely as important as the dragons, ill though she was, Mama might have had a word or two to say about the matter, too. She squeezed her eyes shut to drive away the looming face of that angry dragon and the angry faces of the people that followed.

Once Old Pemberley had died, things should have been easier. And they were, for a little while. Fitzwilliam paid her some notice, which was lovely, but there was that to-do with Wickham.... As soon as the egg disappeared, though, it was as if Georgiana had never mattered, never even existed, in the first place. Just like it had always been.

What sort of way was that to live?

And they wondered why she did not like dragons. Really, should it be any surprise? Why should it be astonishing that she preferred to make her connections in the Blue Order among those who saw the troublesome beasts for what they were?

She certainly did not want to marry a man who would ignore her for the dragon he Kept, and marrying within the Order was her only choice if she were to keep any connection to her brother or to Pax. How could she negotiate a path through the marriage mart under such circumstances?

Fluffy white Pax, her fairy dragon Friend, cheeped softly and nestled closer into her neck. She was the exception, entirely unlike other dragons. She was all things sweet and kind and proper, never once forgetting her Friend in favor of other dragons, or "important" warm-bloods like Elizabeth the Sage or Fitzwilliam or Uncle Matlock. All told, it was a wonder that Pax had been permitted to attend school with her at all, but Georgiana was not about to question that favor. At the moment, her Friend's company was the only thing making this terrible journey bearable.

"Is it true that was the last stop before we arrive at the school?" Georgiana looked back at the little white coaching inn as it disappeared around a bend in the road. Hopefully that did not sound like a complaint. Mrs. Fieldings had proved acutely sensitive about anything that might be construed as complaining, even those statements that were simple requests for information.

"Yes, we should arrive in less than two hours, assuming all things go well." Mrs. Fieldings seemed to use that phrase a great deal—assuming things go well.

Ramrod straight and prim in her seat, Mrs. Fieldings might have been a child-stealing fairy that Georgiana had seen in a book of fairy stories from Pemberley's library when she was a little girl. Tall, willowy, with a fair complexion, blue eyes, and dark hair, she might have been considered pretty in her youth. Before the creases around her eyes and mouth had set into lines and her posture under her plain, dark dresses had become stiff and far too proper. She was one of those women awarded the title "missus" out of respect for her age and position, rather than the more usual manner of obtaining the title through matrimony.

"What are you concerned might not 'go well'?" Georgiana chewed her lower lip. That might not be the right thing to ask, but when Mrs. Fieldings made a statement like that, it was nearly impossible to ignore the urge for further information.

"Were you paying attention to what the operator of the coaching inn said?" Auntie somehow made everything sound like an accusation when she clapped her jaws that way.

"As I recall, he said many things." Many, many, many things. So many things, one could not possibly have attended to them all. He was the sort of man who began a conversation with "Good day, ladies" and ended it with one knowing his entire family tree, the state of their health, and the sometimes-convoluted way in which he was related to everyone in the parish.

"Did you pay attention to the issue of the highwaymen?" Auntie exposed her top fangs. Though Elizabeth insisted it was not bad manners when a dragon did that. Surely an expression that threatening had to be.

"No, I do not recall anything about highwaymen." Could she have been so distracted as to miss something that noteworthy?

Mrs. Fielding shook her head, not quite frustration, not quite disappointment in her eyes. "The innkeeper noted reports of highwaymen active in the region recently, and he suggested the driver take a slightly longer route, one considered safer under the circumstances."

Georgiana pulled her spencer a little tighter to conceal the cold shiver coursing down her back. "Are we taking that route?" That earned another grimace. Surely hers was not so stupid a question, was it?

"Yes, though it will delay our arrival until close to our evening meal. The school keeps country hours, you should know."

That would not be so bad. She was accustomed to that. Pemberley did the same.

"That will make it difficult to orient you to the school before you meet the other students." Mrs. Fieldings laced her fingers and tapped her thumbs.

"Perhaps it would be appropriate to begin the discussion now?" Auntie suggested.

A young lady should not sigh, so Georgiana held her breath. The interminably long lecture would happen one way or another. Perhaps getting it over with now would not be a bad thing.

"I prefer to conduct such a discussion in my office, in a proper, serious environment." Mrs. Fieldings pressed her lips into a tight wrinkle, which seemed to be associated with giving a matter serious consideration. "But under the circumstances, I suppose we can make the attempt now."

Heavens, what did she have to say that required a "proper, serious environment?"

Mrs. Fieldings took a deep breath and folded her hands in her lap. "Tell me why you have been sent to me and why you have been put in the care of Auntie, despite having been ready to make your official come out to the Order."

Again? "We are all quite aware of that situation. Does it really need to be rehashed?"

"Yes, in fact, it does." Mrs. Fieldings crossed her arms over her chest.

Why was she so insistent upon making Georgiana relive her humiliation? "My ghastly brother has banished me to your academy because I am not sufficiently fond of dragons."

"Perhaps this is not the correct environment for this discussion after all." Auntie exchanged pointed glances with Mrs. Fieldings. "I am certain she can skip dinner tonight in favor of a full and proper orientation."

Horrible lizard! "My brother, Sir Fitzwilliam of the Pendragon Knights, has declared I am no longer welcome in his home, and he refuses to see me into my own establishment, although I am well able to pay for it."

"And why is that?"

"He thinks I am a danger to Pemberley and to his family."

"Your tone suggests you do not agree," Mrs. Fieldings said.

Georgiana huffed. "I am no danger to them. They are still my family, no matter that they are casting me off. I would never bring harm to them."

"And you think consorting with a known enemy of the Order is not perilous?"

"I did not know that then." Mr. Oakley had seemed everything charming, and he had paid such lovely attention to her. How was Georgiana to know the secrets he kept?

"But you did know about his dangerous dragon-Keeping attitudes?" Auntie's voice dropped to nearly a growl.

Georgiana's heart beat a little faster. "What of it? A man is entitled to his own opinions! It is not my place to correct them. It is not a woman's place."

"You continued to keep company with the man, even knowing his views would put him at odds with the Order?" Mrs. Fieldings' frown carved deep furrows on her brow.

"Do you suggest that I must eschew the society of anyone espousing notions that might be disagreeable?" She clenched her left hand into a fist.

"When one is a member of the Order, there are certain opinions..."

"I did not ask to be a member of the Order! I never asked to hear dragons. I was forced into this position by an accident of my birth."

"Rather like your connection to the Pemberley family and your rather considerable fortune. You never asked for those, either. Should we understand them to be undesirable as well?" Auntie snorted.

"What is that supposed to mean?"

"It means, Miss Darcy," Mrs. Fieldings leaned forward and gazed directly into her eyes, "that you cannot enjoy the pleasant accidents of your birth without taking responsibility for the aspects that you do not like."

"So claims my brother." Georgiana pressed the side of her hand to her mouth. Bother, she had not intended to say that aloud!

"So declares the Order. By rule of law." How those dreadful words hung in the air.

"If you do not care to abide by those rules, you do have an alternative." Auntie's long talons rasped softly as she tapped them against the rough blue-green scales of her leg.

"I can have my own establishment, I know. But it would mean being exiled to the Scottish countryside, apart from any good society, under the watchful eye of a companion employed by my brother to keep me in line with the Order's mandates. House arrest is the way I would describe it. Not exactly the sort of life I relish."

"But it is an alternative. One that I will not hesitate to recommend should I find you intractable." Mrs. Fieldings stared down her nose, pronouncing the words like a judge's sentence. "Do you understand?"

"You have the power to banish me and ruin the rest of my life. Yes, I well understand."

"Perhaps you should simply do so now and save us all the trouble." Auntie muttered to the side glass.

"Why are we bothering with this exercise, then? You want to be done with me and send me away!"

"There you are entirely wrong, Miss Darcy." Mrs. Fieldings drew in a deep breath and stared at the ceiling as though gathering thoughts and patience in the same breath. "The Order's interests are not served by having one more irredeemable child sent away to be monitored for the rest of her life. The risk that presents and the resources it consumes are considerable. Little benefit to be had in that. No, what I want, what we all want, is to make you a proper citizen of the Order. You do not have to like dragons. That is a matter of preference. But at a bare minimum, you must not be a danger to the Order or its members."

"I am a danger to no one. I would never hurt anyone."

"Not knowingly," Pax twittered.

Georgiana contorted her neck until she could look Pax in the eye. "What is that supposed to mean?"

"You would never knowingly hurt anyone." Pax shook herself out, full and fluffy like a ball of clean, sweet wool.

"There, you see my Friend agrees! There is no need for this entire exercise."

Mrs. Fieldings sighed, deep and long suffering. So much drama. "What Pax has said may be true; however, it is not the complete truth. Is it, Pax?"

Pax twitched her tiny head.

"What your Friend has not said, but is certainly aware of, is that whilst you might not hurt anyone intentionally, you are perfectly capable of wreaking a great deal of harm unknowingly. And that is what must be cured."

How dare Mrs. Fieldings imply little Pax was criticizing her! "Everyone makes mistakes! Why should I be held to a different standard? Elizabeth has made some very great ones—"

"Do not compare yourself to the Sage!" A deep growl edged Auntie's voice. Georgiana jumped back into the squabs.

Mrs. Fieldings looked at Auntie and tsk-tsked. "Such harshness is not appropriate. Remember, Miss Darcy's errors were not the result of malice, but rather indifference to dragons and the dragon state. That is the material point, the one that we hope to alter."

Had Mrs. Fieldings just corrected Auntie and stood up for her instead? "So, it is simply my 'indifference to dragons and the dragon state' that you hope to improve? That is simple. You want me to be concerned? I will be concerned. There. It is done, and we can avoid all manner of unpleasantness." Georgiana dusted her hands together.

"That you think it so simple only convinces me you know nothing of change and how it is accomplished." Mrs. Fieldings huffed, but did not look surprised.

"How do you think it is to be accomplished, then, if the mere act of the will cannot manage it?"

"An act of the will is only the beginning. Without exposure to new ideas, challenges to your ways of thinking, seeing things through the eyes of another, time spent in the company of others who are different to yourself, it will be hardly more than an act, a façade. Your experience at my academy is designed to promote just such experiences to facilitate true and lasting change."

Georgiana fought not to wither under that stern look. "Tell me then, what will these experiences look like?"

"Much like those of any girls' seminary. You have been to school, have you not?"

"No. I have always had a governess to teach me at home."

Odd, the flash of a sympathetic expression that altered Mrs. Fieldings' face for just a moment. "I see. In that case, we will ensure you are well versed in reading and writing your native tongue. History, geography, and literature will be covered, as well as such maths as are appropriate for a lady. You will also be instructed in needlework, music, dancing, the social graces, and the theatrical arts to improve your elocution and overall deportment."

"I expect you mean Blue Order history and literature? Geography as it pertains to dragons? And, of course, social graces include introductions to dragons and the like?"

"Of course."

"I already know a great deal of those things." Georgiana pulled her shoulders back and raised her chin.

"Demonstrate that learning sufficiently, and your tenure here will be abbreviated." Did Mrs. Fieldings just offer her a challenge?

"Just give me the opportunity to prove what I know, and you will see how little time I need to spend at your establishment."

Mrs. Fieldings blinked slowly and nodded in time. "We shall see, then, Miss Darcy; we shall see." How shocking! She did not argue or try to convince Georgiana otherwise. What was this woman planning?

An hour later, Pax twittered and pointed through the side glass with her wing. There, just barely in view, that must be the school building.

"It is called Bennetson Hall," Auntie said softly. "No relation, of course, to the Historian or his family."

But enough to be a constant irritation and reminder of their unwelcome presence in her life. What a cruel joke.

At least the school was not the gloomy Gothic structure she had expected. What else could one expect to house an academy like Mrs. Fieldings'?

Occasionally it was nice to be wrong, though. The house seemed fairly large and modern, stationed in the middle of a pleasant grassy field dotted here and there with fluffy white sheep—probably there to feed the dragons.

She tried to subdue the shudder. Ghastly, watching those lizards eat. Earl, Cousin Richard's cockatrice Friend, was especially horrid!

Though decidedly smaller than Pemberley Manor, the mostly square white stone face of Bennetson Hall had the advantage of being half-covered in purple wisteria vines and possessing a delightful fairytale tower attached to the front right-hand side of the house. It actually made the place seem inviting. Perhaps she might have a room in the tower, like a fairytale princess held captive by a dragon.

"Are the dragons permitted to take nectar from the vines or in the garden?" Pax hovered in front of the side glass, her wings buzzing as they held her aloft.

Mrs. Fieldings smiled at Pax. "You definitely may. When we arrive, I will introduce you to Mercail. She is the head of the small dragons at the school and assists with the young girls and any Dragon Friends who accompany our students. She will be most helpful to you in finding your place among us."

"Mercail is a Friend of one of the teachers?" Georgiana asked.

"Mercail *is* one of the teachers," Auntie snapped.

"We are privileged to have several dragons among our teaching staff. Mercail teaches the youngest students in deportment and social graces. Mica teaches our older pupils in French, dance, and a special salon on the unique responsibilities of Blue Order ladies. And do be sure to pronounce it correctly, 'Meeca', she is quite particular about that."

"Dance? There is a dragon teaching dance?" She did not need a dance master; Mr. Dodge had declared her proficient before the Cotillion.

"She is quite skillful." Mrs. Fieldings glowered. "I expect the same respect shown to the dragon staff as I do to the warm-blooded ones."

"Of course." Georgiana clenched her jaw. She would be expected to sit in a classroom and learn French from a dragon when she had already mastered the language? At least that should not last very long. That would be one more accomplishment that could be quickly ticked off Mrs. Fieldings' list.

Yes, that was the thing. Focusing on how little there remained to satisfy Mrs. Fieldings' requirements would make her feel better about this exile. A good reminder that her exile would be temporary. "What sorts of dragons are at the school or in the surrounding area?"

"Mercail is a fairy dragon, and there is one fairy dragon Friend among our students. A small, wild harem shares the garden with us. Mica, whom I have mentioned, and Gale, who acts as our dragon liaison to the Order as well as an instructor, are minor drakes. And there are two pucks, one a Friend to a younger student, one a Friend to one of the maids." Mrs. Fieldings ticked them off on her fingers. "But alas, no cockatrice nor cockatrix, nor any snake nor wyrm types."

That was a relief. Wyrms tended to be rather horrible.

"Miss Withington is our head girl. She will be assigned to help you adjust. She performs this service for all our new students."

"I am sure I will be fine..."

"It is not an option, Miss Darcy. Managing a school with dragons is far more complex than a traditional girls' seminary. I will not have our carefully balanced community disrupted by a new student's missteps. Given how many dragons live at Pemberley, I should think you rather familiar with the concept. When staff joins the estate, are they not assigned a mentor to watch over them?"

"I would hardly know such a thing. I was not privy to those matters."

"Your mother did not teach you how to manage a dragon estate?"

"No, she did not. To be honest, she taught me nothing." There was that odd little sympathetic look from Mrs. Fieldings again. "When I was young, she was far too busy running the household to be bothered with the likes of her daughter. My governess did not conduct training in those matters. By the time I was old enough to be interesting to Mama, she was already dead, and Mrs. Reynolds, our housekeeper, had taken over all household matters. I suppose it was not her place to tutor the daughter of the house. And since you will surely ask, no, the Dragon Sage has offered no instruction, either."

Why was Auntie frowning again? She had only answered Mrs. Fieldings' question. Was that to be considered wrong now, too?

"We will see that missing portion of your education is remedied. Miss Withington will be able to help you, I am sure. She is the daughter of one of our regional undersecretaries and is well versed in the rudiments of managing a dragon estate."

"I am surprised a girl like that should be a student here. I thought it was only troublesome daughters that burdened your halls."

"Not at all, Miss Darcy. My students are actually rather varied. A full half of them come from half-Blue families where their education in Blue Order matters cannot proceed in the open. Some are the only dragon-hearers in their families, having been discovered by Blue Order members in their communities. And a few come to me because they wish to improve their chances in the Blue Order marriage mart."

"Improve their chances? How?" Perhaps there was something to be learnt here after all.

"Some girls come from good Blue Order families, but have little dowry to bring into a marriage. It is an open secret that there are a fair number of Dragon Keepers who seek women who are well versed in managing a dragon estate and familiar with good Dragon Keeping. Such skills can help atone for the sin of an insufficient dowry."

"How many students are in my... situation?"

"I make it a point not to discuss any of my students' specific circumstances, Miss Darcy. That is tantamount to gossip in my eyes. I will thank you to remember that. If any particular girl wishes to discuss her circumstance with you, then it is up to her to do so."

Georgiana swallowed hard. Perhaps that meant her humiliation would not be widely known. That would be pleasant.

At last, the carriage slowed, then stopped with a stomach-jogging lurch. The driver opened the door and dropped the steps.

"Welcome to your new home, Miss Darcy." Mrs. Fieldings stepped out, Auntie following in her shadow.

Her temporary, very temporary, new home.

Chapter 2

GEORGIANA HUNG BACK AS Mrs. Fieldings and Auntie left the coach. Great merciful heavens, she was stiff! Back, shoulders, hips—everything ached and rebelled against graceful, ladylike movement. But three days in a coach, particularly one with worn springs and thin squabs, would do that to a body.

She stepped down, immediately embraced by late-afternoon sunshine that carried sweet, musky, almost lilac-y scented air wafting from the wisteria blooms that clung to the house in great purple drops. The perfume of the fresh, green grass that surrounded the house mingled with the wisteria in a warm, friendly aura that attempted to reassure her. She paused and breathed deeply. Perhaps this place would only be a little dreadful.

Bennetson Hall rose before her, two white-stone stories high, plus three dormers on a third level. At Pemberley, those rooms would belong to the staff, but here, there was no telling. Maybe the dragons liked the attics.

The house's front elevation was mostly square, except for the octagonal watchtower, which should have belonged to a medieval castle. Faced in dark stone, the tower rose along the right-hand corner. Windows filled the angled walls on each of the three stories, which were topped by a crenellated wall around the roof. There was probably a walkway there and a place to keep watch.

The left-hand side of the building boasted a large bay window on both the ground and first floors. A drawing room and music room most likely resided behind those windows, assuming typical conventions were followed. On the drive in, the house had seemed rather longer on the sides than it was in the front, more rectangular than square. That was pleasing. There was something severe about a completely square structure.

A neat cottage and an equally smart carriage house, both white and covered in affectionate vines, peeked out from behind the house. Though they kept a polite distance, it seemed they were on friendly terms with the main house.

All in all, a rather welcoming sort of place, distinctly different from expectations. No line of servants, staff, and students met them outside, though. Was that a disappointment or a relief? It was difficult to tell.

She followed Mrs. Fieldings and Auntie through the heavy oak door, pausing to allow her eyes to adjust to the dimmer light within.

The open door invited her in politely, decorously. It would be satisfying in an odd sort of way if she could find something legitimate to complain about. Really it would. But the house would simply not oblige. It was determined to be pleasant and proper.

Painted bright white with a polished limestone tile floor, the front hall greeted her with a table bearing a large bowl of fragrant pink roses and a painting of a friendly looking couple. A plaque on the frame declared them to be the original owners of Bennetson Hall. Odd. They did look a bit like Historian Bennet. But that could simply be a trick of the light. Hints of dragon musk blended with the roses, neither pleasant nor unpleasant, a little reminiscent of home, of Pemberley.

A young woman, tall and pale with blond hair, wearing a stylish light-blue muslin gown, met them with a graceful curtsey. A blackberry-colored fairy dragon, with extra-long head feather-scales that looked like a floppy hat, perched on her shoulder. "Mrs. Fieldings, Auntie."

"Miss Withington is our head girl, and her Friend is Berry. May I present our new student, Miss Darcy, and her Friend, Pax." Mrs. Fieldings gestured toward them.

Georgiana curtsied. "I am pleased to make your acquaintance." Perhaps Miss Withington could be an ally in getting Mrs. Fieldings to recognize how little Georgiana needed this place.

Both fairy dragons launched from shoulders and danced around each other mid-air, twittering and chirping. A fairy dragon-sized display of dominance. Finally, they came to some sort of agreement, chirruped, and returned to their Friends' shoulders, but who exactly was the dominant fairy dragon remained unclear. Still, the entire tableau had a rather endearing quality.

"Show Miss Darcy around the school and to her chamber while I gather the staff and students in the drawing room for proper introductions."

Miss Withington curtsied. "Yes, Mrs. Fieldings. Pray follow me, Miss Darcy."

Berry hopped off Miss Withington's shoulder and hovered between them. "I will introduce Pax to Mercail. I am sure she will want to give Pax a proper tour of the school." High and sweet, like other fairy dragon voices, there was also a tart note of sass, reminiscent of April. Hopefully, she would not be a bad influence on Pax.

"Go ahead. You should meet the other dragons here." If for no other reason than it would keep some awful mishap from happening among the cold-blooded residents. Georgiana scratched under Pax's chin and she zipped off behind Berry.

Was it possible to miss Pax already?

Miss Withington turned and headed to the left, down the narrow, dimly lit, white-painted, wood-floored corridor as though she expected to be followed without question.

When she did not look over her shoulder, Georgiana hurried to catch up.

"I understand you are from Pemberley." Miss Withington did not bother looking at her.

Rather high-handed... "I thought Mrs. Fieldings did not talk about her students."

"She does not, but the Darcy name and Pemberley are hardly unknown among the Blue Order. Especially after all the recent goings-on with the Sage's kidnapping and the Cotillion. That news has been the talk of the girls here for weeks." Miss Withington looked over her shoulder and arched her eyebrow.

Somehow, it just made sense that those things Georgiana would rather forget were the things most interesting here. Her cheeks burned, and she looked aside. How many of her details would be common knowledge here, even without Mrs. Fieldings speaking of them?

"Still, if you prefer not to speak of it, I will not. In any case, you will, no doubt, find that the house is smaller and not nearly so well appointed as that to which you might be accustomed. It is, though, quite comfortable to our needs and there is little you should find yourself wanting. Except perhaps for a maid assigned to take care of you and your things. Several of us can claim to miss that luxury. That means you will need to dress yourself, manage your own hair, and do your own mending. There is a charwoman who manages the washing twice a month, lest you think us completely uncivilized. If you have white muslin, though, you might wish to carefully consider when to wear it, as it is difficult to keep clean. The charwoman will expect extra from you if you want her to wash it. Between you and me, she is not very good at managing white garments and is rather hard on them. I reserve my white gown for special occasions."

That seemed good advice, and kindly offered, no less.

"I see that Auntie is with you. I met her during Miss Lydia Bennet's tenure with us. I expect that the arrangements now will be as they were then. If so, then she will be assigned quarters in the Dragon Tower and assist in training the governess students. When you leave the building for any reason, though, I suppose she will be required to attend you."

She would not have to share her chambers with that dreary dragon-governess? Happy news indeed! Mrs. Fieldings could have shared that with her earlier. A little weight slid from her shoulders. Even a modicum of privacy would be a welcome luxury after days of constantly being watched.

"That is the drawing room there on the left, where Mrs. Fieldings will conduct introductions shortly. It is usually used only when receiving guests or new students." She pointed to wide double doors near a tall window at the end of the hallway. Slivers of sunlight peeked underneath. Disappointing that Georgiana could not actually see inside. "Behind us, on the other side of the front hall, is the general parlor, which all students may use when not otherwise occupied in our studies. Mica holds her salons there as well. They are unusually interesting. I hope you will join us for those."

Not if she could help it, but probably best not to say that. Really, what could a dragon understand about the role of warm-blooded women in the Blue Order? Was it not enough to have lived with the Dragon Sage?

They turned right and their steps echoed along the worn but well-polished wood of the hallway floor. Strange that no paintings lined the wall, no gallery of disapproving elders glaring down at them. Georgiana had never liked all those portraits at Pemberley; even worse, the ones Aunt Catherine insisted upon at Rosings Park! One always had the sense she was being watched, judged, and found wanting whilst visiting there.

"Next is the large dining room, where the older students and dragon-companion students gather for dinner. The little girls eat in the common room with the head of little girls and the dragon-governess students. Beside the dining room you see the morning room. We are granted our leisure there until ten o'clock, when our lessons begin. Breakfast things are picked up promptly at ten minutes to the hour, so if you wish to eat, mind the time. No servant will fetch you for mealtimes. We are expected to learn to be attentive to such things ourselves. You will find a clock in nearly every room to assist you, though." Did Miss Withington just sniff at the thought? Perhaps there was a touch of humor in her after all. "The kitchen, scullery, and servants' hall are through that green baize door; students are not permitted there."

Vague odors of food, cooking, and cleaning wafted from that side of the corridor.

Miss Withington turned right down a long passage that seemed to cross the length of the house. Windows that seemed to push out their elbows, demanding more space in the tight hall, struggled to light the narrow space. "The housekeeper's rooms, the headmistress' office, the dragon liaison's office, and the library, which is furnished to accommodate study, are on the left."

Thankfully, the offices each bore a simple plaque with their designation.

They turned right again into a hallway that ended at the tower.

"On the left are the teachers' offices, each with their name on the door. On the right are storage chambers, another place we are not allowed unless sent by one of the staff. In case you are wondering, those doors are kept locked at all times. The headmistress and the housekeeper are the only ones with keys to the storage—although our resident pucks are often secreting the keys away for their hoards. The maid's puck Friend hoards keys, you know, which is awfully inconvenient and something Gale—the dragon liaison—Mica, and Mercail are all trying to train her out of. But it is not easy to get a puck to change her ways."

That was the sort of thing she would probably be expected to remember. "And the tower?"

"The proper name is Bennetson Tower, for the dragon who once lived on the estate here. But we usually call it the Dragon Tower."

"There is a major dragon here?"

"I am not sure what happened to the estate dragon, but there is no dragon assigned to the territory any longer. Such a shame, that. It would have been so helpful to have an actual estate dragon to learn Keeping from. I suppose the school cannot have everything, though. In that dragon's honor, the tower houses the resident dragons, staff on the ground floor, students above. The topmost floor boasts a unique common room, which the dragons share."

Well, that was disappointing. No tower chamber for her.

"Dragon Friends of students are, of course, welcome in their Friends' rooms—they are not banished to the tower! You need not fear for your Friend." Miss Withington laughed. "You should know, though, that students are expected to respect the dragons' territory and to stay out of the tower unless clearly invited by one who lives there. I am sure you understand how dragons can be about their territory."

"Of course. I am well familiar with that." Old Pemberley had taught her that well. She rubbed her upper arms briskly.

"Good, good. Shall we go upstairs now? Students are welcome to use these back stairs, as they are often most convenient." Miss Withington opened a door at the end of the hall, just across from the tower door, to reveal a wooden spiral staircase that smelt strongly of dragons and wood polish.

Where were the main stairs? Oh yes, near front hall. Strange that they had not used those.

They climbed the tight spiral, with fading sunlight streaming down from glass planes in the ceiling above, rather like conservatory windows.

The spiral stairs ended at another door, leading into a narrow, carpeted corridor with windows at either end. Miss Withington turned left. "Along the left, facing the front of the house, are the classrooms. The music room is next to them. We use it for dance lessons as well. The last door on the right leads to the wing with the teachers' quarters and their private parlor."

"And it is off limits to students, no?"

"Of course." Miss Withington winked. That was uncomfortably familiar of her. "In the center of this floor you will find the students' common room, where most of the girls congregate during unassigned time. Since Miss Fieldings is gathering everyone downstairs, it will be empty now, but I will show you." She opened double doors into a large chamber with dark paneling and lit by large windows on the opposite wall. A waist-high wooden banister surrounded three sides of what must be the main stairs, as they opened into the middle of the room.

Several clusters of furniture defined spaces in the common room. A large worktable with chairs around it and atop it, a board game, still in progress, stood near the doors. Three small couches near the windows with workbaskets nearby, likely for sewing. A cluster of chairs in the far corner, probably used for reading and conversation. Another table littered with scraps of paper from some sort of project and a silhouette screen nearby. A few other chairs and small tables tarried in odd spots as though they might float about, moved as would be convenient at the time. One could almost hear the echoes of girls' chatter and laughter within, despite the traces of dragon musk that lingered in the air.

"All of us students congregate. It can get a mite loud and chaotic at times, but on the whole, it is an uncommonly pleasant place to pass the time." She pointed to a door on the right-hand wall near the windows. "That will take us to the end of the corridor, where all our chambers may be found. Come."

The drab brown common room carpet, though a bit worn and even threadbare in places, muffled their steps in a comforting, soothing, if shabby, kind of way. Miss Withington was right. These were not the sort of trappings to which she was accustomed. Mrs. Reynolds would not have permitted such carpeting anywhere inside Pemberley, even in the servants' quarters.

They passed through the door into another long, carpeted corridor, large windows near the doorway still admitting the fading late afternoon sun. The white-painted right-hand wall held two landscape paintings; both looked like images of Bennetson Hall. Plain, painted wooden doors at regular intervals populated the left side.

"This is the students' wing. The younger girls have quarters at this end of the hall. They share two or three to a room. We older ones have the privilege of a room to ourselves. Yours is down at the far end, next to mine." Miss Withington plunged ahead, without a backward glance.

Thankfully, the thin carpet dampened sound, or else it would probably be unbearably noisy when its residents were about. Miss Withington opened the second door from the end on the left. "This will be your chamber."

Georgiana hesitated a moment, then peeked in. It was... a room. Large enough for the requisite furniture: a bed, a press, a chair, and a writing desk. Not a prison cell nor a dungeon, but not at all comparable to any but perhaps the servants' quarters at Pemberley or Darcy House. The walls were painted a faint pink; the bedding looked clean and functional, with sufficient mattresses on the bed to be tolerable, but not luxurious; the curtains seemed serviceable. Dreary, but better than she had expected. This place seemed entirely determined not to be awful.

"I know it is not what you are accustomed to, but once you get used to it, I am sure you will be comfortable."

Comfortable? That might be a bit of an exaggeration. "Will my things be sent up here?"

"Yes, but you will have to do your own unpacking. When you are finished, your trunk will be placed in storage." Miss Withington dusted her hands together. "Well, that is that, then. We should get to the drawing room. I am sure they are all waiting for us now. The spiral stairs are outside the door at the end of the hall. Come." Miss Withington ducked out the door and turned left and through a slim door. Just as promised, there was the door to the spiral stairs.

Down the staircase, Georgiana found herself back where they had started.

"I hear them all in the drawing room. Quickly now! They will be anxious to make your acquaintance. After all, dinner will not be served until you are introduced."

And that, of course, would be the primary reason anyone here would want to be acquainted with Georgiana Darcy—to ensure they got their dinner on time.

She sighed. Temporary; this was only temporary.

Mrs. Fieldings only retained them in the drawing room a quarter of an hour—just long enough to flood Georgiana in a sea of names and faces—all warm-blooded—she would hardly remember, then dismissed the school to their respective dinners: the younger students to the common room upstairs and the older ones to the dining room. Georgiana had not even had adequate time to get a sufficient look at the drawing room to recall what it looked like when Miss Withington appeared at her shoulder to guide her to dinner.

A long dining table, stained to resemble mahogany, but probably some lesser wood, dominated the center of the room. Windows along one long wall poured early evening sun on the warm, burnt-orange walls. The far short wall contained the fireplace, while several matching sideboards and extra chairs lined the remaining walls. Two mirrors, a round one over the mantel and a rectangular one above the sideboards opposite the windows, stood ready to catch the candlelight from pewter candelabras, which would brighten the apartment after sunset—though that would probably only happen for important guests. Candles were expensive, after all. In the countryside, dinner was served early enough to make the most of the daylight.

A crisp white tablecloth and plain, cream-colored china welcomed them. Fragrant aromas wafted from the serving platters. Not to Pemberley's standards, but better than the food at coaching inns. Neither shabby nor particularly noteworthy, the room was precisely the sort that one would hardly notice for good or bad. At least it would not ruin one's digestion.

Mrs. Fieldings took her place at the head of the table, near the fireplace. Miss Bamber, art, theater, and needlework teacher, who looked too young and pretty not to be married to a husband of her own, sat to Mrs. Fieldings' right. English and writing teacher Mrs. Ramsbury, a stocky, cross-looking school matron if there had ever been one, sat at the foot with head girl Miss Withington to her left. With a subtle nod, Miss Withington indicated an empty place on the right side two down from her, for Georgiana.

Where were all the dragons, though? Pax's support would have been invaluable right now.

The girl next to her leaned closer—what was her name? Oh, right, Miss Sempil. Honoria Sempil, the daughter of a spice merchant who dealt with plantations in the West Indies and in India. Unsavory sorts of places that Fitzwilliam eschewed investing in because of their dark practices, despite the potential for profit to be got there. But she should probably not hold it, nor her likely half-Blue family, against the plump, chubby-cheeked blonde whose luscious curls clustered around her face like the wisteria on the front of Bennetson Hall.

"The dragons occasionally take their dinner in the tower dining room. They are with us all day and sometimes prefer to have private time to discuss matters of interest only to cold-blooded society." Something about the way Miss Sempil flashed her brows suggested she might be rather more sympathetic to Georgiana's plight than some of the others were.

"I see."

"You need not worry about your dragon Friend, though. Dragons are treated well here. Had I a dragon Friend, I would be especially satisfied with his or her accommodations." The words hung in the air with unspoken implications.

Mrs. Fieldings announced the dishes as a hostess would. Nothing particularly noteworthy, but nothing particularly unsavory, either. Just a plain, if hearty meal: a joint of mutton, fish, potatoes, cauliflower, pickles, preserves, meat pie of some sort.

"So, why are you here?" Miss Sempil asked as she sipped her soup.

"Why do you want to know?" Georgiana edged back slightly.

"I do not blame you for being wary. I will tell you first, then. This will be my third year with Mrs. Fieldings. My father is a merchant in Sheffield. The 'family dog' took a sudden dislike to me. He told my father that I had suddenly become able to hear him speak, and that was going to cause no end of trouble for his neatly managed family." She snorted and wrinkled her pert button nose. "Once I came into my hearing, it was considered essential for me to acquire an entirely new set of accomplishments so that I could marry an Order man, despite the fact I already had a particularly acceptable beau. There is no hope of me getting him now."

"You were forbidden?"

"Oh, absolutely! And I cannot tell you how I resent that. I am sure there are nice enough Order men about, but Mr. Byrd was quite special indeed. Now I am destined for Mr. Howe, the only other unmarried Order man of my family's acquaintance. Given our circumstances, it should come as no surprise that we do not know many."

"You family is half-Blue, then?"

"More like one-third Blue, I think, but still, the point is the same. Mama, my sister, and two brothers cannot hear, but I can. So, in thanks for being the special one of the family, I got sent away. Do not mistake me, though. The school is decent enough; I do not mind it so much. I have made the best of it and learnt things that I think will help me secure a husband. But I think I should have been much happier doing it in a normal school without the... ah... unusual circumstances one finds here. I heard a rumor about you and the Keepers' Cotillion..." Miss Sempil sipped her wine, staring over the rim of the glass, big blue eyes expectant.

Georgiana's face grew cold. She turned her attention to the sliced mutton and potatoes on her plate. "There was a man that my brother did not approve of. But he was an Order man. It was his Dragon Keeping to which my brother took exception." No need to acknowledge Mr. Wickham at all.

Such fellow feeling in Miss Sempil's eyes.

Perhaps Georgiana would not be as alone as she had feared. "My family is all Blue. Very, very Blue." So Blue it was surprising any other color was allowed anywhere at all.

"Should I understand that you might not be quite so... Blue... yourself?" Miss Sempil's fine eyebrow arched.

"That would be one way to describe it."

"There are a few of us who feel that way, but I would caution you to be careful to whom you express that opinion. You might say it is not an entirely proper one within these walls. If you like, I will introduce you to the others whom you might find sympathetic. We are without our usual cadre of dragon students right now and can speak a little more freely than usual."

"Why? What has happened to them?"

"They graduated from their program—"

Mrs. Fieldings rose. "Our new dragon pupils will be arriving shortly. Our dragon liaison, Gale—"

"Called that because she comes in like a storm and out like a flood, leaving a mess in her wake," Miss Sempil whispered.

Just the sort of dragon Georgiana could do without.

"Gale will be returning with them in a week's time, assuming things go well. A few... complications... have delayed them. So, we will make good use of the opportunity. Starting tomorrow, we will begin a thorough spring cleaning of the Dragon Tower. All students and staff will be expected to participate. Many hands make work light."

Fancy words for mucking out the stables. This is what Fitzwilliam was sending her to school for?

Mrs. Fieldings stared directly at Georgiana. "Have you a concern, Miss Darcy?"

"I... I did not anticipate housework would be part of our curriculum, Mrs. Fieldings."

"In order to manage a household, a woman must have a firm grasp of all the tasks required in the home. Spring cleaning is one of them. And it will be instructive for all of you to see that the management required for a dragon's chambers is little different to our own. Hardly like mucking out a stable—"

Georgiana pressed her hands to burning cheeks. Oh, merciful heavens! Surely, she had not said that aloud? Mrs. Fieldings' hearing must be as acute as Elizabeth's!

All the students groaned.

"And when we are finished, we may have two days off of all work and all lessons."

Squeals and applause followed.

"May we go to the assembly at Chapel-en-le-Frith afterwards?" a pretty ginger-haired girl, whose name Georgiana had forgotten, asked.

"No, none of you are out in society. However..." Mrs. Fieldings held the pause for what must have been dramatic effect. "I think we might hold our own dinner party here one evening. It might not be a public assembly, but an evening of frivolity appropriate to your status."

"Are students here ever allowed to attend assemblies?" Georgiana asked.

"Not usually, Miss Darcy. Girls who are out are generally not in attendance here." Mrs. Fieldings' mild tone belied the reprimand disguised there. "Some evening diversion, though, will be exceedingly welcome. You will all be permitted to dress up, and even help plan the event—except for the guest list; that will be carefully curated, of course. All in all, another excellent learning opportunity."

May 3, 1815

THE NEXT DAY, SURPRISINGLY enough, a team of local girls—mostly relations of the Bennetson staff—arrived to assist the students and staff in cleaning. Georgiana's opinion of the headmistress reformed—a little.

For three days, Georgiana actively engaged herself in spring cleaning throughout the house—everywhere but the dragon tower. Though she would never admit it aloud, the enterprise was proving instructive.

Such things certainly went on at Pemberley, but she had never been a part of them. It was interesting to watch how matters were accomplished, even if she would rather not do them herself. More instructive still, observing first-hand how staff were best supervised. It would have been nice if Mama or Elizabeth had tried to teach her such things. But they were too busy managing dragons.

On the fourth morning, Georgiana staggered off the single mattress tick laid out on the floor, on which she had slept that night, and leaned heavily against the nearby dresser. Stiff and sore from wrestling mattresses off beds and outside for fluffing and restuffing the day before, whatever work was required today to get the beds reassembled would be worth the promise of a decent night's sleep. Clearly, she had failed to appreciate Pemberley's flock and feather mattresses enough! One night on chaff would be sufficient for the rest of her life. Prickly sneezy stuff!

Pax flew circles around her, twittering, as Georgiana struggled into her oldest morning gown. Dusty and smudged from the last several days' efforts, the charwoman might never get it clean again.

"You really ought to stop that. You will exhaust yourself before you even begin." Georgiana pointed at the dresser, where Pax would hopefully settle down and perch. "I do not understand your assignment in the Dragon Tower, but you have been utterly exhausted every single night."

Pax landed on the bedpost that stood sentinel over the empty bed ropes to look Georgiana in the eye. "Come to the Dragon Tower with me today. I want you to see the dragons' common room. Mrs. Fieldings has established lovely accommodations for us fairy dragons. It is unique, and you need to see it."

"I am well aware of the arrangements Pemberley makes for their fairy dragons, which you told me were quite remarkable. What more is there for me to learn? Is the effort of the Dragon Sage at Pemberley not enough?"

Pax scrabbled around the bedpost, climbing a little higher. "This is different to Pemberley. I am uncommonly fond of it, and I want you to see. Please?"

"Then describe it to me. You know my imagination is exceedingly good. I am certain you can tell me everything I need. I will even sketch it all so that you can correct any misunderstanding. No doubt that will please Miss Bamber, the art teacher."

"But I want you to see it. There is too much for me to describe." Pax zipped about overhead. What could possibly put her in such a state of agitation?

"I promised Miss Sempil that I would help her this morning. All the bed ropes must be tightened before the mattresses are returned to their places. If we do not finish that task by nightfall, I will have to sleep on a chaff mattress on the floor again, and I do not relish the thought." She rubbed her shoulders and the back of her neck.

"You are concerned about your own comfort, but not about mine." Pax landed on the dresser and turned her back.

"That is not fair. Your lovely basket is stuffed with your own downy mattress. And you possess a bespoke fairy dragon home of wrought iron, heated with warm bricks and wrapped with a woolen cozy, designed according to your exact specifications. All of that is strictly for your comfort. How can you say I am unconcerned about you?"

"Those are things you chose to provide for me. You never asked what I want."

"That is not what you want? You have always told me you enjoyed warm and soft. I made sure there is plenty of warm and soft for you." Georgiana stepped toward Pax, open hands outstretched.

"Yes, those things are lovely, but..."

Oh heavens! That 'but' was familiar! It was the one she spoke in her own mind when Father and Mother and Fitzwilliam had become high-handed and overbearing in making decisions on her behalf. "I suppose then I must. Pray give me a moment to inform Miss Sempil of my plans, and I will be at your disposal."

Pax twittered happily and landed on her shoulder, nestling into her neck. Georgiana scratched under her chin. Dear sweet Friend.

Pax did not appreciate Miss Sempil's disappointment, but both were sufficiently well-mannered not to create any sort of kerfuffle, which was probably the best that might be hoped for. Miss Sempil's indifference to dragons extended to Pax as well, which, while Georgiana neither encouraged nor appreciated it—after all, Pax was an exceptional Friend—she did understand. Poor Miss Sempil's life had been turned inside out because of dragons that she did not want to hear in the first place. Who could blame her for resenting the situation? It really was something the Blue Order should have more consideration for.

After promising to work very hard when she returned, Georgiana made her way to the Dragon Tower with Pax. She had been curious to see what the structure was like on the inside and it was usually forbidden to warm-blooded students, so this really would be a lovely opportunity to take a peek within. Yes, this would be a pleasant diversion, even if it reeked of dragon musk. She was determined.

The tower's polished oak door, carved with an elegant rose-and-vine motif that scrolled around the door, stood ajar. Sounds of industry poured out to greet them.

"Mrs. Fieldings has such a lovely wing for the resident dragons." Pax sang as she shook herself fluffy with pleasure. "So welcoming. The three staff dragons are assigned lairs on the first floor. Sometimes they entertain visitors there. Those lairs are exceedingly accommodating. Upstairs, there are spaces for the students and Friends, each laid out with the dragon type in mind. The common room is on the highest floor. A common room just for dragons! Not even Pemberley has such a place. That is what I want you to see. Particularly the bower for fairy dragons. I have never seen such a thing!"

A bower? That was indeed unique. It might be nice to know about something Elizabeth did not, to suggest a comfort for the resident fairy dragons that Elizabeth had not thought of. Perhaps a contribution like that might actually be appreciated. What a new and novel thing that could be.

The first-floor corridor that encircled the narrow spiral stairs at the center of the tower teemed with activity. Four open doors off the octagonal entryway poured filtered sunlight into the odd little space. Light seemed to filter down from above as well. Georgiana peered up through the staircase spiral. A frosted glass window, like one from a greenhouse, rained sunlight down from above. That would explain why the tower felt so warm. And why Pax liked it so well. She did like her 'warms'. A steady stream of girls carried feed sacks of old straw bedding down from the upstairs rooms.

Georgiana peeked through the first doorway, into a room perhaps two-thirds the size of her own chamber. The space was oddly shaped, sliced from the octagon that formed the tower. What was the word for it? Rather like a badly cut slice of pie. Yes, that described it well enough. Sheer curtains dressed the window and filtered light on the plain furnishings: a low wooden platform tucked against the inner-most wall—probably where the dragon slept; a standing desk with several drawers stood near the window, a bookcase with freshly dusted tomes, a few that looked like the monographs Elizabeth had written; and a small wooden chest that likely held whatever personal effects a dragon might possess.

What sort of personal effects would a dragon keep?

A maid, on hands and knees, scrubbed the stone floor while the scullery maid scrubbed out the small fireplace near the bed platform. A stone mantel above held a candle and a few jars that looked like they had come from an apothecary's shop. Plain and utilitarian. Somehow, that made her feel a bit better. If the dragon's room had been more sumptuously appointed than her own, she might have been tempted to jealousy. She breathed out a little of the tension she had not realized had been lodged in her chest.

"Berry and I already went through the first-floor rooms looking for mites." Pax twittered from the mantel.

"Mites? Vermin?" Georgiana recoiled, wrapping her arms around her waist. "How dreadful. How dare they ask you to perform such a task?"

"Scale mites are horrid things." Pax landed on the writing desk and shook herself very hard. "I am happy to help rid the place of them. It is a job only fairy dragons can do! There were very few, to be sure. The school is kept very, very clean. I am impressed. The few mites we did find were actually tasty, almost sweet. That also speaks well of the upkeep here." Pax smacked her beaky nose as though she had just enjoyed a treat.

Praising the taste of the vermin found here? Georgiana's stomach knotted and flipped. How utterly revolting. Good that she had not yet eaten breakfast.

"Do not look so disgusted. Some of the foods you enjoy so greatly are repulsive to me, and you do not see me making a dither about it."

"Indeed. What do you find distasteful?"

"Potatoes."

"Potatoes? Why? What on earth is disgusting about potatoes?"

"What is displeasing about sweet little mites?" Pax extended her wings like Mrs. Reynolds lecturing a servant, arms akimbo.

Georgiana's jaw dropped. How did one answer such a question? "I had no idea our tastes were so different."

Pax chirruped rather disagreeably. "Come upstairs." She buzzed toward the stairs. While it would have been nice to peek at the other rooms, Georgiana followed her up the narrow stairs. The exceedingly narrow stairs.

Perhaps it was a good thing that this tower was dedicated to dragons. The steep, irregular steps would have been difficult to manage without careful attention to one's steps. Even then, they were rather perilous. Four feet with talons would probably make for more secure footing.

The wooden treads were worn and gouged by claws, and the banister was similarly scarred, to the point that splinters presented a real obstacle. At least for Georgiana's soft human hands. They would hardly have bothered tough dragon hide.

Pax flew past the students' and Friends' floor, where sweeping and gathering old bedding filled the air with sneezy dust and chaff. A quick glance suggested the rooms were even smaller here, and no better appointed than the ones downstairs. An almost oppressive cloak of dragon musk hung in the atmosphere—rather reminiscent of a barnyard, but then again not. Would spring cleaning remove that, or was it a permanent part of the stone walls, like the smell that pervaded Pemberley or the Blue Order offices?

What did the dragon-deaf think of that scent? Did they even notice it, or were they as oblivious to it as they were to the voices of dragons?

Pax zipped up the topmost flight of stairs. "The common room is at the top of the stairs."

As with the girls' common room, the stairs opened into the middle of a large, open space. Hot and bright. Glass windows covered the exterior walls, reflected by glossy white paint on the interior walls. Window glass set into the ceiling effectively created a small greenhouse. In the center stood a cluster of bulbous clay pots with blooming shrubs and trellised flowering vines. A sectioned iron bench embraced the pots in a loose circle, probably for dragons to sun themselves like they did on garden rocks at Pemberley. Wooden benches lined the windows, probably also for sunning. Here the flowers' perfume pushed away the dragon musk and the sense of a garden prevailed.

"Is it not wonderful?" Pax flew circuits around the edges of the room. "Even better than the morning room at Pemberley."

One could hardly argue the point. A hothouse set up indoors expressly for the use of the household dragons; what was disagreeable about that?

Deep-purple Berry, Miss Withington's Friend, zipped out from the center of the shrubs. "You did come! You did! I knew you would!" she cried as she buzzed happy circles around Georgiana's head.

"Were you in any doubt that I would do something to please my Friend?" Georgiana asked.

Berry did not answer, but caught up with Pax and flew wingtip to wingtip with her around the chamber, singing such a song as she had never heard a fairy dragon sing before. Pax had not exaggerated about how happy this space had made her.

Perhaps in Georgiana's next letter to Pemberley she would describe this room, maybe even sketch it. Elizabeth would probably be glad to hear she had discovered something for the comfort of her dragon Friend that they had not already provided at Pemberley. Yes, that should rather nicely make her case for an abbreviated stay here. Not to mention, it would help her recall the details when she tried to recreate it for Pax. Somewhere. Someday.

"And look here!" Pax flew toward the ceiling window and landed on the edge of a small, straw nesting basket, one of several hung from a rail that traced the top edge of the wall. "A basket in the sun has been provided for each fairy dragon, and there is a large one when we want to nest in company."

Nest in company? Fairy dragons did that? Wild ones hibernated in harem groups, but Friends enjoyed the same kind of company? Extraordinary.

Georgiana walked over to examine the basket hanging just over her head. It was remarkably well made, with a colorful pattern woven into the straw along the sides. "I shall inquire as to where these are produced and how one might be acquired for us when we leave here."

"I would not expect that to happen too soon." Miss Withington stood in the doorway, not quite glaring, arms folded over her chest. She wore a smudged and dusty apron over an equally dingy morning dress. A mobcap covered her hair, though several pale blonde tendrils escaped to cling to her dirt-streaked cheeks.

"Pardon me? I do not understand what that is supposed to mean." Georgiana pulled herself up tall and squared her shoulders.

Pax and Berry squawked and dove into the larger basket, making it swing from the ceiling.

"I am sure you do not. But you should." Miss Withington looked her squarely in the eyes with a look of quiet confidence.

"Pray, then, be clear in your meaning. I am not fond of riddles."

"This is the first time you have set foot in the Dragon Tower, despite the fact that cleaning it is the one specific task necessary to complete before Gale's return with the new students."

"There is plenty of labor to be done, or did you forget that the whole of the house was to be cleaned? You may ask Miss Sempil to vouch for me. I have been hard at work assisting her in the student quarters, not shirking, regardless of the fact that I am unaccustomed to such activity."

"I am quite sure you are not accustomed to this sort of work, any more than I, Miss Darcy." Miss Withington's tone cut with a razor edge. "And I am aware you have been taking part." The way she emphasized that word—the untoward implications! "But that is not the point."

"Then what is the point?"

"Mrs. Fieldings explained to me the special tutoring I am to do with you. It is clear you are trying to avoid it."

"What are you talking about? What special tutoring? I have been told no such thing. I have been doing precisely what I have been asked."

The left side of Miss Withington's dainty nose pulled back in a polite little sneer. "You think you are so clever, do you not, Miss Darcy? You make it appear as though you are doing just as you should be, when you are in fact actively avoiding those precise things that would convince anyone that you are serious about acquiring an education here. You might fool yourself, but you do not fool me."

The gall! The audacity! "How can you possibly judge me like that? You do not know my thoughts."

"I know your actions. Everyone can see them. You have been sent here, above all else, to acquire a proper attitude toward dragons. If you were intent upon doing that, then you would be running toward the tasks related to dragons, not away from them."

Georgiana's cheeks flushed prickly and hot. "I ran away from nothing."

"But you did not embrace them."

"I was working where hands were needed. But if you are so determined that I should work here, perhaps you should explain to Miss Sempil that I will not be assisting her today. Surely you do not want to sleep on chaff again tonight."

"Miss Sempil is hardly the model of student you should be emulating. She has plenty of hands to help her, with or without you. Berry, would you mind relaying to Miss Sempil that I have need of Miss Darcy here?"

Berry poked her head out of the basket, cheeped a grudging assent, and zipped out of the room. She generally kept her distance from Miss Sempil. Come to think of it, so did Pax.

"There. Now, you may assist me." Miss Withington folded her arms over her chest and stared like a cranky old schoolmistress.

"Fine. What is to be done here?" Georgiana glanced around the perfectly maintained common room.

"This room is fine. The dragon quarters below need to be finished, though. The rooms for the new students need to be fitted before they arrive. The old bedding has been carried out and the first two student lairs scrubbed. You will help me move the furnishings from storage and arrange the lairs for occupancy." Miss Withington beckoned her to the stairs.

"Very well," Georgiana muttered. "I do not understand why a dragon lair needs furniture. Old Pemberley's did not. Besides, when they live wild, left to their own devices, they do not enjoy furnished lairs. Why do they need such things?"

Miss Withington stopped and turned to her slowly, like a predator regarding its prey. A little too much like Old Pemberley had regarded her that awful time she had come across his lair. "What would you know of how wild dragons live? Have you ever been invited into their lairs? Have you even met one personally? What do you actually know of them?"

Georgiana sniffed and looked away.

Miss Withington closed the distance between them. "Tell me, whence do you gather that information?"

"From where do you gather yours?"

"As a matter of fact, I have several excellent sources. The Dragon Sage has produced a monograph on the fitting of dragon lairs for the comfort of resident dragons by dragon type and rank. Are you aware that Mrs. Fieldings provided her extensive assistance in writing the document? Or that Barwines Chudleigh has a lair lined with pillows?"

"Have you ever met Barwines Chudleigh?"

"I have not had that privilege; the daughter of a mere undersecretary to the Order is not likely to receive such an invitation. But I would like to. I understand she is quite extraordinary."

"No, you would not. I have met her, and she is a persnickety, cranky old lizard, just like the rest of them, for all her fancy feathers and beguiling looks. She would not have the time of day for you, much less entertain you at tea."

"And how would you know that?"

"I was not invited to the tea party she held in honor of Pemberley and Eliz—the Dragon Sage. If I was not invited, how could you ever expect to be received?"

"You seem rather put out by her neglect."

Georgiana covered her throat with her hand. "Who would not be? It was indeed a cut, intended to make a point."

"And what point was that?"

"What do you think? You do not strike me as a simpleton."

"I think you do not understand dragons well at all if you are trying to attribute human motivation to them."

"What are you talking about? The Dragon Sage is always going on about how their thoughts and feelings and rights are just as real as our own." Georgiana snuffed and turned her shoulder to Miss Withington.

"They are, but that does not mean they are all the same as our own. Have you never sought to understand things from the perspective of a dragon?"

Merciful heavens! She sounded like Elizabeth—think like a blasted dragon! Gah, how disagreeable to be provoked to such language even in one's thoughts. "Why would I want to?"

"Because you might find that many things make more sense that way."

"Then enlighten me, oh wise one!"

"Sarcasm is not attractive in a woman."

"Neither is flaunting knowledge."

Miss Withington closed her eyes and drew a deep breath. "I am not flaunting, Miss Darcy. Mrs. Fieldings asked me to assist you in acquiring the knowledge you want and need in order to make a quick exit from this place. If you care to extend your stay, indefinitely perhaps, you are free to continue in your ignorance. It is of no matter to me."

Georgiana gritted her teeth. Getting away from this school and into her own establishment was the only thing she really wanted and if listening to this arrogant girl would help that... "Very well, enlighten me about the relevance of the invitation, or rather, the lack thereof."

Miss Withington seemed to consider whether to bother answering. "Dominance."

"That is all you have to say on the matter? Dominance? It was a tea party, not a territory battle."

"Everything with dragons is about dominance. And it was a territory battle, after a fashion. The guests of that tea party were no doubt chosen with that in mind."

"Absurd!"

"You think so? Consider this. First, as I understand, that tea party was not held by Barwines Chudleigh, but by Vicontes Pemberley herself."

"What difference does it make? The Barwines is her dragon guardian of some sort. How would you know, anyway?"

"It makes a great difference. Very great. And I know because Mrs. Fieldings had a written account of the event created for study."

That tea party had been made into some sort of monograph? "That is absurd."

"It is a brilliant case study in several things, including dominance. You do understand how both the Barwines and Cowntess Rosings are working to establish Pemberley's dominance among the Order dragons even though she is still too young and small to hold it on her own? There is little precedent for such a thing in any of the historical records."

"Now you sound like Historian Bennet." Disagreeable old curmudgeon.

Miss Withington squeezed her eyes shut and grimaced. A most unladylike expression. "It is rare for major dragons to promote the interest of one who might later be a rival. It is truly important. The guests at that party—"

"—included servants at Darcy House! Servants!"

"Members of Pemberley's Keep who served their major dragon well and deserved reward for that. Such notice is an honor among dragons."

"And Miss Bennet, the Sage's sister?"

"That showed Pemberley's appreciation for the service she rendered to the Sage. It speaks of her strong attachment to her Keeper and signals a means by which to earn Pemberley's favor."

"So, you mean that all the guests—"

"No, not all. There were two classes of guests, those there to demonstrate Pemberley's recognition and acceptance of them, and those to establish her place in dominance. Consider Lady Matlock and Lady Dressler, who are connected to high-ranking officers and dragons in the Order. They were of the latter type."

"I was not invited."

"That suggests that you did not fall into either of those two categories. So, you were as far above her notice as you were below it, neither requiring her recognition nor her need to be recognized by you because of your place in the dominance hierarchy."

Georgiana winced. "But I am family to her Keeper as much as Miss Bennet, am I not?"

"But did you insult the dragon?"

"Insult Pemberley? Preposterous!"

"But you never really tried to be of service to her, either," Pax whispered over the edge of the basket.

"That is not true. When she was first hatched, I worked tirelessly for her comfort. You have no idea what I did for her."

Miss Withington's brow knit and she cocked her head. "You are right. I did not know." She took half a step back and folded her arms loosely across her chest. "What happened?"

Georgiana pressed her arms to her stomach and looked aside, moving several steps away. "Have you ever tried to please a demanding dragon?"

"Not one bigger than my Friend."

"Then you do not understand how all-consuming and how thankless it can be. I did everything I could find in the notes the Dragon Sage provided. Everything. And to no avail. Nothing I did brought her succor, nothing was enough. You see, I was not *her*, and I could not be the Dragon Sage. Nothing else would please the drakeling. So, all my efforts were ignored and deemed insufficient; I was deemed insufficient... what point is there in trying to please a particular dragon when they have already decided that you cannot succeed?"

"You are right. I had no idea."

Chapter
4

May 8, 1815

SPRING CLEANING CONTINUED FOR five full, long days, but at the end of it, Bennetson Hall sparkled from the front hall to the girls' common room and everywhere in between, including the dragon tower. Georgiana's bed, with ropes tightened, mattresses cleaned and fluffed, and made up with fresh linens, might be the most comfortable she had ever slept upon—though it could well be their sheer exhaustion that accounted for that sensation.

Either way, it was still particularly pleasant. Georgiana leaned back into the mattresses—a lovely wool flock one on top. No more sleeping directly on chaff!—and laced her hands behind her head. Staring up at the dust-free ceiling, the afternoon shadows cast by the not-yet-flowering honeysuckle vines danced upon the faded pink walls of her chamber. How delightful it was to be permitted a rest.

Grueling as the exercise might have been, there was something satisfying in the process, in seeing their accomplishments in so tangible a way. And she had a better understanding of what was required for when she was mistress of her own establishment. Though she probably could have figured out most of it on her own, it was useful to have seen it first-hand.

Now, if asked, she could honestly answer that her time at Mrs. Fieldings' had been useful.

It seemed, though, that not everything had gone well. The dragons did not arrive after the expected seven-day, bringing considerable consternation to all the staff and many of the students—apparently, the dragon students were usually quite amiable. Even so, the post still arrived on time, bringing a larger-than-average number of letters and parcels ahead of the new term, if the gossip was to be believed.

That delivery also resulted in great consternation, as Mrs. Fieldings herself went through all of it and decided whether it was appropriate to share with the designated recipient. And if it was not, it would be kept back until an appropriate time.

What a violation! Surely that was against some law, was it not?

Merciful heavens! Georgiana sat up, heart pounding against her ribs, and pulled her knees to her chest, rumpling the plain linen coverlet beneath her. Did Mrs. Fieldings also spy upon outgoing post? Did she read the letters Georgiana had sent to Aunt Matlock and Aunt Catherine? Mrs. Fieldings could not have appreciated Georgiana likening her establishment to a medieval dungeon—which was an exaggeration for effect, of course. She had needed to make a point to her aunts.

Mrs. Fieldings gave no indication that she had read those words. Perhaps that meant... no, no, who was she fooling? Of course, the headmistress had read them, and they would come back to haunt Georgiana at the worst possible time. She had probably just increased her stay at Bennetson Hall by weeks, if not months!

Was that why Mrs. Fieldings had reminded her that "a true lady is mindful of what she says at all times, especially in her correspondence, which her descendants might not be so considerate as to burn after she leaves this mortal coil, preserving hasty words for generations?" It seemed an odd thing to say just in passing.

Georgiana flushed all the way to her shoulders. Now she would always wonder if Mrs. Fieldings was remembering those remarks whenever she looked Georgiana's way. How perfectly dreadful. Never again would she be so thoughtless in her writing. No one else would have such a thing to use against her. Never.

Blast and botheration—no doubt Elizabeth would consider that a worthy contribution to Georgiana's education.

She drew a deep breath, then another. Dwelling upon what had happened would do her no good. No, such attention would probably ensure she would commit some other thoughtless act in her distress. What else could she focus on?

In the three days it took for Mrs. Fieldings to sort through the post, Miss Bamber, the theater teacher, Mr. Elkins the visiting music master, and Mica, the dancing drake, arranged for the girls to have an evening to display their accomplishments as they might be asked to at an evening party once they were out in society. Mr. Elkins insisted Georgiana play for her fellow students, strongly implying that if he found her playing satisfactory, he would declare her sufficiently accomplished to Mrs. Fieldings.

Pleasing though that result might be, Mr. Elkins' suggestion also meant that Mrs. Fieldings had shared at least some of Georgiana's story with the staff. No telling how much, though. Surely enough to color the way they looked at her. What must they think of her?

Mortifying—simply mortifying.

She wrapped her arms tightly around her knees and rocked slightly. There was absolutely nothing she could do about it now. But she would make sure not to give anyone anything to talk about, ever again. This was enough humiliation for a lifetime!

She pressed cool hands to her fiery cheeks and drew in several deep breaths. She was to play this evening, and it would not do to allow herself the luxury of being upset.

Distraction. She needed distraction. Yes! A call upon Miss Sempil would be just the thing.

She made her way down the hall and knocked on Miss Sempil's door.

"Go away. I have no wish for company." Miss Sempil's strained voice barely filtered into the hall.

"It is Miss Darcy. Pray let me in."

After several long moments, the door creaked open, just a sliver, and Georgiana slipped inside.

The chamber arrangement and plain furnishings resembled Georgiana's, except the walls were faded green, not pink. The curtains were drawn, swathing the room in shadows and slivers of light that sneaked in around the edges of the window dressings. Rumpled bed linens suggested Miss Sempil had thrown herself headlong onto the bed, clutching the pillows underneath her. A crumpled letter lay beside the pillows.

"Has there been bad news from home?" Georgiana closed the door behind her. "Is your family well?"

Miss Sempil collapsed, head in hands, on the end of the bed, sobbing. "I am wretched, Miss Darcy, simply wretched."

"What could have rendered you in such a state? Was it something in the letter you received?"

"What else could it be?" Miss Sempil stretched back and brought the worn-looking missive to her chest. "It is the worst news possible!"

"Your father? Something has happened to your father?" Only the death of a husband would alter a woman's life more than her father's death.

"No, no! He is fine and determined I should stay here for yet another term." She gulped back her sob. "I was to leave here soon, to begin my life finally, but now... now... now it is all ruined."

"Ruined? What do you mean?" Georgiana sat beside her. "You have been here for three years now, you said. How can you possibly be ruined?"

"Read this!" She pushed a piece of wrinkled paper into Georgiana's hand.

Smoothing the scrap of newspaper against her skirts, Georgiana read:

Miss Leticia Burk, daughter to Mr. and Mrs. Reginald Burk of Little Dowling, lately married to Mr. Edwin Howe of Overley Park...

"A marriage announcement? I do not understand how this would mean you are ruined."

Miss Sempil looked up, blue eyes flashing over red, chubby cheeks. "What do you not understand? Mr. Howe is the only Dragon Keeper in the acquaintance of my family!" Sobs drowned out the rest of her words.

"Should I understand that some sort of alliance of your two families was in the planning?"

"Yes, yes! The last time I was at home, we were much in company. I know my father approached him with the idea, and I understood it to have been favorably received. Although my dowry is not nearly so generous as yours, it was thought sufficient to ignore my father's involvement in the spice trade. It was all so very hopeful! Mr. Howe was my hope for a future. What am I to do now? I am ruined!"

"There is a significant difference between having a man you like choose another and actually being ruined in the eyes of society." If anyone was aware of that, it was Georgiana. "You must know that. Were there any implications of an engagement between you two?"

"No."

"Any public expectation that there was, or should be?"

"No."

"Then you are hardly ruined."

"That is easy for you to say, you who have connections and others to assist you with introductions to those in the Order. But I am only the daughter of a merchant! Who will introduce me to suitable men within the Order? You seem to think the world is full of Blue Order members everywhere you turn, but I assure you it is not. When one is not connected to Order officers and peers, the rarity of eligible partners is a profoundly real challenge."

Gracious, that thought had never occurred to her. Was it really true? Everyone in Georgiana's world seemed to hear dragons; every place was full of them. But it was also well known that dragon-hearing was a rare trait. It had just never seemed so until now. "You could marry a dragon-deaf man; there are plenty of them. There is nothing to stop that from happening. You do not have a dragon Friend. It is not as though you would lose connection to your family the way I would."

"And risk having a half-Blue family of my own? Risk that my children might suffer as I have? Surely not! When two dragon-hearers marry, their children will hear dragons. I must have that assurance."

According to Elizabeth, it was not always so simple, but now was definitely not the time to bring that up. "The Sage's uncle is in trade and I have made his acquaintance. Perhaps I may be able to ask him to make introductions for you? They have been impressed by Mrs. Fieldings' education of Miss Bennet. That could make them disposed to help you. Or even Miss Bennet herself. I know you have made her acquaintance. She might assist. All hope is not lost. Do not give up."

Miss Sempil pulled a handkerchief from her sleeve. "I suppose you are right."

They both jumped at a sharp rap on the door. Miss Withington peeked in. "Oh dear, it looks like the letter was bad news, just as I feared. Chin up; I am sure Mrs. Fieldings will have some helpful suggestions for you. She always does. If you want, I can help you talk to her when you are ready. I know she can be intimidating, but she really is quite sympathetic. But in the meantime, today's exhibition is still set to begin in a quarter of an hour. You ought to get ready. You too, Miss Darcy." She shut the door behind her.

"How horribly unfair! My heart is broken and yet we are expected to carry on as though nothing has happened!" Miss Sempil dragged her handkerchief over her tear-streaked face.

Now there was something else Georgiana must avoid thinking about tonight. A possibility she had never considered. What prospects did she have in the marriage mart if Fitzwilliam and Elizabeth no longer welcomed her into the family? Would any upstanding Blue Order man of worth marry her if a knight and officer of the Order disapproved of her?

A quarter of an hour later, Miss Sempil, face washed and hair tidied, and Georgiana, Pax nestled close on her shoulder, made their way down the long hall to the music room.

Hardly equal to Pemberley's music room, which housed the pianoforte Fitzwilliam had given her for her last birthday, Bennetson Hall's pale-yellow-walled music room still contained the essentials: a pianoforte stationed in the bay window, a library of music, sufficient space for singers or other performers near the pianoforte, and a triple-row audience of chairs for the observation and admiration of the performers. It appeared those chairs had been designed to stack one upon the other should a dance floor be required. Clever and useful when one did not have a house full of servants to move furniture about.

She swallowed hard and blinked even harder. It had been too long since she had played for anyone. Fitzwilliam and Richard, too, had always had time for her to play for them. Even Elizabeth, when Georgiana had deigned to play for her.

Georgiana and Miss Sempil took seats in the back row of chairs with the teachers, as they were taller than the little girls.

Mrs. Fieldings stood near the pianoforte. "Now that we have all taken our seats, the afternoon's entertainments may begin."

Miss Dunn, the sallow, red-haired, too-thin head of young girls, joined Mrs. Fieldings near the pianoforte. "Mr. Elkins, would you favor us on the pianoforte?"

The visiting music master, a wholly average, unmemorable man with ash-blond hair and no feature to set him apart from any other man, rose from his front-row seat and sat at the equally nondescript instrument.

"Girls, come to the front."

Eight little girls rose from their seats in the front row and arranged themselves between the pianoforte and a pretty painted table lined with a series of wine glasses, each with a different level of clear liquid, probably water, near the angled side of the bay window.

The large window in the center of the bay, facing the drive up to the house, had been opened, allowing the wisteria blossoms to droop into the window and perfume the room. Tiny petals, shed from the cascading vines, wafted in on the soft breeze, landed on the little girls' choir, as though part of the performance.

Mercail, assistant head of young girls, a white, feather-scaled dragon, whom Georgiana had not noticed until now, flew to perch on the table, bowed to the audience and to the girls, then approached the wineglasses. Her feather-scales glistened like a pearl, which was what her name meant. She was said to be a fairy dragon, but her glistening white body was entirely bird-like, down to her slender, beaky snout, similar to a greater cockatrix, but far smaller. She boasted an elaborate head crest of iridescent feathers, lovely and feminine, but subdued compared to the other cockatrix Georgiana had known.

Pax nestled a little closer and whispered in her ear. "Is she not magnificent?"

"She seems small for a cockatrix, all told. Cait is far larger and grander. Her feathers are splendid, so pearly and glittery. And I will grant that her head crest is unique, all fluffed up and standing straight. She is rather pretty."

"Rather pretty? She is exquisite!" Pax pinched her ear with her beak.

What? Georgiana covered her ear with her hand. Pax had never nipped ears before.

Miss Sempil tittered beside her. "Do not let the fairy dragons overhear you say that! What an insult you have offered!"

"I just praised the creature! How is that an insult?"

"Mercail is not a cockatrix! To suggest so is insulting!" Pax hovered in front of her face, eyeing Georgiana's ear menacingly. "She is a fairy dragon."

"That cannot possibly be a fairy dragon!" Georgiana hissed. "She is the size of a large pigeon!"

"You think I cannot recognize one of my kind?" Pax twittered.

"We are told she is a unique form of fairy dragon, called a 'queen fairy dragon' or some such thing. They are known to commune with a variety of cockatrix who looks extremely similar, so your confusion is really quite understandable." Miss Sempil tossed her head. "Mercail is much revered by the little girls and the local fairy dragons. I, though, cannot see much to be impressed with."

Pax huffed and flittered off to a wisteria branch poking in through the window, where she could more closely admire Mercail. As far as Georgiana knew, she had not yet drawn up the courage to speak to the queen fairy dragon, despite Berry having introduced Pax upon their arrival. Pax had always been the retiring sort, but this was excessive, even for her.

Mr. Elkins cleared his throat and nodded at the little girls. He played a few opening notes. As the girls adjusted their posture to sing, Mercail hovered a hand span above the table. How did a creature of that size hover like a tiny fairy dragon? How could she move her wings that fast?

Mr. Elkins played a light country ballad, and the girls sang along. Mercail pecked at the glasses, producing a bell-like harmony to counterpoint Mr. Elkins' melody.

Georgiana closed her eyes, swaying softly with the music. Lovely, simply lovely. The odd, ungainly fairy dragon and the little girls created unique, ethereal sounds that Georgiana had never heard. Though she did not prefer to sing herself, it might be worth learning from a music master who could craft such harmonies.

The piece ended to rousing applause.

Mr. Elkins stood and bowed to Mercail. "Credit where credit is due. The arranging of this piece is entirely Mercail's work."

Pax chirped and twittered enthusiastically. Georgiana blushed—such effusiveness was hardly considered polite, even if the performance was notable.

Mercail hovered beside Mr. Elkins and faced the audience. "Thank you all for your support in this little musical experiment. As promised, I will submit a full report to the Order Council of Arts. I hope that what we have done here will be considered for the next Symposium of Collaborative Draconic Arts."

The little girls gasped. Did they not know they had been part of some sort of draconic experiment?

"You have suggested we might sing for the Symposium?" the tallest of the little girls exclaimed. "You think us that good?" She seemed genuinely pleased.

Mercail cooed a bit too sweetly.

The girls crowded around her in a rather juvenile show of affection and excitement.

Was this the kind of behavior that Mrs. Fieldings taught? Certainly not appropriate to the class of student Georgiana had thought would be in attendance.

Perhaps it might be helpful if she provided an example of good breeding to the others, making herself appropriately useful within the group. She might supply what the teachers could or did not. Mrs. Fieldings would certainly approve.

Mrs. Fieldings rose and dismissed the young girls to their seats. "Now we shall enjoy the final concluding exercises by our more advanced students. Miss Sempil, Miss Withington?"

They joined Mrs. Fieldings at the pianoforte. "As our most advanced students, you will demonstrate what the others have to look forward to. Miss Sempil, you will begin, then Miss Withington."

Miss Sempil's posture and fingering at the pianoforte were certainly adequate. Georgiana closed her eyes to listen carefully. The piece was suitably complex for an advanced student, the sort that sounded more complex to play than it actually was. There, yes, she missed several notes and failed the change in dynamics. She was hardly as advanced as Mrs. Fieldings thought. Adequate, yes. Pleasant to listen to, yes, one who would be agreeable in drawing rooms and domestic music rooms. Exactly the variety of accomplishment that would suit Miss Sempil's station. But hardly a true proficient.

Georgiana clapped politely when Miss Sempil stood.

Miss Withington was a mite better. Her fingering sure and her mastery of the dynamics solid, she only lacked a certain connection to the music that would have set her aside as a truly accomplished musician. More polite applause.

"And finally, our newest pupil." Mrs. Fieldings took to the center of the room once more. "Miss Darcy. I have heard you are an accomplished musician yourself. Pray share your talent with us." She gestured toward the now-empty stool before the instrument.

Georgiana rose with as much grace as she could muster and made her way to the front of the room, ignoring all the eyes turned toward her. This was not the sort of audience that should intimidate her. No reason for her face to burn and her heart to race. None at all. Deep breath, and another. This was her place of mastery, where she was most comfortable and assured.

She ran her hands over the keys, taking a quick measure of the instrument and getting a feel for its action. Two deep breaths to settle into place and find the melody in her head. There, that was it. Her fingers settled into motion.

Gracious, how good it felt to be in the midst of something familiar and soothing, the most comfortable she had felt since she had come to Bennetson Hall. The second movement began, and the music shifted into a minor key, her favorite section.

Wait, what was that? What a horrible, rude noise! Was someone tromping up the stairs? Eyes turned away from the piano and toward the back of the room. No! How ghastly unfair, not during the best section of the piece.

The door creaked open and far too many noisy feet scrabbled in.

Georgiana looked to find the doorway was full of minor drakes and stopped playing.

"Please do continue." The largest drake, deep grey, almost black, with sweeping, wispy clouds of white and pale grey along her sides and back, stood on her hind legs. "I love that piece, and you are making an excellent show of it."

"Welcome back, Gale. Pray take a seat, all of you, and join us." Mrs. Fieldings waved them in.

Gale led a parade of six smaller, probably younger, drakes to the empty seats at the far right of the audience. Each one perched politely on a chair, graceful, even rather ladylike. That was probably supposed to be a good thing, but it seemed rather uncomfortable with their thick tails in the way. Elizabeth never insisted on dragons using furniture in warm-blooded fashion. There was always a ready supply of stools and poufs and pillows for them to perch upon.

Georgiana drew a deep breath and settled her hands on the keyboard once again. Where had she left off? Second movement, yes, that was it. Just start that over again. That made sense.

The music flowed through her fingertips once more. The minor notes bubbled up and filled the space, the emotion matching her own mixed feelings, feelings no one at Pemberley would acknowledge, feelings no one understood or accepted her having. Perhaps that was why she liked this composition so well.

Someone sneezed, an odd, snorty breed of sneeze. And again. And a third time. Her fingers tangled and tripped over the chord. She recovered, but not without cost: her momentum lost, the evocation of emotion ruined. More sneezing. Louder.

Dragon sneezes.

She scanned the right side of the audience. A black-and-white-speckled drake whose hide looked as though it were covered in sparkling glass beads dragged her forepaw across her snout. "Your pardon, Miss Darcy."

Not again. Not twice in a single sitting. Too much to be borne!

"Pray continue, Miss Darcy. I will excuse myself..."

Georgiana rose. "No, I will." Head high, shoulders back, she strode from the room, quietly shutting the door behind her.

5
Chapter

May 10, 1815

Georgiana kept to herself the rest of the evening. No one came to correct her for escaping the music room. Nor did anyone comfort her for the humiliation suffered at the hands of the dragon student. It was almost as if it had never happened. A relief, to be sure, but also rather lonely and isolating, leaving her with just a touch of melancholy that lingered through the formalities of Sunday church and dinner with the Blue Order vicar that followed.

According to Miss Withington, the start of a term was always marked with a special event. A little frivolity, a little ceremony, and a little reminder of the expectations of society, all rolled into one, would set the tone for their studies quite appropriately, or so Mrs. Fieldings said.

For the little girls, the event would be a tea party, with good china and fancy cakes, welcoming the new dragons who would be studying to become governesses to Blue Order families. The remainder of the term, the little girls and those dragon students would take their dinner early, in the students' common room, rather like what children did with their governess at home.

For the older students and the companion-dragon students, a fancy dinner of sorts would be held Monday evening, with pretty china, dinner dress, and time spent in the drawing room with parlor games and opportunities to exhibit their accomplishments. Excellent practice for social life after school—or at least that was the theory. But since most dinners in society did not include dragons—except for Pemberley's dinners, of course—the resemblance to an actual society dinner would be limited.

Hopefully that meant the dragon students would learn to eat in a civilized fashion, from the sort of dishes that were usually served at warm-blooded tables, not the gruesome chunks of raw meat that found their way to the table at Darcy House when Walker and Earl were about. While Georgiana was not terribly particular about food, bloody, hacked cuts, some still with feathers or fins attached, piled high on a platter, were simply not an appetizing sight. If Mrs. Fieldings managed to teach her dragon students some proper table manners, then she definitely would be doing some good in the world.

"It is not so bad, eating with the dragons." Miss Sempil tittered as they made their way down the wide, wooden main stairs to dinner. Her pale-pink muslin gown complemented her peaches-and-cream complexion, making her positively pretty tonight. "Mrs. Fieldings insists they eat with proper cutlery and it is rather amusing to see them try to use a knife and fork."

Oh, that would be a sight! Georgiana giggled behind her hand. Such a thing would never happen at Elizabeth's dinner table. She would consider it the height of rudeness to inconvenience the dragons that way.

"You must never laugh at them." Miss Withington hissed as she came up behind them. How much more pleasant company she would be if she were to develop a better sense of the ridiculous. "We may not laugh at other students here. Would you have liked to be laughed at when you fumbled at the pianoforte?"

Georgiana glared over her shoulder. "I did not fumble. I was distracted by the rudeness of the audience. That is hardly the same thing."

"Mr. Elkins says only weak musicians conjure such excuses for their own mistakes. An excellent musician can ignore everything around them and focus on their performance."

"As if your own performance were so accomplished." Georgiana sniffed. "There were multiple places—"

"I do not recall asking your opinion of my performance. I am well aware of my own shortcomings, thank you." Miss Withington's face flushed, and she pushed past them, down the stairs.

"She is quite high and mighty tonight, is she not?" Miss Sempil just barely sneered.

"I wonder what has stirred her up so."

"I imagine it is the companion-dragon students."

"I do not understand." Georgiana paused and caught Miss Sempil's eye. "I understood she was paired with a dragon student last term and found the experience quite satisfying."

"She was, and she did. The partnership was extraordinarily successful. That dragon graduated and immediately acquired an excellent placement with a prominent Blue Order family. That is the problem."

"Pray be plain. I do not understand at all."

"Although the partnerships will not officially be announced until the drawing room tonight, she has heard who she will be partnered with."

"And that is a problem because?" Pray she come out with an answer this time.

"Are you so simple you have not figured it out? It is Bede. She is partnered with Bede."

"The sneezy dragon who interrupted me?"

"The very one. The same one who continually interrupts everyone, corrects everyone, and appears to know everything."

"The one who argued with the vicar over the history of the parish church during Sunday dinner?" Georgiana gasped. Pax and Berry had taken tea with the little girls, ostensibly to enjoy the abundance of sweet dainty things served them, and now were sleeping off full bellies in the bower in Bennetson Tower. The truth of the matter was that it was a convenient way to avoid that dragon, whose entire demeanor made them uncomfortable. "Oh heavens! Even our poor Neville Withington does not deserve that!"

"No one does. I do not understand how Bede was admitted into Mrs. Fieldings' academy. I cannot fathom a creature less suited to being a lady's companion than she. Can you imagine spending your time with someone who thinks they know everything, questions and criticizes everything you do, and has little time for you otherwise?"

Georgiana pressed her hand to her constricting chest. "Yes, actually I can. Not a fate I would wish on anyone."

"I do not know what Mrs. Fieldings is going to do with her. Can you imagine what being partnered with her will be like?"

"I suppose Miss Withington's dudgeon makes much more sense now." Poor thing. It was a great deal to ask of the poor girl. Thank heavens it would not be asked of Georgiana.

After dinner, Gale withdrew with the rest of the dragons while Mrs. Fieldings directed the girls to remain, rather like when the ladies would remove to the drawing room and the gentlemen would remain in the dining room for cigars and port, only reversed.

The maid brought out a tray of dainty cakes decorated with flowers and feminine colors, likely from the confectioner's shop in Chapel-en-le-Frith. The little girls had probably enjoyed a similar offering at their tea this afternoon. Georgiana's mouth watered as she caught the scent of currants and berries from the array of tiny tarts. No wonder the dragons had left. The elegant tiny bites were definitely not suited to the taste of most drakes.

Were they enjoying some manner of dragon dainty in the drawing room? Was it the sort of thing that Mrs. Fieldings would not prefer served in her dining room?

As the sweet course was served, Mrs. Fieldings stood. "Girls, grant me your attention."

Various conversations faded away and silence crept across the room. That cold, uncomfortable flow of silence that ushered in a wave of polite foreboding.

"Tonight, we have the pleasure of welcoming the newest class of companion-dragon students to our fold. I expect you to demonstrate the utmost respect for these young dragons, who have chosen a life of useful employment in the warm-blooded world. It is not a common choice among dragons. They must give up a great deal in order to do so, as you have already seen at our table. Though they handled the demands of unfamiliar food and manners with aplomb, you must remember that the transition to life amongst warm-bloods can be very difficult, and the training is arduous."

Considering how much adjustment Georgiana had to make in living with so many dragons, it seemed only fair, if a little surprising, that it actually went both ways.

"Even if you are not partnered with one of them, you are a vital part of their education. I caution you, though; I will not have you lording that over them. Treat them as you wish to be treated. Be kind and courteous and remember the tenets of the Blue Order at all times. I will announce training partners this evening. Should you be fortunate enough to be assigned a dragon partner, your new class schedule will be explained to you tomorrow morning."

"She has never said that before. I am certain it is because Bede is causing offense wherever she goes." Miss Sempil's lips pressed into a delicate little frown.

Poor Miss Withington.

"Let us withdraw now and enjoy the rest of the evening with our new students." Mrs. Fieldings led the girls out.

Candles—tallow, not wax, from the vaguely bacony smell of them—in large pewter candelabras in each corner of the drawing room made the robin's-egg-blue walls more green than blue. It was one of those colors that was much prettier in the daylight; unfortunate, because so many drawing rooms, usually seen only in the evening, were painted that color. Two mirrors on the walls at either side of the large bay window brightened the room with reflected light.

Matching oak curiosity cabinets provided inspiration for conversation underneath each mirror, with clusters of striped blue upholstered chairs and couches nearby. The group nearest the fireplace on the far wall had almost half again as many chairs as the other. A card table painted with vines and flowers and surrounded by plain wooden chairs took up the center of the room. Not as fine as any Darcy drawing room, to be sure, but adequate to the purpose, rather like the rest of Bennetson Hall.

The silver tones in Gale's black and grey scales, brought out by the candlelight, glistened as though she were in a silk evening dress. She stood on her hind legs as the students entered in Mrs. Fieldings' wake. Gale's dark eyes sparkled above her short, round snout that seemed to conceal her fangs better than most drakes managed, giving her a rather more gentle, friendly appearance that belied her storm-and-strife reputation.

Gale and the dragon students curtsied to Mrs. Fieldings in the fashion of a proper lady. Such a strange sight, it nearly hurt the eyes. Elizabeth always insisted that dragons be greeted in their own 'tongue,' so to speak, with every manner of odd gesticulations that rendered the exchange all things odd and unexpected. This tortured display, though, was hardly better. Perhaps Elizabeth had a good point in not insisting that dragons be polite in ways that forced their limbs into unnatural contortions.

"It is a pleasure to have you return." Mrs. Fieldings matched Gale's gesture, her willowy figure ever graceful. Was that her knees popping as she did, though?

"My students are honored to be accepted into your lair." Three young drakes gathered and curtsied deeply, some managing the awkward motion better than others. Poor Bede nearly toppled over, catching herself against one of the other drakes, almost knocking them all over. "May I introduce Coxcomb—" A slender, yellow-brown drake with a distinctly triangular head stepped forward. The tufty crest of feather-scales around her head and her long eyelashes bobbed as she attempted another curtsey.

"Quicksilver—" An odd drake took Coxcomb's place.

From her midsection up, she was several shades of bright blue, with a pattern of golden-brown diamonds running down her back beside a blue spinal crest. Her throat appeared goitered; probably a pouch that would expand if she felt angry or threatened. "Thank you for your welcome." She curtsied, but her knee buckled and she caught herself on the floor with her front paws. Suddenly her color changed to fiery red from the tip of her nose to her spinal ridge, with the diamonds along her back turning black.

Gale touched Quicksilver's shoulder gently, and she stepped back while slowly shifting back to blue. What a trial it must be to blush so dramatically. It was bad enough when Georgiana felt her checks burning, but it could be nothing to such a color change.

"—and Bede."

Bede stepped forward without a curtsey. With tiny black spots, she looked like she was covered in miniature glass beads. Even the black irises in her unsettling red eyes were lined with tiny white dots. So striking! "Forgive me, but I am confused as to the propriety of the introductions here. I would have expected—"

"I am pleased to make your acquaintance." Mrs. Fieldings' voice carried a note of warning and Gale pulled Bede back.

Mrs. Fieldings introduced each of the girls in turn.

Coxcomb and Quicksilver sucked in a sharp breath at Georgiana's name. They probably recognized her connection to the Dragon Sage. Hard to predict precisely what that meant, though.

Greetings complete, the company broke into conversational clusters. Miss Sempil and Miss Barton—dressed in pale green and hailing from Derby. Her father had a modest estate and kept a wyvern; she was here to improve her attitude towards dragons, or so Miss Sempil said—drew Georgiana away to a small card table in the far corner.

"There are only three of them this term." Miss Barton glanced back at the dragons. Her drab brown hair seemed in keeping with her square, sturdy figure, giving her the look of a milkmaid more than a young lady of the gentry.

"Perhaps you will not be burdened with a partner this time, Annabelle. You have already done your duty." Miss Sempil sniggered.

"One can only hope." Miss Barton offered a well-practiced, long-suffering sigh.

"What is it like, having a dragon student partner?" Georgiana asked.

"Dull, dreadful, and drowning." Miss Barton muttered. "There is no getting away from them. They are at your shoulder all day and half the night. If you are lucky, she will leave you alone when you are sleeping. If not, you might find a dragon-musky pallet dragged into your room and a snoring dragon to keep you up at night."

"Whatever for?"

"Apparently, dragon companions are often wanted for trouble-some Blue Order daughters, the kind who cannot be trusted not to run away with some unsavory fellow. Such charges must be guarded every moment of the day, and some of the dragons like to practice that." Miss Sempil said behind her hand.

"I've heard some girls can be stupid enough to be talked into elop-ing without proper marriage articles in place. Dragons or no, I would never risk my future on an elopement." Miss Barton sneered.

Georgiana's face burned. There was no way these girls could know her history. Besides, she most certainly had never intended to run off with Mr. Oakley. A spot of fun sneaking into the Cotillion, yes. It was dreadfully unfair for Fitzwilliam to deny her the Cotillion. But running off to Gretna Green? No, absolutely not! Even if he preferred hibernating dragons, a Dragon Keeper like Mr. Oakley was most assuredly not the sort of man she wanted to marry.

"It was not really so bad with my partner Autumn last term. Gale told me to make a game of it to see if I could sneak away from my companion. All told, it was rather fun to try to do so. I managed it twice before my partner learned to watch carefully enough. She was so embarrassed by her failures. I would not mind doing that again." Miss Sempil winked.

That did sound rather amusing. It would be an interesting turn of the tables to demonstrate a dragon's flaws for once, instead of having all her own pointed out.

"Do you think Mr. Elkins will excuse you from further lessons on the pianoforte?" Miss Barton nudged Georgiana's elbow.

"I made such a hash of it, I think not. I place the blame squarely on the new dragons." Georgiana jerked her head toward them. "I am quite put out, and I will not be dissuaded from my resentment of them."

"I am most sorry to hear that."

Georgiana jumped and turned to look over her shoulder. Where had Gale come from?

"Oh, I, excuse me, I did not mean that—"

"You meant exactly that. You just did not mean it for my ears." Gale stared down at Georgiana. "A lesson you will soon learn is that no spoken word is truly safe. Nor is any written one. If you want something kept truly private, it needs to remain in the confines of your own heart. Once released, you never know with whom it might end up, warm-blooded or cold. If not with dragons, there are always servants."

Georgiana winced. Had Gale heard of her letters to her aunts, too? "You are, of course, correct."

Gale's brow ridge lifted high, and she cocked her head. Grudging approval, perhaps?

"I have been sent to invite the three of you to join in a game of hot cockles."

Hot cockles? Certainly not. Parlor games were rather horrible and… the look on Gale's face made it clear: "no" was not an acceptable answer.

Georgiana followed Miss Sempil and Miss Barton back to the rest of the group near the fireplace. Her only hope now was to blend into the background and avoid notice.

All the students, dragon and human, formed a loose ring around a single wooden chair. Miss Withington sat down and beckoned Miss Barton to take a dark-colored scarf and sit at her feet. Blindfold tied, Miss Barton placed her head in Miss Withington's lap.

Miss Sempil pressed her finger to her lips, tiptoed to Miss Barton, and tapped her shoulder.

"Miss Darcy?" Miss Barton said.

"No, try again." Miss Withington laughed. Pointing with her chin, she indicated one of the new dragons, Quicksilver, and the short, dark-haired girl in dark blue—was that Miss Grant?—standing next to her. They both crept up on Miss Barton. Then Quicksilver touched her, but the girl ran away.

Clever ruse.

"Miss Grant?"

"Not me!" she giggled.

Miss Withington prompted Bede and Coxcomb, the other two new dragons, to converge on Miss Barton while the rest of the group marched in place. Clearly, this was a favorite game.

"Gale?"

"Not I."

Miss Withington signaled Georgiana, who tiptoed around to the opposite side and barely tapped Miss Barton.

"I know that perfume! That is definitely Miss Darcy!"

"Correct!" the entire group cried, clapping as though they were pleased with Georgiana's defeat.

No, that probably was too personal an interpretation, but it certainly felt true.

Miss Barton rose and untied the blindfold. "Your turn."

No, how utterly dreadful! This is why she avoided playing parlor games. They were just an excuse to make fun of others. Now everyone was going to stare and laugh at her. How mortifying!

Miss Withington helped her tie the scarf and settle into place.

What kindness! Miss Withington had left a tiny gap in the blindfold. Georgiana need not be stuck in the middle forever. She could decide how long to endure the torment. Yes, it was typical in such games to do so, but somehow it was touching that Miss Withington would have offered such mercy. Perhaps this could be a spot of fun, after all.

The first tap on her shoulder she recognized immediately. The sharp fingernail must belong to the mousy girl who liked to sew and always caught her nail on the fabric. Bless it all. What was her name? Miss Reed? Perhaps it was just as well that Georgiana was unsure of the name. It would ruin the fun if she guessed too quickly. "Miss Sempil?"

"Not me!"

Two sets of feet approached right and left. The slipper on the left belonged to Miss Barton, whose name she called when her left shoulder was tapped. But apparently, it was the girl on her right who tapped her shoulder.

Dragon feet neared, white, with black speckles. A human-feeling tap on her shoulder, but no girl's feet could be seen. "Bede!"

"Yes!" Miss Withington laughed as she helped Georgiana stand.

Georgiana smoothed her skirts and breathed a discreet sigh. She had done her duty to her company and now she was free.

Bede stood on hind feet and worried her front paws together. The top of her head reached Georgiana's shoulder as the drake looked up at her. "I do not understand."

"What do you mean, Bede?" Miss Withington asked. "I know this is the first time you have played this game, but I thought you understood the rules of play."

"I thought the object of this amusement was to guess without the use of all one's senses." Was that a remonstrative look Bede cast Georgiana's way?

"Yes, that is why the blindfold is used."

"But it was not tied properly. The young lady could still see."

Georgiana's face colored painfully.

"Well, the blindfold can be imperfect."

"Then the correct thing to do would have been for her to confess the issue and to retie the scarf, or perhaps just to close her eyes."

"I suppose, but—"

"Is cheating to be expected in all games warm-bloods play?"

Cheating? How dare that awful little dragon accuse her of cheating? Darcys did not cheat! How insulting that it could even be considered! much less spoken aloud! No wagers were made on this game. It was only in good fun, exactly what was expected in every drawing room—

"Students, pray grant me your attention. Come join me." Mrs. Fieldings called from the center of the room.

Georgiana lagged behind with Miss Withington as the girls made their way to Mrs. Fieldings.

Miss Withington leaned close and whispered, "Do not feel bad about what she said. Do not take it to heart. No one thinks you are a cheat. Though it was tactless of her, do remember that dragons often have a challenging time understanding—"

"Why are you making excuses for her? Had a warm-blooded student said that, she would have been reprimanded for making accusations. Why not Bede? Why do the dragons get special privileges that always mean I am slighted?" It was difficult to keep her voice down when her heart pounded loud enough to drown it out.

"I am sorry you feel that way. But it is not intended, of that I am certain. Perhaps you have a certain prejudice of your own in how you see them."

"If you had spent your life slighted because there were dragons to be attended, then perhaps you would understand."

"Perhaps I would, I grant you. It is more often the case that dragons are ignored in a home or on an estate, so that is what I am familiar with."

"I find it difficult to believe."

"Perhaps as difficult as your own situation is to believe." Miss Withington raised an eyebrow and walked on.

Even if it were difficult to believe, that did not make Georgiana's experience any less true or real. Did it? She sniffled softly and took a place at the back of the loose ring around Mrs. Fieldings and Gale near the fireplace.

"Now, for the part of the evening I have most looked forward to. It is time to announce who has received the privilege of student partnerships this term. Those of you chosen will embark upon a unique and instructive exercise in your education, an exercise in the sort of partnerships fundamental to the Blue Order way of life. I cannot stress enough the honor conferred in being selected. Step forward when I call your name. Miss Withington, Miss Grant, and Miss Darcy."

Could she have heard that correctly? Her name was called?

The three dragon students drew close to Mrs. Fieldings. "Quicksilver, you shall be with Miss Grant. Coxcomb, with Miss Darcy—"

Yes, relief! With her dainty face and long eyelashes, Coxcomb's disposition seemed gentle. Pax liked her well enough. Perhaps this might be tolerable...

"—and Bede—"

"Pray, Mrs. Fieldings," Bede waved a front paw, then returned to worrying them together.

"Yes, Bede?"

"I know I do not have the dominance to make such a request, but may I make one even so?"

"I will listen." Mrs. Fieldings nodded, some tension in her lips.

Gale bared her fangs just the slightest bit. Interesting, and a mite unexpected.

"May I please be paired with someone else?"

Miss Withington gasped, her posture becoming rigid.

"Do you find fault with the student I have selected?" Mrs. Fieldings crossed her arms over her chest, pulling back her shoulders to stand a little taller, a little broader.

"No, madam. I just thought, perhaps... I would very much like to work with Miss Darcy."

6
Chapter

May 15, 1815

FIVE DAYS! FIVE DAYS of Bede at her heels, shadowing every foot-step, questioning her every move, demanding explanations and justi-fications for everything, and now this? It was not to be borne!

Georgiana glanced around at the shambles her room had become. The neat order and tidiness that had made it a cozy haven of peace, overturned in a flurry of new furniture and rearranging. None of it at her request! A bookcase with "appropriate volumes for study" borrowed from the library; a larger desk and a second chair; a standing desk so Bede could "study with her"; all this she had accepted with as much grace and goodwill as she could muster. Even the pungent smell of Bede's unique dragon musk she had tolerated with forced goodwill. But this? Now Bede had gone too far.

Georgiana grabbed the half-size, chaff-filled mattress tick, wrestling it out of Bede's paws. "No! No more. I will not tolerate it."

"But what will I sleep upon?"

"The platform in your own lair! Your accommodations in the dragon tower are more than adequate. There is simply no need for you to move into my chamber."

"But how else am I to come to understand how a young lady of quality lives?"

"The same way the other companion-dragon students do. Not by invading my chambers and making yourself at home without so much as a 'by your leave, Miss.'" Georgiana threw the mattress into the hall and slammed the door.

"But it is to be a part of my education. How else can I learn how to prevent a recalcitrant hatchling from escaping her parent's dominance but by preventing you from doing so?"

"In the first place, my parents are dead. They have no dominance—"

"Your guardians, then, whoever has dominance over you." Bede's eerie red eyes bulged.

"And in the second place, on what grounds do you believe I would try to escape this place? Auntie, my assigned companion, does not believe so. She gave me leave to walk the school grounds and even go into town without her watch. I certainly do not deserve such scrutiny from you. Now get out!"

Bede stood tall, puffed her chest, and inflated her throat pouch, which matched her scarlet eyes. Was she mimicking Quicksilver now? "I do not offer you a choice, Georgiana—"

Georgiana stomped three steps, nose to nose with Bede. "Miss Darcy! I have not given you leave to call me by my Christian name!"

"But you are not dominant. Therefore—"

"How have you come to that conclusion? I do not accept your dominance. Not under any circumstance!" She stepped forward, pulling back her shoulders and rising to tiptoe, as she forced Bede back.

Georgiana's door flew open and Miss Withington pushed her way in, a flurry of pale-green muslin and good manners. "Bede, stand down. You are not the dominant here."

"You should not intrude in a confrontation outside your own range." Bede hissed and snapped as she darted around Georgiana toward Miss Withington.

"As head girl, this is my territory. You are infringing upon it. This is your last warning. Stand down. Return to your lair in the dragon tower at once!" Miss Withington stamped and looked ready to spit.

Bede stared at her for a moment, dropped to all fours, and scrabbled out with a peculiar pacing gait that appeared natural on horses but comical when done by a dragon, especially one so low to the floor.

Miss Withington closed the door softly.

"I will not have it! I cannot!" Georgiana whispered, trembling. She slowly collapsed on the edge of her rumpled bed, face in her hands. "She is utterly impossible. Coxcomb, I could have managed. At least she is polite and even good company at times. But this? Bede is too much."

Miss Withington sat down beside her and laid a gentle hand on her shoulder. "For the little that it is worth, I could not have tolerated Bede as a student partner either, and this is after several training partners in my tenure here. I have never encountered a dragon like her. All my other partners were sympathetic and polite, even if stubborn. I wonder that Gale approved her for admission to her training program."

"I wonder to whom she is connected. If she were warm-blooded, that would be the most likely way she would have gotten into a position where she did not belong."

Three sharp raps and the door opened just enough to admit Mrs. Fieldings. In her severe, deep-blue headmistress dress and with dark hair pulled back to match, her dark expression was more somber than usual.

Georgiana and Miss Withington jumped to their feet and curtsied. Weak knees did not make for a graceful gesture.

"I do not suppose you are surprised to hear Bede has come to me with yet another complaint." Mrs. Fieldings clasped her arms loosely across her waist.

"Yet another?" Miss Withington winced.

"I am afraid so. She seems to believe that you, Miss Darcy, are willfully interfering in her training and refusing to provide her with the necessary experiences for her to succeed as a companion."

Georgiana drew breath to fuel many, many words, but clamped her jaw shut. Who was it who had advised her to count to ten before she spoke? "With respect, Mrs. Fieldings, you often say there are at least two sides to any story."

"Would you care to present me with yours?"

She actually wanted to hear it? Georgiana's eyes widened. "Yes, madam, if I may."

"Pray, sit down and explain." Mrs. Fieldings gestured toward the bed.

Georgiana perched on the edge of the slightly lumpy, flock-filled mattress, hands braced to steady her. "It is my understanding that we are not required to share a room with our training partner. Have I violated the school's rules and now require constant oversight?"

"No, you have not, Miss Darcy. There is, though, an element of a companion's education—"

"As I understand it, that is a limited exercise which is agreed upon by both parties, not demanded or enforced."

"Your understanding is correct." Mrs. Fieldings clasped her hands behind her back.

"If I may, Mrs. Fieldings," Miss Withington took half a step forward. "I know I am not involved in the matter, but having had several training partners, I think I possess some insight here. It is quite clear to me that Bede is not nearly at the point in her training for such an exercise. She does not yet understand young ladies well enough to actually discern the difference between an escape attempt and sneaking into the kitchen in a late-night jaunt to sate the stomach wyrms. What good is there in forcing Miss Darcy to endure the consequences of such errors, especially since Auntie has permitted her all the privileges of a trustworthy student? It seems like a decidedly poor way to reward that achievement."

"It is a privilege to be part of a companion-dragon's training."

"Assuming things go well, as you are apt to say, Mrs. Fieldings." Such boldness from Miss Withington! "Miss Darcy's experience with dragons has not been an easy one. Bede's temper and character are so... so... different from those who are usually in service as companions. To be frank, on the best of days she is quite off-putting, and to leave Miss Darcy with no respite from her difficult ways would hinder Miss Darcy's progress at best, and at worst—well, I would prefer not to speak of that."

What was that? Had the head girl actually taken her side in an issue with a dragon? Such support, even praise, in an odd, sideways sort of fashion, but praise nonetheless!

Georgiana clutched handfuls of the coverlet in tense fingers. "Pray, forgive my question, Mrs. Fieldings, but why would Bede insist upon being paired with me when Miss Withington is an experienced training partner and so much better suited for the task?"

Mrs. Fieldings pressed her lips into three different frowns before settling on the one best fitting the occasion. "I believe she thought, because of your family connections, that you would be the most dominant student in our academy."

"What gave her the standing to make such a request? She does not seem to be the dominant dragon amongst Gale's students this term," Miss Withington asked.

"I believe she thought, assuming things went well, the association with you would raise her low-ranking standing." The admission seemed to cost Mrs. Fieldings.

"I have been a pawn in a dragon dominance game?" The words came out in an angry squeak.

"It is no game, Miss Darcy, and you have been no pawn. Affiliation with you has already raised Bede's esteem amongst the other dragon students."

"Is that why you assigned her as my partner? To improve her standing?" Georgiana was on her feet before she realized it.

"No. I had hoped that Bede would become more tractable in a partnership that she had requested."

"Tractable is not a word I would use to describe her. Especially after she has driven Pax to distraction. Have you noticed how she is keeping to the bower in the dragon tower recently? Is it fair for my Friend to be driven away?" Georgiana swallowed hard. "Pray do not require me to share quarters with Bede as well. Being alone here is one of the few times I can be assured of Pax's company."

Mrs. Fieldings held up an open hand. "I will consult Gale's opinions on the matter. I will let you know my decision after Mica's salon, which I assume you both will attend?"

"Absolutely, Mrs. Fieldings. I look forward to it." Miss Withington looked genuinely excited as she cocked a warning eyebrow at Georgiana.

"Yes, madam, I will attend as well." At least it would offer a welcome respite from Bede's attentions.

The parlor door had been thrown wide open, allowing the soft hum of conversation to pour into the corridor. From the sound of it, a substantial group had already gathered inside. Miss Withington had not exaggerated the popularity of the event.

Georgiana swallowed hard. The crowd meant she would probably be required to say little, which would suit her well indeed.

"Mica—and do remember to say it 'Meeca'. She hates to be mixed up with the mineral, mica," Miss Withington laughed at her own joke, though it really was not very funny. "Mica usually begins the salon with tea and greetings, then poses a question which we are all to ponder and discuss. Do not hesitate to join the discussion. She really does welcome all points of view."

A nice sentiment, but one that probably would not stand when tested. Most overestimated their tolerance for unpopular opinions. Today would not be the day Georgiana tested anyone's tolerance.

Miss Withington led the way into the crowded parlor, plunging in to claim a space amidst the chatter. Georgiana lingered in the doorway. Loud, busy rooms were always disorienting, and she found it advisable to take a moment or two to plan the least obtrusive way to enter.

The two large windows that faced the front drive welcomed sunlight, filtered through a screen of wisteria blossoms, to fill the room. Slightly faded burgundy curtains attempted to keep the sunbeams in good order but failed, as shadows and sunlight danced across a disorderly mob of chairs and settees with cushions to match the curtains. For every place to sit, a small table bearing plates of biscuits and pitchers of some herbal water stood ready and within reach to provide refreshment, implying a level of relaxed merriment that made it easy to ignore the tired and dusty white-and-gold striped paper-hanging on the walls. Eight girls, six student dragons, two teachers, and Mercail, in all her white-feathered glory, paused their conversation to look at Georgiana as Pax and Berry twittered a greeting.

"Miss Darcy!" Mica, a tall, slender drake whose pinkish-sand color with lacy pattern on her face and shoulders reminded one of a lady hosting an afternoon tea in her finest half-dress gown, approached on two legs. Her teeth were particularly small, her fangs not pronounced like other dragons, making her smile far warmer and friendlier than any other dragon—save the fairy dragons, of course—Georgiana had known. "I am so glad you have joined us. Do come in. I reserved a seat for you next to me, in the hopes that you would attend."

"Oh, heavens. There is no need for that."

"Of course, there is." Mica looped her front paw in Georgiana's arm. "I am honored to receive you at my little gathering. I like to recognize all my first-time guests this way." She drew Georgiana in.

While the sentiment was pleasing, to be sure, unless Georgiana was behind a pianoforte, the front of the room was the last place she wanted to be. Especially when it meant she would be hemmed in on all sides by the student dragons, who were also at their first of Mica's salons.

As Georgiana sat down, Mica clapped her paws together. "Attention, attention, everyone."

The parlor stilled, and all eyes turned toward Mica's sweet voice—was it possible for a voice to sound like the wisteria smelt? Probably not, but somehow it seemed so.

"I would like to welcome all of you to my first salon of this school term. I hope that these gatherings will be as helpful and informative this term as the previous ones."

General sounds of assent resounded as girls and dragons found their seats.

"Please extend a special welcome to our first-time guests today," Mica gestured toward the seats nearest her and polite nods and soft words of welcome followed. "For their benefit, and our own, bear with me as I remind us all of why we are here and how we are to conduct ourselves." She waited until the room stilled. "Our purpose here is to explore the role of females, warm- and cold-blooded, in the Blue Order, especially how it might differ from that same role in the world at large. All questions are invited, with the understanding that oftentimes there might be few definitive answers. All discussion and opinions are welcome, but must remain decorous at all times, with respect given for all parties involved. No unkindness, shows of temper, or contests of dominance will be tolerated in this room and could result in the loss of attendance privileges, yes?" Her teeth showed a bit, suggesting she was serious about civility in her salon.

"Yes, Mica," the audience intoned, but the sentiment sounded sincere.

"With that out of the way, pray help yourselves to the chervil water and shortbread, both of which smell utterly delightful, even from here. We will begin today by considering a question brought up at the end of last term which we did not have an opportunity to properly reflect upon, something we have never considered before: the role of the female dragon both in the Blue Order and in dragon society at large."

Female dragons? Really? How unusual. The topic had never come up in Georgiana's hearing, but it was rather interesting.

With all the grace and poise of a society matron, Mica took a seat beside Georgiana. "As you know, unlike warm-bloods, whose female roles appear to be established more by the political and cultural dictates of geographical regions, for the female dragon, role is determined by type and species."

That made sense, or at least it seemed to.

Pax and Berry launched from the table, near where Mercail perched, and hovered mid-air.

"Yes. Pray. let us hear from our fairy dragon friends." Mica gestured at them.

"Amongst fairy dragons, there are three or four hens hatched for every cock." Berry twittered.

"Males are so rare. They must be shared if we are all to be able to bear a clutch." Pax added. "A young fairy dragon cock was instrumental in the recent rescue of the Sage. I know him. He is an admirable creature."

Georgiana blushed—in no other company would this conversation be considered proper for young ladies, much less those not yet "out" in society.

"I am sure he is," Berry snapped tartly, "but that would make him an exception to the rule. The males I have known are egotistical despots who would bring as many into their protection as they could whilst doing as little as possible for their care and comfort."

"Well, Phoenix has not gathered his first harem yet, so I do not truly know how he will behave then."

"Perhaps his connection to the Sage will make him more tolerable." Berry tilted her head in a rather conciliatory way and flew a lopsided circle around Pax.

"Are your ties to the male permanent, like marriage?" Miss Grant, Quicksilver's plain and sensible partner, asked.

"An excellent question. Berry? Pax?" Mica smiled broadly. Even without bared teeth, the expression remained a bit disconcerting.

"A harem does not represent a legal binding to a male, if that is what you mean," Berry returned to hover at Pax's side.

"It is more a matter of who he can convince to stay with him because of the territory he claims and his own qualities that would produce strong chicks that keep a harem with him," Pax added.

"In the wild, few chicks survive their first year. Many eggs must hatch in order for even a few to fledge into maturity." Berry's head and tail drooped.

So high a mortality rate? How tragic. All the hatchlings from Phoenix's and Pax's clutches had survived and thrived. Not even the bestiaries Elizabeth had recommended mentioned such grim realities for the dear sweet dragons.

"What happens if a hen wants to leave?" Miss Barton, a dumpy girl with a generally whiny attitude, asked.

Berry flew higher over the girls' heads. "It depends on the male and the size of a harem. In a small one, it is more difficult to leave, especially if the male's dominance in an area might be threatened by the loss of the females. If the harem is large, then she might slip away relatively unnoticed. Particularly if the hens are the squabbling sort. He might spend so much time trying to keep them from pecking each other's eyes out that he might not notice her departure."

"How do so many females in the same space get along?" Miss Sempil glanced at Miss Barton and Miss Grant, who had had more than their fair share of squabbles even in the short time Georgiana had been there.

"It depends on the personalities." Pax sang a few calming notes. "There is usually one leading hen and the others rank below her. Her temperament generally determines how congenial the relations are."

"And what role do females play in the society of fairy dragons?" Miss Bamber, who looked more like one of the upper students than the needlework teacher, seemed utterly fascinated.

"The males hold the territory, but the females are called upon to help defend it." Pax seemed uncomfortable with the notion. "If a male cannot attract strong hens that help him hold his boundaries, it will not be his for very long. If another male takes it, then the harem will probably choose to follow the stronger male."

Georgiana stared at Pax. What sort of life was that? Continually fighting for one's home, uncertain who the master of the territory would be tomorrow. What else did Georgiana not know about her little Friend's world?

"And the chicks? How are they cared for?" Miss Bamber asked.

"Eggs that are laid in the communal nest are cared for by all the dragons of the group, which is particularly helpful when hatching hunger is at its peak. Some prefer their own nest, and in that case, they are responsible for their own chicks. Only the strongest and the most foolish reject the harem's assistance," Berry said.

What did Pax expect for her future? Would she join a harem, like April, her brood mother, did? Even if just temporarily, it would be difficult to lose her companionship.

"Mercail, I believe you are in a unique position to help us understand." Mica turned to the glorious white queen fairy dragon. "How does this differ from the role of the cockatrix?"

"My experience with cockatrix is somewhat more expansive than the average fairy dragon's, since some cockatrix persuade warm-bloods that they are the same sort of pigeon that my own species prefers to use in persuasion," Mercail managed a sweet laughing sound. "While male fairy dragons are uncommon, it is the female cockatrice, the cockatrix, who tends to be rare. In general, there are three males to every female; and that is after you consider the young, foolish males who get themselves killed in their quests for dominance. The lesser cockatrix, whom you might not even recognize as a cockatrix for her plainness, outnumbers the spectacular greater cockatrix by a similar ratio. So, the males must compete to court the greater females, convincing them they are best suited to father offspring, establishing extensive boundaries and bearing gifts to prove the point. The greater cockatrix has the upper wing, as it were, in negotiations, and since mating pairs do not live together after a chick has fledged, she is free to choose another mate or not, as she wishes."

"What about territory? Does she hold her own territory?" Miss Withington scribbled something in a small notebook.

Were they supposed to be taking notes during the salon?

"Absolutely; a cockatrix holds her own territory, and it remains hers even after she chooses a mate. Males will occasionally concede part of theirs to her as a means of courting." Mercail gestured for Pax and Berry to perch beside her again.

A female could hold property on her own? How interesting. It did explain a great deal about Aunt Catherine's Friend, Cait, though. They were quite similar in many respects, come to think of it. Aunt Catherine had never remarried after Sir Lewis' death. Aunt Matlock thought Aunt Catherine chose solitary widowhood so she could maintain control of her own fortune, rather than sign it all over to a new husband once the marriage lines were written.

"These tendencies contrast with those of most minor wyrms, who mate for life and share territory as a cluster. We minor drakes," Mica gestured at herself and the student dragons, "often live in communities, with pairs together maintaining territory within that community. Individual females, if strong enough, may hold their own territory if they do not wish to share it with a mate. Those who cannot hold their own, male or female, may share the communal asset, but enjoy only minimal status in the community."

"Is it different for major dragons?" The words slipped out before Georgiana could stop them. It was a fascinating, if frank, discussion.

Brilliant-blue Quicksilver puffed her throat pouch slightly, a red flush rapidly spreading across her face down to her shoulders. "Major dragons of all types are large predators and require substantial lands to supply their needs. The land can only support a few major dragons, so they do not mate nearly so often as we minor dragons, and rarely for life. Consequently, they tend to be solitary creatures, with females holding territory and establishing dominance much like the males."

"Dominance is a key factor in most dragon interactions, one which many warm-blooded members of the Blue Order, especially the female ones, underestimate." Mica's brow ridge rose just so.

"We do not vie for dominance like dragons; how are we to understand it accurately?" What was that ginger student's name? Stay, Stone... no, it was Sweet, Miss Sweet. Ginger-sweets, that was how Georgiana would remember it!

"No, no, I am certain that is not the case at all. You must be quite mistaken." Bede stood, chest puffed, which looked silly and exaggerated on her slender form. "What I would like to know is if dominance is established among warm-blooded females differently than among dragons?" She rose on her toes, trying to look big again.

Georgiana sighed softly.

"Ladies do not squabble for dominance like dragons do." Miss Sempil adjusted her sleeves and tossed her blonde curls with a huff.

"What say you to that, Miss Darcy?" Mica asked.

She gasped and pressed a hand to her chest. "Pray, excuse me, but what would I know of that?"

"As I understand, you were lately in London, and are familiar with the Cotillion board, who are some of the highest-ranking warm-blooded females in the Blue Order. What can you tell us about their dominance structures?"

Merciful heavens! What did Mica know of her time in London? "They... they... I think they would not consider dominance at all. They look at one's rank in society."

"But what is that rank based on?" Bede widened her stance and folded her forelegs across her chest.

"One's birth, one's connections."

"Are not the wealth and territory a family holds part of that consideration?"

"Yes, that is part of social rank."

"Is that not essentially hoarding and holding territory?" Bede lifted her snout high.

"I think they are noticeably different."

"But how?" Bede's taloned toes scratched at the faded carpet.

Georgiana's face grew fiery as she stammered. "I think... I mean, it would seem to me that hoarding is rather a different thing than gathering wealth. As I understand hoarding—"

"What do you know about hoarding?" Bede clapped her jaws like a judge banging his gavel.

Oh, that was too much. Such cheek was not to be borne.

Georgiana slowly stood. "Quincy, a hoarding puck, is the butler's Friend at my aunt's estate. He hoards buttons. He would steal them off my gowns when I would visit. My brother would bring buttons specifically for Quincy so that he would not ruin our clothes." The room tittered. "And there is a puck on staff at Pemberley who hoards paper. Part of the written contract with her includes what paper she may hoard and how she may acquire it. I have seen rather a lot of hoarding behavior and hoarding hunger and hoarding ecstasy."

Pax trumpeted a shrill note of agreement. She and Quincy often squabbled over Georgiana's buttons.

"There are dragons on staff at Pemberley?" Miss Sweet's green eyes grew wide. "Is the paper-hoarding puck a Friend of one of the Staff or there on her own?"

"Is it usual for dragons to work at estates?" Miss Sempil asked.

"Those are all excellent questions." Mica raised her forepaws. "But let us hold them off for another afternoon and stay the course we have begun. I believe the question was regarding hoards and how that parallels the accumulation of wealth among warm-bloods—"

"And how that relates to dominance." Bede finished for her. "I believe you just made my point. Hoarding of wealth is part of the dominance display among warm-bloods."

"Humans do not display hoarding hunger or hoarding ecstasy, which is much like what an opium-eater craves. At least that is how the Dragon Sage explained it to me. I must maintain that seeking wealth is inherently different. The warm-blooded do not fight for dominance like dragons do."

"Oh, yes, you do." Bede took several steps toward Georgiana.

"We do not puff up and snarl and hold heads above each other to determine who is better and stronger among us."

"Of course you do. I have watched that happen many times."

"I have no idea what you mean." Georgiana turned her face aside, but Bede sidled into her line of sight.

"All human females do it when they enter a room." Bede turned to the rest of the students. "All of you do it, every single one of you, teachers, students, all of you. You preen and primp and display your hair and your gowns and your finery to show your dominance, just like greater cockatrix to a lesser cockatrix. You snap and snarl and backbite to prove who is over whom. I have even heard females plot against each other to establish dominance. It is all so very clear. The problem is that none of you can recognize it. I think it altogether deceptive and disingenuous."

A collective gasp rose. The other dragon-students pulled their chairs back, away from Bede, teeth bared and low growls rumbling in their throats. Mercail began a soothing song. Pax and Berry joined in.

Georgiana trembled, but that was not fear. No, it was anger. Good sense dictated she jump back to join the others, but enough was enough. She would stand her ground.

"Bede! That is enough." Mica interposed herself between them. "Whether your argument has merit or not, your incivility just violated the fundamental rules of our salon here. I must ask you to hold your peace." Mica's sandy-pink scales flushed deeper and darker, almost the color of dried blood, and white rings appeared around the dark of her eyes, as though her sweetness were being shed and a new creature standing in her place.

"I do not understand. How is it that honestly examining the warm-blooded condition is so wrong or so forbidden? We have examined the state of dragon society with quite unbridled scrutiny, and yet the same courtesy is not extended to us dragons seeking to interpret humans? Is that not hypocrisy?"

"That is unfair!" Georgiana snapped.

"Dragon society was criticized and its members were not referred to with respect. How is this any different?"

"Honest examination is hardly the same thing as badgering and belaboring your point until all are too weary to disagree." Georgiana slipped half a step closer.

Mica held her front paws over her head and clapped several times. "That is quite enough, Bede. You must leave the salon. We will discuss later the terms under which you might return, if you are ever allowed to do so again."

Bede grumbled deep in her throat, lowered her head, dropped to all fours, and scrabbled out of the parlor.

7

Chapter

May 22, 1815

FOLLOWING MICA'S MEMORABLE SALON, Mrs. Fieldings and Gale agreed that Bede's request to share Georgiana's quarters was ill-advised. An excellent turn of events, considering sharing a chamber with Bede might have been the very thing to push Georgiana into running away after all. At times like this, it seemed Mrs. Fieldings really knew her job.

Gale, Mica, and Mercail assigned Bede several remedial assignments related to her outburst during the salon. Which, naturally, she loudly bemoaned as unfair, since the same tasks were not given to Georgiana. Gloating was not considered ladylike or polite, but it was difficult to refrain, given the circumstances. But Georgiana put forth the required effort to demonstrate appropriate decorum during the entire episode. One would never regret ladylike behavior—or so Aunt Matlock insisted.

It was not entirely proper to be so relieved to be free of Bede's company, but there it was. Georgiana could hardly change her feelings about the matter, nor the quiet satisfaction that came from seeing the rude, unmannerly dragon dealt with in a fair and appropriate fashion.

A few days of rain followed, trapping everyone inside, fraying nerves and shortening tempers. Bede's fall from favor left all the dragon students and several of the staff dragons edgy and looking over their shoulders, probably wondering if they would all end up paying for Bede's transgressions. Even Pax and Berry seemed nervous, though they had nothing to do with Bede.

Despite Georgiana's and Miss Withington's reassurances, they were spending more time in the dragon tower now, in Mercail's soothing presence. It was difficult not to be a little jealous, both of the hours Pax spent with Mercail and of Pax having the sort of motherly mentor that Georgiana would have liked to have herself.

Georgiana buttoned her dark-pink spencer and pushed open the heavy front door. It shut softly behind her as she stepped out and drew a deep breath. Wisteria perfumed the late-spring breeze with hints of green, mud puddles, and a touch of sheep riding on the wind. What was it about the air after a rain that made it so appealing?

Sun peeked through clouds and dappled the path that circled Ebbing and Flowing Well before turning toward Chapel-en-le-Frith. Not quite the pleasing, shaded, and far more private footpaths of Pemberley, but fresh air and freedom were not things to complain about. Better yet, fluffy white Pax flew twittering circles overhead, her spirits sufficiently raised to be acting like herself once again, finally.

"Might we join you for your walk?" Miss Withington and Cox-comb, the gentle-tempered, pretty drake with long eyelashes, hurried out to join her.

"If you are up to a long walk, I would enjoy the company. I have just finished the required essay on the history of the Accords and the historical relevance of Dewi's exclusion of minor dragons in their earliest forms of the documents. Pax and I desperately need fresh air and an ample stretch of legs and wings."

"Indeed, we are. For all its books and knowledge, the library is cramped and stuffy, with little room to fly, few good places to perch, and nothing soft!" Pax warbled as she lit on Georgiana's shoulder.

Berry zipped out from behind Coxcomb and into the conversation. "We should petition Gale or Mercail to add a basket to the library."

"That would be a splendid idea. For now, though, I should like some fresh nectar. The highest blossoms on the wisteria are especially sweet in the sun. We should enjoy them while they are still available!" Pax launched and beckoned Berry to join her aerial swoops and swirls overhead.

"May we join in your pursuit of fresh air?" Quicksilver's vivid blue face appeared over Coxcomb's shoulder, with short, sensible Miss Grant not far behind. Where had they come from?

"I hope you do not mind a little more company." Miss Grant said, rather wistfully, though her brown walking dress and matching spencer suggested she had expected to walk, regardless.

"We shall be a merry party. Come, let us not waste another moment of this fine weather. The rain is so fickle, it could return at any time." Georgiana offered an arm to each human companion, and they set off.

Though a solitary walk, full of quiet reflection and contemplation, had been her first desire, perhaps, all things considered, this would not be entirely disagreeable. Coxcomb and Quicksilver's company had become far more tolerable over the past week. Who would have thought companion-dragons might be so sympathetic to her feelings about Bede? Miss Withington had become less of an acquaintance and more of a friend recently. The first real friend of her own age Georgiana had ever had. There was something a little sad in that. Even sensible Miss Grant's company had become increasingly satisfactory, even though she resembled Mrs. Collins in her attention to rather pedantic details.

"Now that the dreadful essay is complete, will Mrs. Fieldings keep her promise and allow us to plan an actual dinner party?" Miss Grant asked.

Georgiana lifted her nose and looked down at Miss Grant, pinching her voice into a parody of Mrs. Fieldings'. "Remember, it is not a real dinner party, but a limited social occasion intended to give us the experience of having planned such an event without losing sight of the fact that none of us are out. So, no eligible young men, or even any young people at all, will attend from the neighborhood. Only respectable, mature, Blue Order members of whom our families have already approved."

Miss Grant giggled. "I do not care if it is not a real dinner party as long as it is something other than this dreadful book work and essay writing!"

"Remember, we have not yet read our work aloud to one another and Mica has not conducted the requisite discussion over all the points made and missed in the essays." Miss Withington said with a small sigh.

"We are not done with the assignment?" Georgiana tried not to whine with little success.

"An assignment is never done until it has been talked to death." Miss Grant whispered behind her hand, as though someone might overhear.

"I do not grasp the human penchant for so much talk." Quicksilver swallowed back a small snarl. "It seems to take a great deal of time to accomplish very little."

"It would be so much more straightforward if they would simply state the correct answer, fact, or opinion and get on with things." What a powerful statement for the normally soft-spoken Coxcomb. "You will not find dragons discussing a thing to death."

Miss Withington pulled herself up ramrod straight, into a posture so much like Mrs. Fieldings that Georgiana had to look twice to be sure the headmistress had not suddenly appeared. "There is little to be gained in merely being told the correct answer. Such information is quickly dismissed in favor of what one experientially feels to be true. In order to learn, to change, to grow, one must experience new material, wrestle with ideas, live with the internal conflict, and resolve it within. That is the thing that will change you."

"Oh, heavens, you sound just like her." Miss Grant pressed her hands to her face.

"And do you believe that sentiment?" Quicksilver's wide eyes and gaping jaw were almost comical.

"That is a good question." Years fell from her shoulders as Miss Withington's posture returned to normal. "While I find it as dreary as you do, yes, I truly think there is something to be said for her methods. As I look back on it, I can hardly think the way I did when I first came. The world looks so different now. I am quite sure that I could never believe those old things again."

"One can only hope that Bede experiences such a transition." Quicksilver snorted and pawed the soft ground.

Georgiana gasped.

"I am sure Missus would not find that an appropriate comment," Coxcomb's voice masked a low hiss. "Gale has emphasized how important it is that we learn to curb our directness around the young ladies with whom we are in company."

Quicksilver's muscular blue tail lashed hard enough to brush Miss Grant's skirt. "That is one thing I will never understand about warm-bloods. Why must everything be so indirect that it is nearly impossible to discern? Are your constitutions so weak that you cannot tolerate truth? The slightest bit of clarity, of honesty, seems to send you all into a flutter."

"I believe it is considered being polite." Miss Grant raised an eyebrow to Quicksilver.

"How is making things less clear, pretending problems do not exist, polite?" Deep red bloomed at Quicksilver's cheeks and slowly crept across her face as her throat pouch swelled. "I was under the impression politeness should smooth interactions between warm-bloods, not make them more difficult and so fragile that a dragon must coddle them like hatchlings! Do you realize how difficult these displays of 'politeness' make it to respect all of you?"

"You do realize there are those warm-bloods who appreciate directness. Perhaps they are not the most common types, but they do exist. I have heard the Sage is exceedingly direct. Is that true, Miss Darcy?" Miss Withington asked.

Georgiana swallowed hard. Direct was the most politic way to put it. "Indeed, she is. As forthright as a dragon, in many cases."

"Do you not find that refreshing, so much easier to deal with than all the subtleties that could mean one thing in one situation and entirely another in yet a different one? And still another thing from each person who says or does something similar?" Quicksilver cocked her now brilliant red head so far to the side, she resembled a fairy dragon.

"That inquiry is too direct." Coxcomb slapped her tail on the ground.

"Perhaps it is, but it does not alter the fact that I would very much like an answer." Quicksilver puffed out her throat. Asserting dominance? Or just her right to ask an honest question?

"I do not mind answering." Georgiana drew a deep breath, a useful way to stall for time while gathering one's thoughts and words. "Be assured, I would not speak ill of someone so highly ranked as the Dragon Sage. And in fact, she herself would wish to answer you plainly, so I will endeavor to do so. The truth of the matter is that her directness does have unforeseen consequences. While she gets on well with dragons of all sorts, in my experience, those skills have hampered her ability to deal with other warm-bloods. Amongst our kind, she can be considered rather cold and unfeeling, even neglectful at times, especially when she does not attend to our expected social conventions."

"Indeed?" Quicksilver edged back several steps. "I expected her to be highly regarded for being able to bridge the gulf between dragons and warm-bloods."

"She is, by some." Just how much dare she, should she, explain? "But I do not think that trait is as widely admired among our kind as perhaps it should be."

"But you hold her in high regard, do you not?"

"She is my sister by marriage, my family."

"That did not answer the question." Quicksilver stepped forward again.

"It is the only answer I shall offer." Georgiana pulled her shoulders back and stood erect.

"That means you do not regard her as highly as we do." A soft growl rumbled in Quicksilver's throat.

"Quicksilver!" Coxcomb hissed and sidled between Georgiana and Quicksilver. "That is certainly enough. She offered you a truthful answer. It is disrespectful to press her thus. Pray forgive us, Miss Darcy. We are still trying to learn the fine points of these interactions."

Georgiana released a slow breath and relaxed her shoulders.

"They are difficult, are they not?" Miss Grant forced a smile, carefully not showing her teeth. "Learning to manage distinct personalities can be quite challenging, even among warm-bloods, and across species even more so. It seems you dragons handle that better amongst yourselves."

"Only because we have teeth." Quicksilver tried to smile, but only succeeded in looking menacing.

"I rather think a clear understanding of dominance helps us navigate those situations." Coxcomb scraped the back of her front paw across her jawbone in an expression similar to Miss Withington's.

"Knowing who has the right to bite whom makes things far clearer." Quicksilver nodded.

"How do you determine who has dominance over whom? To be honest, I should think wealth and social class are a much easier way to ascertain rank," Miss Grant asked.

Coxcomb snorted and shrugged. "Demonstrating strength and the willingness to use it is far easier to recognize than the intangibles you rely upon."

"Even then, though, there are those who refuse to acknowledge proper dominance. They always cause trouble, upset the order of things." Quicksilver glanced over her shoulder toward Bennetson Hall.

"Like Bede?" Bother! Georgiana had not intended to say that.

Quicksilver turned to Georgiana, eyes wide, jaw gaping. Throwing her head back, ruby throat pouch fully extended, she coughed out a chortle that sounded more like a strangled sheep than actual laughter.

But she was clearly laughing. "So, you can be direct when you wish to be. I knew you had it in you."

"That is a compliment, by the way, Miss Darcy," Coxcomb nodded with nervous rapidity.

"It was vulgar of me." Georgiana pressed hands to prickly, burning cheeks. "I pray you forgive me for saying such a thing and forget I said anything at all."

"Why should we do that?" Quicksilver laughed again. "It is an interesting question. I am sure every warm-blood—and cold-blood, for that matter—in the school has wondered about her."

Georgiana slipped back into line with the other girls and glanced from one to the other.

"Bede is rather different to every other dragon student." Miss Grant whispered as she shrugged.

"That she is. And we would all be glad for you to recall that and not apply your judgment of her to us." What a strong opinion Coxcomb had—how surprising.

"You find her objectionable?" Miss Withington asked.

"There you go, returning to your polite and concealed ways again."

Coxcomb mirrored her partner's posture. "Bede is rather a challenge to all the dragons of her acquaintance."

"How is it she came to be here, then? Is it not a privilege to attend this program? What's more, she does not seem disposed to being a suitable companion." Miss Grant rubbed her throat and looked aside.

The two dragons shared a glance and chittered something no one else could interpret.

"I am under the impression that she is a distant relation of Gale's," Coxcomb said.

"They look so different. I would not have expected that." Miss Grant's brow furrowed in thought.

"The family lines are rather confusing. Perhaps it is better described as more of a connection than a relation. She is part of a community that Gale's sire once led, before he left to serve the Order. Bede did some sort of favor for the new dominant dragon, and Gale was asked to repay the favor."

Clearly, there was more to the story than that. But it would be impolitic, though probably appropriately draconic, to ask.

"By taking Bede in as a student?" Miss Grant whispered.

"Essentially."

"Surely it could not be that simple, even for dragons." Miss Withington crossed her arms and pulled back her head slightly.

Quicksilver laughed and the back of her head turned red. "Well put, Miss Withington. You are correct. Bede was a problem for her community."

"So few dragons live in communities. What sort of problems come up?" Miss Withington asked.

Coxcomb glanced at Quicksilver and cleared her throat. "Dominance usually resolves matters fairly quickly. But Bede does not seem to comprehend dominance. I have never met a dragon more oblivious to the signals and more unwilling to abide by them."

"Under more typical circumstances, she would have been put out or simply eaten," Quicksilver muttered. "But she protected the dominant pair's eggs from a marauding band of hungry wyrms—stupid, foul creatures; they have their reputation for a reason. That earned Bede an unprecedented amount of tolerance. So instead of putting an end to the problem, as would usually have been the case, she was given an opportunity to make her way outside the community."

"Gale was supposed to ensure Bede's proper behavior..." Coxcomb's voice trailed off.

"That makes me glad we are not hosting an actual dinner party here, just going through the motions." Miss Grant still sounded unhappy about the matter.

Quicksilver sucked in a sharp breath and clapped her paw to her mouth.

"What have you heard? You must tell us." Miss Grant laid a hand on her partner's striking blue shoulder.

"They will figure it out on their own soon enough. They are hardly simpletons." Coxcomb looked away.

"There are, in fact, going to be important guests at the dinner?" Georgiana whispered.

"No young gentlemen, to be sure. None of you are out, but..." Quicksilver leaned closer and cupped her mouth with her paw, "I have heard you are to invite Blue Order landowners and well-to-do merchants from as far as Hazel Grove and Bakewell. I know as fact a number of them have sons in need of competent Blue Order wives."

8
Chapter

May 27, 1815

THAT EVENING AT DINNER, Mrs. Fieldings announced that the
essays on the Accords were 'adequate,' though they should expect
an extended discussion on the issue to continue into the following
week. Nonetheless, since all parents and guardians had given their
approval, the planning for the dinner party would commence immediately. That news raised a small cheer around the dining table. But the
most stimulating news came from a partial guest list. The names were
largely unfamiliar to Georgiana, but excited discussions after dinner
revealed a rather significant list of eligible connections related to the
guests—just as Quicksilver had revealed.

More evidence to prove Elizabeth's observations correct. No one
paid attention to what was said around dragons, and one never really
knew when a dragon might be listening to a conversation, so it always
behooved one to watch their words. Odd that Mrs. Fieldings was not
more cautious about that.

Unless she was and Quicksilver—no, that was not only uncharitable, but probably unfair as well. It was Bede who was the problem, not the others.

Would any of the guests have heard about the debacle at the Cotillion? That she was not presented, though she was to have been? Or was it possible that little Pemberley's presentation garnered so much attention, no one paid any notice to her? Could she be so lucky?

Perhaps Miss Barton would allow her to borrow her recently arrived editions of Mrs. Pendragon's scandal sheet—horrid publication though it was. If Georgiana did not appear in those columns, then it might be possible that her reputation was unscathed.

She pressed her hands to her cheeks. How could she ever show herself in public again if that were not the case, though?

It took three days for Miss Barton's parcel containing six weeks' worth of *La Gaucherie: Tales of the Blue Bloods of the First Order* to receive Mrs. Fieldings' approbation and finally reach Miss Barton. Another day passed before Georgiana could wrest the fateful pages out of Miss Barton's hands.

At last! She clutched the battered parcel to her chest and scurried to her room. She shut the door behind her, pulled her small wooden chair up to the neatly made bed, and spread out the issues on the coverlet, to be kissed by the sunlight, before she grabbed them up and sucked in every word like a drowning woman breaking the surface for air.

Great merciful heavens and dragon bones!

Talk about words fit to drive a dragon to distraction! Every detail couched in vagaries and innuendo. Tantalizing talk that did not easily give up identities, while it freely offered details of gowns and jewels, humiliations and speculations. There was little Pemberley on those pages, daughter of Lady R. And Elizabeth, the Lady D. But nothing about Elizabeth's sisters... nothing alluded to Georgiana at all. But perhaps in one of the later editions.

Slowly, the stack of volumes to be read dwindled.

Mrs. Pendragon required three volumes to contain the intrigues of the Cotillion. Apparently, an engagement was broken and a breach of promise suit pending, two betrothals announced, a dust-up between gentlemen ended before it came to fisticuffs by what seemed to be dragon intervention, and a knighthood awarded to someone who sounded much like Elizabeth's Uncle Gardiner.

But not a word about anyone who was supposed to have been presented and was not.

Georgiana collapsed in her chair and allowed her head to fall back. Was it possible her shame was not significant enough to have been splashed far and wide through the entire Blue Order membership? No doubt there was someone who knew, but here, so far removed from the intrigues of London, if Mrs. Pendragon did not carry the tale, no one else likely did, either.

Perhaps she could make a good impression upon those at the dinner. Her chances in the marriage mart were not ruined. She might still make a respectable home for herself, a family, and have those things she had always wanted. Mayhap this small start, a little country dinner party, could be the beginning of that.

Hot trails ran down her cheeks. Now she was simply being foolish. Did grown women weep when they weren't mentioned in the society pages? Certainly, they did not. But just this once, she would permit herself the luxury of her relief before she read every volume.

Dragging the back of her hand across her eyes, Georgiana opened the final remaining edition of Mrs. Pendragon. No!

She gasped as her lungs refused to draw breath. Her clenched hands trembled, wrinkling the paper to keep from dropping it.

Mr. O.

That had to be Mr. Oakley.

Mr. O. had met an untimely demise, thrown from his horse during an ill-advised race. His estate would be inherited by a Mr. P, whose excitement over his good fortune, and, of course, grief over the loss of his cousin, were obvious in equal measure to his friends and family.

Was Mr. Oakley actually dead? And if so, was that how he died? Or had he met his end in some judicial action prescribed by the Blue Order court? There was no way she would ever know. Nor was she sure she even wanted to.

Cold settled into her chest. She wrapped her arms around her ribs and shivered. All he had done was dislike Dragon Keeping, no? Surely that was his only real crime.

But Fitzwilliam and Richard had spoken of Mr. Oakley's association with the snapdragon symbol... and all that might mean. All the terrible, frightening things it might mean, things that seemed so much worse now than they had before. Maybe it was really true that he was a criminal. It seemed he had paid the price for it.

Was she guilty of contributing to his demise? Had it been her fault the Blue Order turned on him? He might not have been caught except for his risky visit to Darcy House the night of the Cotillion.

But then again, why was he really there? Had it only been for her, or were there other motives afoot? Motives associated with the snapdragons?

Certainly, if visiting her the night of the Cotillion were his only transgression, Fitzwilliam would not have turned him over to the Order. Though protective, Fitzwilliam was not entirely unreasonable. Even Mr. Oakley's bad Keeping would not have been enough—or so Richard insisted.

It was the association with the criminal snapdragons that was the issue. Poachers and smugglers, enemies to the Order, stealers and killers of dragons like Coxcomb and Quicksilver, who were becoming her friends, who treated her with respect and kindness. He was the sort of man who would harm them for profit.

She shuddered again. Cruel and ugly and heartless—how had she seen Mr. Oakley as anything else?

A soft knock at her door caught her attention. "Come in." She laid the scandal sheet aside and tried to arrange her features into something pleasing.

"It is time to go to the classroom and write out invitations," Miss Sempil said softly. "I feared you might be late, all distracted by Miss Barton's newspapers."

"Thank you, yes. I am coming." Mr. Oakley had made his choices.

Now she would make hers.

May 30, 1815

Three days later, Pax and Berry summoned Georgiana in from her walk in the garden just beyond the house, with the news that the upper students were to meet Mrs. Ramsbury in the classroom. Mrs. Ramsbury's lessons on writing were never particularly interesting; copying bits of letters from deportment books could hardly be called stimulating. But she permitted the girls to enjoy conversation as they wrote, so all in all, it was hardly as dreadful as it might have been.

Why had they been directed to the classroom now, though? Surely, there could not be more to write after all the invitations had been finished.

"She did not seem pleased," Pax twittered as she and Berry hovered over the sunny garden, on her way back to Bennetson Hall.

"Not at all. I thought I heard Gale grumbling as well." Berry wove through stately stalks of pink and purple delphiniums, chasing a few small, and apparently tasty, insects from the blossoms. "I could not make out anything about what bothered her, though."

"Were you invited to the conversation?" Georgiana asked.

"No, but neither was I eavesdropping." Berry swooped across her face.

Georgiana stopped short, nearly stumbling into the flowers. "Do be careful. I nearly ran into you."

"Do not accuse me of eavesdropping."

"I made no accusation. I merely asked."

"You can hardly fault me for hearing what was being said while I was minding my own business finding nectar in the garden." The saucy little berry-colored fairy dragon dove back into the lilac-colored blooms. Was she ignoring Georgiana or hiding from her?

"Perhaps not." Georgiana stopped and folded her arms across her chest. "Perhaps it is too much to expect you to demonstrate the maturity and decorum to remove yourself from such a situation when it becomes clear you are listening to something not intended for you."

"But they were intruding upon us! We were in the garden first, before they were in Gale's office." Pax landed on Georgiana's shoulder.

"True politeness—"

"Politeness to a dragon or a warm-blood?" Berry dove toward Georgiana's ear.

Oh, no. She was not having that! Covering her ears, she harrumphed a growly sort of sound that Gale used to get the fairy dragons' attention. "You do not think it impolite?"

Berry ceased her assault. "Gale should have closed the window if she did not want to be overheard. She did not; therefore, how were we to know we were not to listen to the conversation? She well knows there are fairy dragons in the house and in the garden. She is responsible for guarding her words."

"Pax, pray understand that while this may be appropriate to your kind, in any home with me or my family, it would be appreciated if you conduct yourself with greater self-control. That is how the Sage has trained the staff, and the family's behavior should be no less than that of the staff."

"If you do not approve of my behavior, then say so directly." Berry snorted and swooped.

What could have gotten into the normally sweet little fairy dragon? "I do not approve of your behavior. And while it may be tolerated here, should you ever find yourself in my territory, I would expect something more from you."

Berry squawked and zipped away.

"Do you think I hurt her feelings terribly?" Georgiana asked as they continued inside.

"No, she just recognized your dominance. It was exactly as I told her it would be. But I think she does not like you having a sort of dominance her Friend does not, even though she is head girl." Pax stroked her fluffy head against Georgiana's cheek. "I like that you are showing dominance."

Dominance? Georgiana was demonstrating dominance? What a very odd thought that was. Certainly not something she had ever intended to do, but it seemed right under the circumstances.

Plain, worn, long wooden tables and chairs filled the classroom, lit by bright sunlight, unfiltered by curtain or shade, their surfaces marked by generations of students past. Even the wisteria dared not droop across this window, lest stern schoolmistress Mrs. Ramsbury deem it inappropriate. A globe on a tall stand took up one corner near the front of the room, next to a low bookcase with maps and histories for classroom exercises. A sun-faded teacher's desk cut off the opposite corner at an angle, allowing its occupant to survey the room in a single glance. Without carpeting or curtains, sound bounced sharply throughout the space, making it feel occupied by many more than were actually in the room. Pax flittered to the windowsill to perch with Berry, where they could at least smell the wisteria, if not easily snack on its nectar.

"Where is Mrs. Ramsbury?" Miss Reed, a tall, willowy girl with a voice like a spring breeze, scanned the room as though eager not to be caught out of place.

"It is not like her to be late." Miss Sempil sat at her favorite table, a spot she guarded with draconic territorial instinct.

"No, she is usually very punctual." Miss Reed glanced over her shoulder.

That was an understatement. Mrs. Ramsbury rivaled Fitzwilliam in her love of punctuality, as the large mantel clock atop the desk testified.

And it was just as annoying in a woman as it was in a man.

"I hear someone approaching, and there are dragons with them!" Miss Barton, looking dumpier than usual in a brown and pumpkin-colored, roller-print gown that did not suit her at all, scurried into her seat near Miss Sempil, who turned aside and winced. Miss Barton was not her preferred desk mate.

Mrs. Ramsbury, stocky and blocky in what might well be a new, dark-blue gown—her favorite color, it seemed—swept in, looking more cross than usual. "Good afternoon, girls." Her voice was high and tight and displeased.

Gale stalked in behind her, her expression suggesting Berry had been accurate about what she had overheard. Bede, Coxcomb, and Quicksilver followed her in, heads down, tiptoeing so softly that even their talons did not make a sound on the hardwood floor.

Pax and Berry chirruped and went remarkably pouffy. Sensitive little creatures.

Bless it all! Georgiana perched on a chair at Miss Withington's table and they shared a quick glance. This would not be pleasant, whatever it was.

"Good afternoon, Mrs. Ramsbury. Good afternoon, Gale," the girls intoned as one.

Mrs. Ramsbury glanced at Gale, tight lines across her forehead, and nodded as she took her place behind her desk.

Gale, her dark-grey scales rather like pewter in the sunlight, scooted in front of the desk and cleared her throat. "As you girls know, my students are here to complete their education as companions for young ladies of the Blue Order. In light of your activity in planning for this dinner party, we have decided to take this opportunity for them to practice evaluating the accomplishments of young ladies. Companions are expected to assist a young woman in properly presenting herself to society. What better way to do that than in a setting designed to mimic the sort of activities a young lady would actually engage in?"

The student dragons were going to evaluate their work? Georgiana held her breath, but several of the others had far less success in stifling their groans. Pax and Berry flittered to their Friends' shoulders, protective and alert.

Dragon's blood!

Mrs. Ramsbury rapped on her desk with her knuckles. "None of that, girls. None of that. We should all embrace the opportunity for improvement, no matter whence it comes." The way she said that—she did not appear to approve of this interference in her classroom.

"Mrs. Ramsbury, Miss Bamber, Mr. Elkins, and Mica have all graciously agreed to allow my students access to this rare window into the lives of young ladies. We are most grateful." Gale smiled one of those particularly disturbing sorts of dragon smiles Georgiana would rather not see. Pax leaned in close to Georgiana's neck, her sharp toes prickling her shoulder. "To begin this exercise, my students have examined the invitations you girls penned and evaluated them against the standards for penmanship widely accepted among warm-blooded kind as the most accomplished."

Mrs. Ramsbury pulled a bundle of papers from her desk. The said invitations, no doubt.

"Whilst there are a few which attain acceptable standards, and may be posted, quite a few did not." Gale pulled back her shoulders and looked down her nose.

Mrs. Ramsbury's deepening frown suggested she did not agree with the assessment. Still, she held her peace. Was that her choice, or did Mrs. Fieldings insist upon it? Interesting.

And disquieting.

Gale distributed papers to the three student drakes. "As your name is called, please attend the one who calls it and you will receive a critique of your work with specific instruction on improvement."

Coxcomb stepped forward, head down, shoulders slumped. Not the posture of a dominant dragon at all. No, she was miserable in this situation. What was it Elizabeth said about such dragons? That one should handle them gently, for they were fragile in such a state. Poor creature.

"I limited my remarks to the contents of the invitations themselves. With respect, Miss Sweet, there was a word left out of your invitation, and it would seem most appropriate that it is rewritten."

Miss Sweet, the ginger-haired girl who lived up to her name, collected the invitation. Coxcomb pointed out what must be the missing word.

"Oh, gracious! Thank you, you have saved me no small amount of embarrassment!" Miss Sweet hurried back to her seat, cheeks the color of her hair.

Quicksilver stepped forward. "Like Coxcomb, I limited my remarks to matters of fact, not opinion." She cast a side-eyed glance at Bede. What a different sort of effect that expression had when one's eyes were affixed on the sides of one's face. "Miss Reed and Miss Barton, I have consulted two dictionaries, and they both agree. Each of your invitations includes errors in spelling. *The Polite Lady* suggests these are quite normal and natural in correspondence, but perhaps on a formal invitation requires correction."

Miss Reed and Miss Barton collected their work from Quicksilver, blushing as the misspellings were pointed out to them.

"I cannot believe I made such a mistake," Miss Reed whispered, palm pressed to reddening cheek.

"Thank you for granting us the opportunity to correct these," Miss Barton mumbled as she returned to her desk.

Bede stepped forward and cleared her throat, settling into a dominant posture that always signaled bad things from her. Pax and Berry flittered to the desk their Friends shared, pouffed a little larger and opened their wings. "The remainder of the invitations do not contain factual errors, as Quicksilver described them. I have striven to enhance your instruction by reviewing the manner in which the letters have been formed, the pleasingness of the penmanship that has been displayed."

Gale turned her face aside as though trying to conceal a too-telling expression.

Oh, feather dust!

"Miss Grant," Bede all but tapped an impatient foot as Miss Grant made her way up, her steps more lumbering than graceful. "It seems you have received improper instruction in using the long 's'. You have begun several words using a short 's', when clearly a long 's' is dictated."

Quicksilver's face scales reddened, and her throat pouch enlarged.

"But—"

"Are you making excuses, Miss Grant? Can you tell me I have seen your work inaccurately?"

"No, and yet–"

"Is arguing considered ladylike behavior?" Bede asked.

"No."

"Then I urge you to stop it immediately." Bede turned her shoulder on Miss Barton, who still stood slack-jawed at the front of the room. "Miss Sempil and Miss Withington."

They went to the front, standing straight in their most dominant postures. Berry hovered nearby.

"It is clear both of you have studied English Round Hand, but clearly you have not mastered it."

Miss Withington colored. To be honest, she had few real flaws, but vanity about her handwriting was one of them. She raised a hand for Berry to perch upon lest the protective little dragon fly at Bede.

"Miss Withington, you do not appear able to control your pen properly. The joins between several letters are stilted and artificial. You have failed to achieve the necessary hairlines throughout, with far too much thickness in many of the strokes. Miss Sempil—"

Miss Sempil actually winced.

"It is obvious you have studied Running Hand and Round Hand. While you have produced an attractive page, you have freely combined the letter forms of Round Hand and Running Hand, creating an improper hodgepodge of letter forms that does no credit to you or the education you have received."

Miss Sempil opened her mouth, presumably to speak, but drew a deep breath and shut it instead. Probably the wisest choice, all things considered.

"And Miss Darcy."

Pax squawked her displeasure.

Of course, her turn would come. Georgiana rose slowly and encouraged Pax to her shoulder. What was it Elizabeth had said? Match your posture to the dragon's and get bigger if you can. Look down at them, if possible. It is a quiet show of dominance. Since she was nearly a foot taller than Bede, she would happily stare down at her, even if her heart raced, her hands sweated, and she could hardly breathe.

"I hardly know what to make of your efforts. I understood your hand was quite accomplished upon your arrival here. But I am sure that assessment was indeed incorrect. None of your lettering conforms to the expected style or forms. I suggest you begin by refreshing your understanding of Round Hand from the beginning. I am available to tutor you personally—"

Georgiana stared at her and counted to three, four, five. "You do not recognize the forms because I used Italian Hand, not Round Hand."

Bede snorted and waggled her head. "Why would you do such a thing? It seems rather arrogant and self-aggrandizing to change the parameters of an assignment based on your own whims."

Stare and pause again. Soothe Pax lest she lose her temper. Only a threatened dragon answered quickly. "Because Italian Hand is considered a more elegant, if more advanced, style than Round Hand. Since the invitation is to a formal occasion, or at least that is what we are attempting, it seemed most appropriate to use the most elegant script at my disposal."

"But the assignment was—"

Georgiana rose slightly on her toes. On her shoulder, Pax did the same. "It was to write an elegant invitation to our event, conveying a personal greeting, the details of the event, and a request for a response, on a designated piece of writing stock. That was all."

"But clearly it would be assumed—"

"Mrs. Ramsbury," Georgiana turned to the now quietly smiling teacher, "did my approach to the assignment violate either the explicit directions or the implicit expectations?"

"No, Miss Darcy, it did not. In fact, I considered your work exemplary, actually above and beyond the expectations of the assignment."

Bede shifted her weight from right to left. "But that is not what I understood. It was clear to me—"

Pax and Berry twittered, but it was difficult to parse the meaning of it.

"You told Miss Grant arguing was unladylike. I expect that as companions, you are enjoined to model correct behavior at all times." Georgiana mustered all the sharpness she could find into her voice.

"Miss Darcy makes an excellent point." Gale mimicked Georgiana's posture. Was that encouragement?

"And on the subject of Miss Grant. Her use of the long 's' is actually correct. Different rules apply depending on whether a piece is printed or handwritten. So might she be excused from redoing her assignment?" Must not look smug, but the tight smile would not retreat from Georgiana's lips.

"I... I... is this true?" Bede stammered, clacking her jaws. "That two sets of rules apply?"

Mrs. Ramsbury nodded once.

"Why was I not told? Why was this information withheld?"

Pax cuddled into Georgiana's cheek, soft and warm and satisfied.

"And regarding your advice to Miss Withington, perhaps you might demonstrate for us all the proper way to manage a pen and make those strokes so that the hairlines are acceptable in all letterforms?" That was probably too bold, but Pax and Berry chirruped their approval.

Bede inched back and glanced at Coxcomb and Quicksilver, who shook their heads and stepped away from her.

"I cannot offer any advice on the matter," Coxcomb stared at the floor. "My use of a pen is far from proficient."

"Are you able to teach Miss Withington to improve her writing as you suggest?" Gale asked.

"I understand the theory of what must be done." Bede wrung her front paws.

"But the practice? Can you train her in the practice?" Gale's voice turned deep with a growly edge.

Bede shuffled back again. "No."

"Then it might be wise of you to limit your critique to what you can adequately instruct."

"But those were not the parameters of the assignment you gave us."

"Perhaps you should attend me. We will review those parameters together." Gale glared down at Bede, who dropped to all fours and scrabbled out with Gale following.

9
Chapter

MERCAIL FLEW IN MOMENTS later and led the dragon students away, inviting Pax and Berry to join them, which they did. Mrs. Ramsbury did her best to reestablish order and decorum in the classroom, though she only managed for a quarter of an hour before dismissing them for the rest of the day. What lesson could take place after that display? Considering how hard her heart thundered and her hands trembled, Georgiana certainly would have learned nothing more this day.

The upper students gathered in the common room, stunned into a silence uncommon for a group of young women. Shortly thereafter, Mrs. Fieldings herself came in and announced that instead of a formal dinner tonight, a cold supper would be offered in the dining room and the girls could bring trays upstairs to their rooms.

Unheard of! Such a privilege had never been extended before, making it difficult to know what to think.

About half the girls assumed it meant that the teachers had to gather in an urgent meeting to decide how to handle the latest challenge Bede presented. The rest believed it an unspoken reward to Miss Darcy, who had successfully stood up to Bede's arrogance with a proper draconic display of her own.

Neither explanation left Georgiana comfortable, and the second was far more distressing than the first. Heaven forfend that the others look on her as some sort of model for dealing with troublesome dragons.

Yes, it was satisfying to see Bede's errors corrected, but the whole situation bore little resemblance to how dragon relations should run.

After half an hour of debating the issue, the upper students trailed downstairs to gather their meals. Supper trays in hand, they crowded into Miss Sempil's chambers—she was always ready to host company, and the more the better. Several dragged in chairs from the other rooms to accommodate everyone, even if it was in a shoulder-to-shoulder sort of way. Miss Sempil shared the edge of the bed with Georgiana and Miss Withington. The place of honor, it seemed.

One Georgiana would happily have done without.

"I still cannot believe that happened." Miss Barton poked at a slice of cold chicken.

"It was unprecedented. Mrs. Fieldings has such superb control of everything in her domain—I can hardly imagine how Bede was permitted to just go off like that." Miss Sweet shrugged and looked from Miss Sempil to Miss Withington as if hoping for answers.

"I am not sure who was more distraught, us or the dragons. Who would have expected that they would have concerned themselves with such matters, though? What is your opinion, Miss Darcy?" Miss Reed nibbled a buttered roll rather like a mouse watching for a cat.

"I do not know what to make of it." Georgiana chewed her lip. "The Dragon Sage has a book in her library about drake communities. She made me read it. It talked about how minor drakes are apt to form communities wherever there were sufficient numbers of them gathered. She thought that their community-mindedness was one reason that all the dragons on Pemberley seemed to get along well."

"Quicksilver certainly is upset. She could hardly contain herself." Miss Grant dragged her chair nearer the bed; she seemed to enjoy remaining close to those with higher status. "I cannot understand why Bede is even here."

"Truly! She does not even seem to like young ladies. Why on earth would she be trying to be a companion?" Miss Barton rarely agreed with Miss Grant, especially regarding the student dragons.

"I suppose because she has not the skills to be a secretary." Miss Sempil sniffed. "She can barely write and has not the patience to assist the mistress of an estate."

"More likely it is because she has issues recognizing dominance and acting accordingly." Miss Withington's expression seemed so thoughtful.

"Dominance? I do not understand." Miss Grant did not seem to understand dragons well on the best of days.

"It is like social rank to them. It governs all their interactions." Miss Withington glanced at Georgiana. "You said Pemberley Keep has many dragons who manage to live together peaceably. How does it work there?"

How? Did anyone but Elizabeth really understand that? "Pemberley Keep is difficult to explain, even having lived there all my life. And I am not sure things run as smoothly as you expect. When I was born, Old Pemberley, Vikont Pemberley, was still alive. He was a cranky old firedrake. No one wanted to cross him, so all the dragons were rather walking on eggshells, as it were, minding their manners with him and one another. I doubt he would have hesitated to eat anyone who crossed him or caused any sort of trouble." She cringed a little. "In fact, I think that may have actually happened."

The girls gasped.

"And now?" Miss Reed hid her mouth behind her hand.

"Well, since his death some years ago, things have been different. Especially after the theft… did you realize Vicontes Pemberley's egg was stolen from the Keep after the vikont died?"

Another gasp.

"I had heard rumors, but hoped it was not true." Miss Withington whispered without making eye contact.

"My brother had no choice but to go in search of it. I am not familiar with all the details, but with the Dragon Sage's help, he recovered it."

"Was that why he was knighted?" Miss Sempil asked.

"That and other things. After she hatched and was returned to Pemberley, all matters at the estate were rather turned upside down."

"Did you help take care of the hatchling?" Miss Withington asked, as though she had been waiting to ask that question for quite some time.

"I did the best I could."

"What an honor, caring for a baby dragon." Miss Withington said.

"It did not feel like such an honor. She was a most unhappy infant. Nothing seemed to please her."

"One of my little brothers was that sort of baby." Miss Sempil's lips wrinkled into a frown at the memory. "They called it colic. He did nothing but cry for the first two years of his life, and no one but my mother could soothe him. It was dreadful."

"That is exactly how it was. I did not know human babies could be like that, too. I have little experience with infants, as I am the youngest in my family. It is interesting to consider that dragon babies can be like human ones." Georgiana rubbed her knuckles along her jaw. "Things were difficult not only because she was a troublesome infant, but because—in retrospect it makes sense—the entire line of dominance was disrupted. There was general uneasiness in all the dragons. Perhaps it was because they had no basis in what to make of a Keep without a dominant estate dragon overseeing the territory."

"Was there a great deal of squabbling and fighting among them?" Miss Sweet layered cheese and meat on a slice of bread.

"No, no, there was not. Which, as you mention it, is very interesting indeed. Perhaps it was because there were large minor dragons on the estate who oversaw matters during Old Pemberley's decline and continued to do so until Young Pemberley was ready to take over. I never really appreciated the role they must have played in keeping the territory running until little Pemberley could manage. That surely cannot be the way estates usually run."

"It is not the way of my father's." Miss Barton shook her head. "The wyvern my father Keeps barely tolerates the minor dragons there, and they rarely do as she asks."

"Nor mine. The minor dragon who lives on our estate is constantly in conflict with the Keep dragon, like a tenant squabbling with a landlord." Miss Withington caught Miss Barton's gaze for a moment. "As I understand it, if the Keep dragon were to meet his demise, the minor dragon would try to grab as much territory as he could for himself. It would not be a pretty situation at all. I fear the Order would have to step in, and there might be bloodshed."

"I believe that several other Derbyshire major dragons tried to challenge Pemberley for her territory recently. Two were denied the challenge because of a legal technicality which I do not understand, and the other resulted in bloodshed." Georgiana shuddered.

Miss Reed gasped. "What happened? Did you see an actual dragon battle?"

"No, I did not. But the Sage's sister recently wrote to me about it—and a number of other things." Miss Bennet's letter had been quite thoughtful and thought-provoking. "Bolsover challenged Young Pemberley to fight, but my brother stood up against him. He used the Dragon Slayer to defend his Keep dragon. Nonetheless, he was overpowered; one man against an angry firedrake, even a small one, is hardly a fair fight. But instead of conceding dominance, Pemberley went against Bolsover herself. All the minor dragons of her Keep in attendance went to her defense as well. Together, they overcame Bolsover and retained her territory. As I understand, though not entirely unprecedented, such things have rarely happened. As a result, both dragon and estate are recognized as quite remarkable. That event established her dominance in the estate, over all the minor dragons in the Keep, even though they are bigger than she. I have been told that the large minor dragons are being particularly supportive in assisting with managing the territory, and things are settling down to something more normal."

"Normal? Nothing of what you have said is remotely normal." Miss Withington laughed ruefully. "It is most extraordinary, to be sure. You are so fortunate to be connected to such a place. Such an advantage that must give you in the Blue Order marriage mart."

Only if Georgiana had not ruined that for herself already, something only time would tell. "I had never really considered it that way."

"That the minor dragons on Pemberley could work together so well—" Miss Barton chewed her cheek. "It really does not cast Bede in a favorable light at all, does it?"

"I am quite certain the other student-dragons do not regard her highly. Whispers behind her back say that a fight for dominance would be in order. But I do not expect that Gale, who, as I understand, is the dominant dragon here, would tolerate it." Miss Reed rubbed her arms briskly.

"But why not? Is that not the way of dragons? Would it not settle matters? Maybe even make Bede more tolerable?" Miss Sweet asked.

"Gale's mission is to help the student-dragons to manage girls and young ladies in the warm-blooded world. Since we do not fight for dominance, at least not in a draconic sort of way, she will not want to reinforce that behavior amongst her students," Miss Withington said, as though she had actually talked the matter over with Gale. Had she?

"There was a girl like that back at home. I met her at lessons with the dance master." Miss Sempil stared at the ceiling. "She did not seem to naturally understand social rank or identify the necessary social cues in group settings. She made constant gaffes. It was so bad that I saw her cut by her superiors in the street. Eventually, she was sent away to live with a relative in another county in hopes she could make a fresh start. I would have felt sorrier for her if she had not been so annoying."

Miss Withington harrumphed. "I am sorry, but I cannot feel sympathy for Bede at all. Not after she humiliated me in front of everyone over a few strokes of the pen. That was uncalled for and completely inappropriate. I cannot help but imagine you, Miss Darcy, are even more put out after she criticized you for nothing at all."

"It was impressive the way you took up for yourself." Miss Sempil said. "I did not think you had it in you, to be honest. You seem rather the meek and mild sort."

"I suppose, having watched the Dragon Sage, I have learned a bit." Georgiana looked aside. "It probably was not proper of me to react the way I did. I am not sure what is proper when dragons are involved with young ladies. It all seems rather muddled, and I never am sure of which set of rules to follow, cold-blooded or warm."

June 6, 1815

A week later, just after the breakfast things were taken up, the upper students hurried upstairs to the music room in a tight little knot.

"Can you believe that Mrs. Fieldings actually gave us all leave to go to the haberdasher to place our own orders for ribbons and roses and laces for our gowns?" Miss Sweet tittered as she clasped her hands before her chest, beaming. She was one of those people who seemed to be happy with her entire being.

"I had not expected such a privilege. She must be pleased with our efforts on the menus and plans for decoration," Miss Reed whispered behind her slender hand. "It was so helpful knowing what Darcy House and Pemberley would serve!"

Georgiana climbed the final step. "I am only glad to have been able to help. It is not as though I had any opportunity to assist in the planning myself or attend any of the events at Pemberley or Darcy House."

"But you will once you are out, and that will be so amazing. You are so lucky to be connected to such a Dragon Estate." Miss Withington paused near the railing around the stairs in the middle of the common room and glanced about, as if checking for eavesdroppers. Not an unreasonable practice for a fairy dragon's Friend.

"Pardon me for asking, but how is it you came to be here at Mrs. Fieldings'?" Miss Barton's close-set hazel-green eyes narrowed just a bit and her tones suggested one looking for juicy gossip.

Georgiana swallowed hard. "My brother and the Sage felt I had a rather skewed perception of the Blue Order world and hoped I might learn other perspectives from being here." There. She had not lied, but neither had she offered information that was unnecessary.

"That makes sense, considering what a unique place Pemberley is." Miss Sempil seemed a little disappointed there was nothing more interesting in her explanation. "You are noticeably different from Miss Bennet, whom they also sent here—at least that was how I understood the situation."

"Is that a compliment or a criticism?"

"Neither, really, just an observation. I knew Miss Bennet as quite a lively girl, always speaking her mind, even when it was silly indeed. You rarely offer your opinions, unless pressed hard. It is difficult to take your measure."

"Oh, do not be so serious, Miss Sempil. The haberdasher was able to take her measure for new ribbons and buttons quite well, indeed!" The other girls laughed as Miss Grant pressed her shoulder to Georgiana's. "Those white porcelain rose buttons will be so beautiful on your gown. I am ever so jealous, and I have not even seen it yet!"

"It is not a true evening gown, to be sure. The dresses for the Cotillion were so striking. Order Blue, every one of them, and the Sage's Uncle supplied so many gorgeous trims for Miss Bennet's, Mrs. Collins', and Miss de Bourgh's gowns. I should have liked to have seen a ballroom filled with gowns of that color."

"You and Miss Withington, and maybe Miss Barton too, are probably the only ones amongst us who might dance at a Blue Order Cotillion someday." Miss Sempil looked at her feet. "My father is hardly important enough to be invited to attend. I shall try not to hate you for it."

She would definitely have to speak to Mr. Gardiner—Sir Edward now—about an event for less prominent Blue Order misses. Surely something might be arranged.

"I doubt that my father can afford a London season for me, even if I am invited to the Cotillion." Miss Withington said. "But I am determined to make the best of things while I can, which is why I am here."

"Is there a particular Dragon Keeper—or rather, his family—you are trying to impress with the prowess Mrs. Fieldings instills in you?" Miss Barton asked.

Miss Withington blushed and looked away.

"I knew it! I knew there was someone. Can we guess who?" Miss Sempil turned to Miss Barton and Miss Grant.

"Listen. Are those Mr. Elkins' warm-up scales? We should hurry lest Mica become impatient." Georgiana glanced at Miss Withington and hurried on ahead.

Miss Withington followed with a little sigh that sounded much like relief.

The music room chairs had been pushed aside, stacked atop one another in the window bay near the pianoforte. The carpet had been rolled up and shoved against the long wall. Shadows from the fading wisteria blossoms and sunlight already danced along the yellow walls and now-bare wooden floor.

"Hurry along, girls, hurry along," Mica called from near the pianoforte. "We have much to learn today, much to learn." The morning sun glistened on her pinkish scales, turning them a rather peachy tone, and emphasized the lacy pattern on her face and shoulders, giving the effect of a fine morning gown. With her soft voice and polished manner, she radiated ladylikeness in a way few human women did.

The companion-dragon students, all of them, formed a loose ring around Mica. Bede stood a step back from the rest. The girls assembled near the dragons.

"I have something new on the agenda today. We have been focusing on longways dances recently—"

"We are to learn a waltz?" Miss Barton giggled.

"Silly girl, of course not." Mica clapped her jaw several times. "That is hardly considered appropriate! No, no, no, today we shall work on learning a cotillion. Since these dances will be included in the Blue Order Cotillion, it seems only right to ensure you are properly taught."

"But they are not so new, are they, Mica?" Coxcomb asked.

"Whilst they originated in France, the first collection of English cotillions was published in London in 1767." Bede muttered to her clasped front paws.

"That is correct, Bede." Mica's voice took on that too-patient note that did not bode well when spoken by anyone, least of all a dragon. "They have been popular in public and private dances for some time. You girls might even have been taught a cotillion by a master hired by your parents. However, the one you shall learn today is the specific cotillion written for the Blue Order Cotillion, the one that will be danced at many Blue Order events throughout the coming year."

General excitement rose all around. All the girls had the potential to be invited to a ball or party hosted by Blue Order members.

Mica clapped. "Who can tell me the basic form of the cotillion dance?"

Bede stepped forward into the group. "A cotillion is a dance involving eight dancers in four couples, standing in a square formation. The dance is made up of changes, which vary on each repetition of the tune, like the words of different verses, while the figures are repeated after each iteration, like the chorus of a song. Figures make up the core of the dance itself and are taught in advance to be memorized by the dancers. This stands in contrast to the country dance, in which the calling couple, the first couple, selects the figures immediately before the dance begins."

"Thank you, Bede." Mica's voice turned even more patient, which seemed hardly possible.

"Often the first and final change of a cotillion is *Le Grand Rond*—"

"Which is..." Mica turned her shoulder to Bede and looked at the girls.

"A slipping circle right and left." Bede did not miss a beat. "It is crucial that dancers keep time with the music so as not to end a figure too early or too late. Although Monsieur Gherardi, in 1767, required that the musicians vary the speed of playing to avoid confusion for the dancers, he was criticized for this position. Thomas Hurst, in 1769, offered a softer instruction, merely that the musicians should play their tunes in a true 'British Taste' as expressively as possible. While Giovanni Gallini, in 1776—"

"That is sufficient, Bede." Mica held up an open paw and barely exposed her small fangs.

Merciful heavens! Georgiana had never seen her do that before.

"Cotillions are regarded as too complex for ordinary dancers, thus the delay in their acceptance at Almack's and the Blue Order Cotillion. Thomas Hurst offered a simplified version of many cotillions in 1769 in—"

"Bede! Your answers have been quite sufficient. Entirely sufficient for our purposes."

"But, Mica—"

Coxcomb and Quicksilver growled softly, deep in their throats. The sort of sound one felt more than heard.

"Girls, arrange yourselves in a four-couple square set. Quickly, quickly." Mica clapped and pointed.

Miss Withington grabbed Georgiana's arm and pulled her to the top of the set, their backs to the pianoforte. "Did you learn some of the Blue Order Cotillion whilst Miss Bennet and the others were learning it?" she whispered.

"I did."

"Good, perhaps that will spare us Bede's scrutiny." Miss Withington glanced over her shoulder toward Bede.

"You do not think that Mica will allow—"

Mica stood by the couple at the bottom of the set, facing Georgiana and Miss Withington, and cleared her throat. "Mr. Elkins, play the music through once for us; the first change requires a full sixteen bars to complete and is a Grand Rond."

Lively music flowed from Mr. Elkins' fingers. Come to think of it, Mr. Dodge, the dance master in London, had always taught without music. Georgiana had never actually heard the tune before. Very pretty.

It would have been nice to enjoy it at an actual Cotillion. Would she yet be able to do that? Or even at a lesser Blue Order event, that would be welcome, too.

"Now you have heard the music, keep that in mind as we review the steps. All of you recall the slipping circle? Slide your feet together with each step around the circle. Excellent foot position at all times! Then the figure begins with the first and third couples, those at the top and bottom of the set, turning to their corners in the second and fourth couples, and taking that dancer's two hands around. Yes, yes, walk through that now. Excellent. Now two hands to your partner and around."

Straightforward and easily accomplished, even with corners who were not so certain of themselves on the dance floor.

"Now we become a bit more complex." Mica signaled for them to stop and look at her. "Turn to your corner and we will do changes of rights and lefts. Is there anyone unfamiliar with that figure?"

Miss Reed raised her hand. She probably knew it, but the poor girl was so unsure of herself that she did not want to take a chance of being mistaken.

"Very good. We will walk through it, then. All dancers turn away from your partner and to your corner. Now offer that dancer your right hand and pull by to take their position. Yes, yes, quite like that. To the dancer you meet, offer your left hand. Left, left! Start with the right, then the left! Offer your left hand and pull by to take their place. Now the right hand again, pull by. You should meet your partner on the opposite side of the circle. Is everyone there? Yes?"

Georgiana and Miss Withington dipped in a tiny curtsey as they met—not part of the dance, but somehow fitting for Mica's narrative.

"Offer two hands to your partner halfway around to meet your next corner with a right hand and pull by. Repeat until you meet your partner in your home position. No, Miss Reed, wrong hand. Always begin with the right, then left. Let us walk that again, shall we?"

Three more walk-throughs were necessary to get everyone in their correct places.

"Good, good. Now the second half of that figure. Remember, you will do both the first and second half of the figure after each of the changes—the chorus coming after the verse."

Miss Reed's forehead creased in deep thought. For all her height and willowy figure, she struggled with grace.

"In this second part of the figure, the first couple, the one with backs to the pianoforte, promenade down between the third couple, directly opposite you. After you split through between that couple, the one dancing the man's role, dance to the left, woman to the right, outside the square to the second and fourth couples. Split between them and meet your partner in the middle of the circle to promenade to home place."

It took a moment to sort out the promenade formation, right hand to right hand across their waists and left to left behind the lady's back, but Georgiana and Miss Withington made a credible show of it.

"Each couple repeats the sequence in turn. Second couple to the center, split your opposite couple. Each up the sides and through those couples to meet in the middle. Yes... yes... back to home. Third couple. Now fourth. Well done, well done! Finish that figure with a promenade with your partner around the entire circle and back to home. And that is the full figure."

Not the most complex dance, by any means, but especially for the less experienced, there were many places to get confused.

"Now that you have walked it through, are you ready to do that with music?" Mica clapped.

The girls nodded, Miss Sempil quite vigorously; Miss Reed only because it was proper to do so.

"This time you shall dance to the music." Mica turned to the dragons. "As they dance, watch for those marks of excellent dancing: posture, footwork, tension in your arms, your expression."

Silent groans and looks of misery passed among the girls.

"If you will play us two measures to begin, Mr. Elkins."

He played the opening measure.

"*Grand ronde.*" Mica prompted, and they began their slipping circle.

"Figure, starting with two-handed turns with corners, then partners. Rights and lefts, half turn round with your partner, rights and lefts. Back to home and first couple promenade."

Miss Withington proved quite a credible partner. Perhaps they would escape Bede's scrutiny.

"Second change. Ladies to the center with right hands to make a star and once around. Back again with the left. Now to the figure. Remember to begin with corners."

Turn round the corner. Turn round the partner. Georgiana's corner then offered her left hand instead of the right. Georgiana reached for her right hand instead, to leave her ready for the next move in the progression, and Miss Barton recovered nicely.

"Wait, wait!" Bede burst into the set, breaking into the couples and ruining any chance to continue. Mr. Elkins stopped playing. "Miss Darcy, you have made a grave error."

Mica waded into the chaos. "Bede, I instructed you to watch and wait through the dance before we discuss."

"But she made a serious error." Bede pointed at Georgiana. "The figure was to offer right hand to the corner, then left to the next person. She was offered a left but refused and took the right instead. A clear violation of dominance."

"How do you determine that?" Did Mica roll her eyes? Were dragons even capable of that?

"She was dancing the female role, which by definition recognizes the dominance of the male role." Bede lashed her tail, its swish across the wood floor an angry hiss.

Dragon's bones! This was a dance floor, not a dominance battle!

Miss Barton edged forward. "The error was mine, not hers. I offered her a left instead of a right."

"But as the non-dominant dancer, she should have—"

"No." Miss Barton crossed her arms over her chest and stepped closer to Bede. "Miss Darcy was being a considerate partner by quietly assisting me through an error and setting me up to be correct throughout the rest of the figure. It is the mark of an advanced dancer to quietly and without embarrassment guide another through a misstep without disturbing the flow of the dance."

"I do not understand!" Bede stomped toward Georgiana, teeth bared. "Why is she infallible?"

"What are you talking about?" Mica stepped between Georgiana and Bede.

"Every time I find fault with her, all of you come to her defense to prove me wrong. Why does she never make a mistake? You never permit her to be corrected. Is it her connection to the Sage that makes her so perfect? Or is it my lack of dominance in my community that always makes me wrong? I thought humans and dragons were to be equal here. Or is that not the case? Is she simply considered dominant over us all because of her connection to Vicontes Pemberley? What is the rule of dominance here?"

"This is not a matter of dominance, Bede." Mica hissed. "This is a matter of etiquette and of factual error."

"What error? Explain to me how I am in error. The figure of the dance specifically said—"

Mica laid her paw across her snout and snuffled a sort of sigh.

"Miss Darcy, explain this to me. Defend your actions. I must understand." Bede sidestepped Mica and leaned into Georgiana's face.

Georgiana jumped back, gasping, but it sounded like a hiss.

Mica threw herself between them, front legs open wide. "Girls, you are dismissed. We will resume again tomorrow. Bede, to my office."

10
Chapter

June 13, 1815

A WEEK LATER AND Coxcomb, Quicksilver, and the governess student-dragons were still going out of their way to apologize for Bede's — in their words—inexcusable outburst. Apparently, her demand for Georgiana to defend her actions was tantamount to one man challenging another to a duel! The student-dragons tiptoed about, seemingly afraid that the warm-blooded students, and teachers as well, might consider them parties in the challenge.

According to Pax and Berry, who had managed to overhear a discussion between Gale and Mrs. Fieldings, Bede had been regularly provoking the other dragon students to assert dominance, which was not only rude but exhausting among the dragons. Apparently, once dominance was established in a community of dragons, it was expected to be respected without further challenges until a material change occurred which would specifically influence dominance. The details were hazy still, but the overall concept was clear. Bede was stepping on as many dragon toes as human ones.

The dragon-students were indeed weary. A candid conversation with Coxcomb, which required no small amount of decidedly un-draconic delicacy and tact, revealed another troubling aspect of the problem. The student-dragons were part of Mrs. Fieldings' academy only with the approval of the parents who sent their daughters there and of Lady Astrid, the Blue Order Scribe, who was in charge of all educational endeavors connected to the Order. They feared that the upper students might complain to their parents, or even the Scribe herself, and they would be withdrawn from the academy.

Apparently, Coxcomb, Quicksilver, and the other student-drag-ons—how did Coxcomb put it?—bore a heavy responsibility to prop-erly represent their kind among the warm-bloods, and being re-moved from the academy would be seen as failure. Such failure in the cold-blooded communities, as in the warm-blooded, would result in a loss of status and all the things that went with that. Humiliation was not easy, no matter what your species.

Though it was good to understand the dragons' fears, they had become too careful in Georgiana's presence. Presumably, with her connections, Georgiana was perceived to be the one whose complaints would most likely be acted upon, therefore the one on whose right side it was most important to stay. Georgiana missed the easy compan-ionship she had enjoyed with Quicksilver and Coxcomb prior to the "music room incident," as it was called. Their discomfort seemed con-tagious, and the entire atmosphere at Bennetson Hall seemed slightly stale and tainted.

When Mrs. Fieldings suggested the upper students visit Chapel-en-le-Frith in the company of Ewe-Minder, one of the shep-herding drakes rather than the student-dragons, they energetically availed themselves of the opportunity, intentionally ignoring the implications of the privilege.

Soft clouds floated across the skies, veiling and revealing the sun in a playful game of hide-and-seek. Warm breezes carried the fragrance of wildflowers and field grasses, along with the ever-present odor of sheep, whose soft bleating punctuated the songbirds' melodies. Though not as lovely as Pemberley, to be sure, the walk to Chapel-en-le-Frith had its beauties. Ewe-Minder kept her distance, trotting along as though escorting sheep.

"How long will it take you to finish your dress, Miss Darcy?" Miss Reed had a great love for sewing and fashion. And rather a good eye for it, as well.

"That is an excellent question. Will you hate me if I say I have rarely made alterations to my own clothes? That is not to say I do not sew, to be sure. I do, really, I do. But my brother has always insisted my gowns be ordered from my mother's favorite shops." Georgiana swallowed back the knot in her throat. How she had loved sitting with Mama when the modiste visited Pemberley. "Since I am not out, none of my garments are designed for an event like the one we are hosting. Neither my brother nor his wife expected me to need an evening sort of dress, so this will be my first attempt at retrimming a gown. I can only guess as to how long it will take."

"Truly?" Miss Sempil gaped at her, a tinge of sympathy in her round, blue eyes. Enviable, fat blonde curls bobbed beside her face.

"Pray, let us help. There is nothing quite so much fun as turning a plain gown into something rather special. I love to do it." Miss Reed clasped her hands together.

The others echoed the sentiment.

"You would help me? I thought your own gowns would keep you busy."

"I trimmed out a gown whilst at home between terms. Mrs. Field-ings hinted at such an event before the last term ended, so there is little to do for my own. Save, of course, making sure the charwoman does not get hold of it. She is a fright with delicate fabrics." Miss Withington chuckled, though it was clearly a disguise for her pique over the damage to a favorite dress.

"There seem to be many people out and about in town today." Miss Grant scanned the modest main street before them, lined with a mix of two- and three-story stone houses and shops, broken up by narrow lanes.

"What do you suppose is going on at the town hall?" Miss Sweet pointed just beyond the haberdasher's shop, to the group of men entering the structure across the street, bearing a large sign reading "Town Hall" in dark gold letters.

"I should very much like to know." Berry murmured from Miss Withington's shoulder.

"I shall go with you." Pax launched from Georgiana's market bas-ket.

"We did not ask you to go." Georgiana said. "In fact, I do not think it is a good idea."

"But the hanging baskets on that building contain some lovely looking pot marigolds just blooming, and I fancy a taste of the nectar." Berry zipped away, Pax on her wing.

"It must be nice to have a little Friend to go spying for you." Miss Barton murmured, lip curling back in a very ladylike sneer as she crossed her dumpy arms over her chest.

Miss Withington and Georgiana gasped.

"No, it is not like that at all." Miss Withington caught Georgiana's eye.

Yes, this was a notion that needed to be nipped in the bud immediately. "It is considered bad manners to have a dragon spy on your behalf—as impolite as listening in yourself, if not worse."

"But dragons are independent thinkers, with minds of their own. Fairy dragons thrive on gossip as much as they do their sweets, so they may go in search of it, whether we wish them to or not. And whatever they bring back must be taken with a grain of salt. Or rather, a spoonful. In their excitement over a morsel of hearsay, they are apt to confuse details rather badly. One should never take information from fairy dragon chatter without some other confirming source." Miss Withington pressed her fingertips to her lips.

Miss Barton snuffed. "You are just saying that so we do not—"

"Berry told me you were spreading rumors about me. Telling the lower students that the Head Girl was bossy and selfish and not to be trusted, for she would take all the information received to Mrs. Fieldings. That was how she got to be Head Girl, after all." Miss Withington cocked her eyebrow as she met Miss Barton's hazel-eyed gaze.

"You could not have believed that of me, could you?" Miss Barton, pale on the best of days, turned ghostly white.

"No, I did not, because I understand my little Friend's nature and limitations. We all have them, and it is important to remember those when dealing with anyone."

"Especially dragons?" Miss Reed whispered.

"I would say with anyone, warm- or cold-blooded." Dragons were not the only ones with limitations, to be sure. Certainly, Elizabeth showed plenty of draconic limits herself.

"Then let us not stand around here babbling about fairy dragon gossip. I want to see what new ribbons Mr. Felton has." Miss Sempil, who had little fondness for fairy dragons overall, opened the door and led the way in.

The large pewter bell on Mr. Felton's Haberdasher's door tinkled a welcome into fairyland. Replete with tiny drawers and shelves and boxes, all filled with beautiful things, often unlabeled to encourage the shopper to explore on their own. Small vases of flowers dotted the shop, lightly perfuming the sun-warmed air. An overstuffed golden-yellow couch sat, squat, near the front window with a pudgy brown-and-white puck sleeping in the middle of it. Biggles, who passed as a pug to the dragon-deaf, was the reason Mrs. Fieldings preferred the girls to frequent this shop. Order members were supposed to support their own, after all.

Biggles raised his head and scurried up to them, wearing a pug-like grin.

"Yes, Biggles," Miss Withington crouched down to scratch under his proffered chin. "I brought something for you." She reached into her reticule and pulled out a handmade fabric flower. "Here you go. I made it just for you."

Biggles's eyes bulged wide and round, and his tongue hung out. Breathing hard, he took the flower in his paws and turned it round and round. He fell to his side, rolled to his back, and held the offering in the sunlight, admiring every angle, twice. At last, he scurried away behind the counters, probably heading to his secret hoard.

"You have made my Friend an exceedingly happy little... pug." Mr. Felton smiled as he approached. With his shopkeeper's apron, he was rather

ordinary-looking, except for his long, waxed mustache, unlike any Georgiana had ever seen before.

"He is truly dear, and his enjoyment is worth the effort." Miss Withington said.

"Your offering is much appreciated. The anticipation has kept him from pilfering my latest orders. You have come to pick up yours, I gather? Give me just a moment." He ducked behind the counter and retrieved several brown-paper-wrapped bundles, laying them out on the pale-green-painted counter. "Here you go, ladies. As much as I would love to see you linger here and spend your pocket money with me, I am a father of a daughter and would not want to see her lingering about in town right now." He pointed with his chin, through the window, toward the now-larger crowd outside of Town Hall.

"Gracious, some of them look furious. Do you know what is going on?" Miss Reed covered her mouth with her hand.

"The damned highwaymen—forgive my language, please." He cleared his throat. "It seems a band of the blackguards has been harrying travelers on some of the nearby roads. I worry about you walking out alone without your... guard dogs. Pray tell Mrs. Fieldings that you should not go out without a... dog... capable of guarding you until those ruffians are stopped. In fact, you wait here while I get the butcher's boy to accompany you home. I know he has a delivery for Mrs. Fieldings. I cannot in good conscience see you girls leave here all alone." He tipped his head and hurried out the front door.

"Perhaps we should have mentioned Ewe-Minder. It is not as though we are without escort." Miss Withington chewed her lower lip.

"Is it that dangerous?" Miss Reed whispered. "Perhaps two dragons would be better."

"We saw no sign of anything while we were on our way here. Besides, what could those ruffians want with us? Clearly, we are not likely to be carrying any appreciable amount of money or other valuables." Miss Barton waved off the idea. "We should go before Mr. Felton returns and avoid the butcher's boy's dreary company."

"Would such men would advertise their presence? Call attention to themselves? As for what they might want, it seems it would be far more dangerous to assume that we would be of no interest than to take precautions as though we might be. I am certain Mr. Felton is right." Miss Withington positioned herself in front of the door.

"Yes, that is sensible. I should be excessively glad for an escort home. I hope Pax and Berry return soon!" Georgiana peered through the window. It seemed wrong to leave the fairy dragons alone in town, although they could care for themselves quite well.

Mr. Felton shambled in through the back door with the butcher's boy and a large drake. "May I present Andrew and his Friend Bones."

The imposing brindled drake, with a square head and a broad, bow-legged stance, was probably named for a proclivity to chew large bones, given the prominence of his teeth.

"We'll be walkin' ye ladies home." The young man hefted a large, paper-wrapped bundle to his shoulder. "Not because things are that dangerous, mind you, but he might want to walk out with Ewe-Minder."

"That is not information to be shared." Bones grumbled and bared his fangs, but the tip of his tail twitched the way the household drakes' did when anticipating something.

Andrew scratched behind his ears and laughed. "As soon as them fairy dragons know, there are no secrets."

Bones shook his head and growled. "Let us be off; I believe the cook needs that joint this afternoon." He trotted out the door.

Pax and Berry met them near the front door of Bennetson Hall, twittering between themselves. Andrew headed for the service entrance at the back of the house while Bones followed Ewe-Minder into the fields. Mrs. Fieldings greeted them in the front hall.

"I am glad you have returned safely. A messenger from town brought word of the danger whilst you were gone, but assured us you would be properly escorted home." The assurance must not have been wholly comforting, considering Mrs. Fieldings' expression.

"We bring news!" Berry twittered.

"Berry, Pax, please come with me to tell the rest of the staff what you have learnt. And I am sure you found this out of your own accord. Yes? I am glad you are perceptive enough to know what will be of importance for us and our students." They followed Mrs. Fieldings out.

What an odd exchange. Odd and unsettling. What sort of secrets were being kept? And would Pax tell her about them once they were in private?

"Come, let us go upstairs and work on your gown. There is nothing to be gained by standing around here stupidly waiting for news that may or may not come to us." Miss Withington headed for the main stairs.

She was correct, of course. Better to stay busy under such circumstances. Bother; how much this felt like the days in London after Elizabeth had been taken. That sense of helplessness and dependence on forces so far beyond her. This time, though, Pax was in the thick of it, not simply minding the nursery. Was that a good thing or not? Difficult to tell. Very difficult. Miss Withington was right. Keeping busy was an excellent option indeed.

"Let us fetch our sewing baskets, and we will join you shortly." Miss Reed dashed upstairs, anticipating her favorite pastime.

Georgiana trudged along behind. Sewing would not come easily, but perhaps it would be distracting. She opened the door to her room and ushered Miss Withington inside.

"No! Pray no! It cannot be." Miss Withington staggered back into Georgiana as they heard the scrabbling of taloned feet.

"What has happened?" Georgiana surged forward, but stopped just two steps in.

Shambles! Her room was in shambles, clothing strewn about from one wall to another. Over the furniture, on the floor, even hanging across the rod with the curtains. Chemise, petticoats, stockings, nightgowns hung about as though it were laundry day. And her gowns!

Dragon's blood! Her gowns!

Her prized green lawn was heaped in the nearest corner. The pink calico—the expensive calico ordered from Mr. Gardiner—no, he was Sir Edward now—draped over the back of a chair and dragged on the floor. And her navy spencer stuck full of pins—whatever for? Was that...yes, it was! Dragon's blood! Was that her beautiful white muslin...

One sleeve lay across the bed. The other was spread across the writing table, while the rest of the bodice dangled from the drawer of the press. And the skirt! Laid out on the floor, marked with dragon footprints and talon tears. Even if she could put the garment back together, the fabric was utterly ruined.

Ruined.

"What have you done?" Georgiana gasped. "Why do you single me out for such treatment?"

"I am going to get Mrs. Fieldings." Miss Withington dashed out.

"I... I... I was only trying to help." Bede tossed aside the fabric in her paw.

"Tearing apart my best gown is trying to help? In what way could you possibly construe this to be helpful?"

"I thought I might help you to remake it like you and the others were talking about yesterday."

"So you expected to simply march into my chambers unbidden, into a place where you knew you were not welcome, to go through my things. To destroy what did not belong to you? And this was a good idea?"

"I destroyed nothing. I only unraveled it. It can be sewn together again." Bede dangled a sleeve from her talon, tearing it.

"Look what you have done. You just made it even worse. That sleeve might have been salvageable, but now... now... nothing can be done. And the skirt! It is utterly ruined. There is nothing to be done for it but to make rags! Rags! You reduced my best gown to rags!"

"I am sure it is not nearly so bad. And it can be replaced. It is only a garment." Bede's large red eyes widened as though frustrated.

"Only a garment? Do you understand how much a garment like this one costs? How long it takes to have one made? The fabric alone would have to be ordered from a warehouse in London. And then there would be multiple fittings to ensure it was made properly. The embroidery? It is easily the work of a month, if not longer. Even if there were money for it, which there is not, there is no time."

"What do you mean? Why does that matter?"

"Our dinner! Now I have nothing to wear for it."

"What do you call those?" Bede pointed to the rumpled, though still intact, gowns around the room. "Wear one of them."

"You hateful, awful creature! Not one of those is appropriate! If I wore something like that, it would be utterly disrespectful to Mrs. Fieldings, to everyone here. I cannot. I cannot! After all the work, all the effort, and looking forward to it all, you have taken from me the one thing I really wanted. Just like your kind always does. You always ruin everything! Get out! Get out!"

"I was only trying to help. I studied the latest fashion plates. It did not seem so difficult to remake the dress into something more fashionable. I was only trying to help."

"Do you know anything about sewing, anything at all?"

"No, but it did not seem so difficult."

"Well, it is. The skill of years. Did you actually believe you could simply walk in here and master something so complex?"

"It did not appear complex to me."

"It is not my fault that you were wrong. And your good intentions have ruined everything! Could you not be content with your insults and criticisms of me? Was it necessary to destroy my property as well?"

"I was only trying to make up for my past indiscretions. Trying to make it up to you."

"Pray never try to do me another favor. Get out and stay away from me."

"Pray do not tell Mrs. Fieldings to cast me out!"

"That is not her decision." Mercail, in her glittering white majesty, swooped through the door. "Go to your lair in the tower and wait for us there."

Bede scrabbled out.

Mercail twittered a sweet sound as she landed on Georgiana's bed, careful to avoid the devastated gown.

"Pray, no, do not do that. Pax comforts me in that same way, but I do not want such comfort now. I am angry and I have the right to be angry. Allow me the dignity of my own feelings. Unless you, too, will insist that I have no right to be put out or harbor negative feelings toward dragons. And if that is the case, then I respectfully ask that you leave me alone right now. I do not wish for such company."

Mercail extended her wing. "You have the right to feel whatever way you do."

"That is not a popular opinion, in my experience."

"You have experienced much grief because of the dragons in your life."

"How would you know anything of that? Has the Sage written to you to tell you of my intractable resentment and seek your assistance in correcting it?"

"Not at all. Pax and I have had many long discussions on the matter." Mercail cocked her head. "You might find it interesting to know she agrees with you."

Georgiana sat beside Mercail. "We have never really discussed those things."

"Why might that be?"

"I assumed, hoped, that she would understand me, and it did not need to be spoken. It is such a difficult concept to explain resentment toward her species. I do not want to risk losing our Friendship over that."

"And you think she is not sensitive enough to notice such a thing?"

"She is extraordinarily perceptive. I am certain she has been aware."

"And she has never scolded you about it? Never let on that she might be disturbed by it?"

"No, she never has. She is particularly considerate and hates anything which brings conflict. I assumed that kept her from mentioning it."

"Perhaps there could be something more?"

"I dared not consider it." Georgiana pressed her elbows to her knees and cradled her face in her hands.

"Why not? Would it not be comforting to trust that your Friend understood and supported you?"

"It is far too dangerous to believe such a thing. To do so and discover I was wrong would be more than I could bear." Georgiana swallowed back a lump in her throat.

"Oh, my dear girl, I am so sorry."

"Do you really mean that, or are you saying that as a matter of form because it is something that one is supposed to say to a distraught young lady?"

Mercail leaned into her side and cooed—a sound Georgiana had never heard a fairy dragon make before. It was wonderfully soothing, not in the persuasive sort of way, but in the way of a dove's gentle coo. "I am sorry that you are so wary of a modicum of comfort, but I do understand. You have good reason for feeling the way you do."

"Forgive me if I find it difficult to believe you are saying that to me. I have never heard that from anyone, least of all from a dragon."

"That is deeply unfortunate." Mercail cooed again. "I am slightly acquainted with your brother, and I met the Sage in London during a salon held by Lady Astrid. They are unique among warm-bloods."

"That is one way to put it."

"I can easily see why they get along so well with the dragon side of the Blue Order. They both seem to navigate the relations with the cold-blooded well."

And since that was the most important thing in the world...

"But I have observed that they do not manage nearly so well with the warm-blooded. In that, they are well-suited for each other."

Georgiana giggled. "I had not considered that, but you are quite correct. They are well matched. Few men would tolerate the Sage's single-mindedness and devotion to dragonkind. Some say that he married a warm-blooded dragon."

"I believe that distinction was offered as an honor, but it is rather a two-sided coin. Your brother is much like her in his own way. That could not have been easy to live with."

Had Mercail actually said that? "Hardly. What am I to do? I assure you, these sentiments toward them are not welcome anywhere."

"That is a complicated question, to be sure. But since you ask, my advice is that you acknowledge your feelings for what they are: an indicator that you were hurt and that the situation is less than perfect. Then forgive them for their mistakes. Choose not to continue to hold it against them and move forward."

"So, you suggest I just pretend that it did not happen, then? They get off and pay no price whilst I am—"

"Not at all. They have damaged their relationship with you in a real way; lost all that it could bring them. That is a real price. Whether they know or understand that is another matter, but it is a price they will continue to pay. Much like the price you pay." Mercail draped her wing across Georgiana's back. "Do you want to continue to live in that resentment, making every decision, subjecting every feeling to the wrongs you suffered? Or do you want to dust off your skirts and decide who you want to be and how you want to go from here? That is in your power. Leaving them to the consequences of their actions and doing what is necessary for you to be strong and sure of yourself. That is what I am suggesting."

Was that even possible? It was a very interesting thought indeed.

11
Chapter

June 14, 1815

That evening, Georgiana begged off dinner—how could she possibly tolerate company or questions after such a trial? Surprisingly, Mrs. Fieldings not only permitted her to be excused, but sent up a tray for her to take in the privacy of her room. The privilege was appreciated, but also worrying, as, according to Miss Sempil, unless a girl was quite ill, such things were never allowed.

What did that say for the situation with Bede?

Dragon's blood and bones! What was to be done about that? Thankfully, it was not her job to decide, so she choked down a few bites and crawled into bed as soon as the sun had set.

Sunrise demanded she rise and dress—with so much of her life having been spent in the country, she could hardly refuse the demand, though today it was sorely tempting. How did ladies in town ignore it?

Perhaps she would never find out. Still, that was an issue for another day. Today had enough questions on its own.

She made her ablutions and pulled on a morning dress, one that Bede had not ruined. The remains of her white muslin were still strewn about the chamber, bits of sleeve hanging from furniture, the skirts still draped across the end of the bed. Was that the bodice lying crumpled in the corner? Best gather it all up. Maybe it would look more salvageable in the fresh light of day.

She pulled the chair near the window and smoothed pieces across her lap. Faint traces of dragon musk, Bede's distinct odor, wafted up from the muslin. Her stomach clenched, and she swallowed back rising bile. Never having appreciated dragon musk in the first place, would it now sicken her every time she encountered it?

That would make living at Pemberley, or even visiting there, difficult. At least Pax always smelt of flowers, not musk. The little dear was still sleeping in her basket of softs on the dresser. She had worked herself into quite a lather when she had learnt what had happened—ready to peck out Bede's eyes over it. Had it not been for Mercail's calming presence, she might well have done it. She was a stalwart Friend.

In the unflinching rays of morning, further damage to the muslin became evident. Small tears and pulls on every piece, besides the large rips and talon holes. Nothing but the magic of a fairy story would repair that mess. She clutched the ruins to her chest.

It was only a dress. Just a dress.

Bede had argued that, and after a fashion, she was right. Georgiana had other gowns. It was not as though this would leave her running naked in the street. If she wrote to Fitzwilliam, no doubt he would see the garment replaced as soon as possible. Not even Elizabeth would take Bede's side in this matter, at least according to Mercail.

And she was probably right.

That thought was satisfying. Not so much that Bede would be in trouble, but that Elizabeth would take her side on any matter. Maybe she could do as Mercail had suggested and simply let the wrongs of the past go and get on with her life.

No, it would not be simple at all. How could it be? But it would differ from dwelling on the anger and resentment. And different might be a start to something better.

Perhaps it would be worthwhile to try.

She opened the window and drew a deep breath, fresh and dewy and grassy. Maybe she could face the day after all.

"Is it true?" Miss Barton, hazel-green eyes hungry for gossip only slightly less intriguing than Mrs. Pendragon's, caught Georgiana just before she stepped into the morning room.

On the best of days, Miss Barton was irritating, and this was not strictly the best of days. "Is what true?"

They walked into the already bustling morning room. All the upper students save Miss Withington filled plates, sipped tea, and chatted quietly. Sunshine and the perfume of warm buns filled the air. Georgiana's stomach grumbled. Buns, bacon, and berry compote would be most welcome after her abbreviated meal last night. She sat beside Miss Sempil. Unfortunately, Miss Barton took the seat beside her.

"About Bede. Did she really destroy your gown?" Miss Barton nudged her with an elbow as she reached for the platter of fresh Bath buns.

"Did she go into your chambers and take it? Actually steal it from you?" Miss Sempil whispered.

There was no way around it. The subject would have to be addressed. Best get it over with now. "She took nothing from my chambers."

"But she tore it apart, shredded it?" Miss Reed asked from the far side of the table, her face turning pale.

"My gown is currently... disassembled."

"So, then it is not destroyed?" Miss Sweet bit her lip, sounding hopeful. The morning sun caught her ginger hair just so, rendering her quite pretty early in the day. "It might be remade?"

"The fabric is torn and not likely to be mended."

Miss Barton rapped on the table. "Why are you dissembling so? Why do you not come out and say what she did to you? You cannot be any less upset with Bede's transgressions than the rest of us are."

And why did Miss Barton not recognize dissembling was tantamount to saying she did not want to discuss the matter? "What have you to be upset about?"

"Our doors do not lock. How can we protect ourselves against such malicious action?"

"Why should we have to?" Miss Reed shuddered.

"No dragon has engaged in 'malicious action' against anyone." Georgiana met every gaze at the table. Perhaps a draconic tactic would quell the conversation?

"You do not consider Bede's outbursts attacks?" Like a dog with a bone, Miss Barton was today.

"Hardly. When a dragon attacks, one is quite certain of what has happened." Georgiana turned her glance aside with a small quiver.

Miss Barton barely concealed her sneer. "And you have seen so many of those things happen, you would be the expert on it."

"Members of my family have been the unfortunate participants in more than one such episode." Georgiana clutched the edge of the table and squeezed her eyes shut to drive away the frightful images of Vikont Pemberley. "I am quite certain a ripped dress does not constitute an attack."

Dragon students filed in just behind Miss Withington and took the open seats near the window, where the cold-blooded students could best enjoy the first rays of warm sunlight.

"Pray forgive me, Miss Darcy, but I must beg to disagree." Coxcomb rested her front paw lightly on the table, eyes down.

"What do you mean?"

"As a dragon myself, I think I have a bit more insight on the matter. And yes, I would consider this a form of aggression, not so much in the sense of an attack, but in the sense of establishing dominance."

"You see, I am right!" Miss Barton rapped the table as she crowed.

"Not precisely, Miss." Coxcomb glanced up. "When a dragon actually attacks, it is a life-or-death matter, so it was not an attack in that sense. But it was, in my opinion, absolutely an attempt, if rather ill-founded and backwards, to establish dominance."

Quicksilver cleared her throat. "Even in that, it is not in the usual sense of dominance, but more an act of desperation. When a dragon is of very low status—lowest status, really—sometimes they feel threatened, and when they do, they may desperately try to demonstrate their value—which is an aspect of dominance. Especially toward high-ranking members of the community."

"You suggest I am high-ranking?" Georgiana tried to cover her astonishment in a clumsy cough.

Quicksilver bobbed her head vigorously. "You are connected not only to one of the Pendragon Knights and to the Dragon Sage, who is a most remarkable personage in the Order, but also to Vicontes Pemberley, Cowntess Rosings, Cownt Matlock, and the Chancellor of the Order. Any dragon with sense enough to preserve their hide would think long and hard about crossing a dragon with your bloodline connections. If she could prove her value to you, then she would have greater standing amongst other dragons as well."

Interesting. Was that what had driven Bede to protect the dominant's nest from harm?

"Are you saying that the rest of us are safe from her, then?" Miss Reed pressed a hand to her throat.

Miss Barton flushed angrily. "That we are not well connected enough—"

"Not dominant enough to be of interest to her?" Miss Sweet offered, clearly trying once again to keep peace.

"I do not know if I should be relieved or offended." Miss Sempil sniffed and smiled.

"There is nothing offensive about this." Miss Withington folded her hands on the table and pulled her shoulders back. "Social rank is a fact of life of which we are all aware. We recognize rank every day, thereby making it no different to draconic dominance."

"If it were one of us who did such a thing, we would have been sent away, I am sure of it." Miss Barton met Miss Withington's gaze in challenge.

"I am not." Miss Withington shook her head. "Certainly, if it had been vindictive, that could be the case. But even then, I rather think Mrs. Fieldings would have come up with some sort of plan for the debt to be repaid first. But if the act were not vindictive, I am sure no one would be sent away."

"You think so?" Coxcomb blinked several times, her long eyelashes nearly brushing her cheeks. "That is interesting."

"It seems a different standard is applied between warm-bloods and dragons." Mercury-red flush crept along Quicksilver's jawline. "If a dragon in service makes such a mistake, he or she would be sent away, regardless of the intention. No one would even consider their motivation."

"But that is not the same situation." Miss Withington turned to Quicksilver. "A human in service would be dismissed as well, possibly even charged with a crime. So in that, it is the same. But we are not in service here. We are students. That is a material difference."

"But we are students who are studying to be in service," Coxcomb asked. "Which form of dominance comes into play?"

Quicksilver leaned in closer. "Students have dominance over staff, yes?"

"After a fashion, but the senior staff are dominant in their own territories," Miss Withington tried to catch Georgiana's gaze, as though hoping for her assistance in the explanation.

"I do not understand human territories." Coxcomb snorted. "Would not Miss Darcy's chambers be considered her territory? Did not Bede trespass upon it? Does not that present a challenge to dominance?"

"Oh, heavens! I can no longer make sense of any of this." Georgiana pressed her palms to the sides of her now-throbbing head. "Pray forgive me, I must go."

She ran out, lest she be intercepted, and dashed out the front door.

Oh, yes! Quiet! Solitude!

Birds twittered in the sunshine, beckoning her to walk the field near the house. How much better the gentle swish of grass against her skirts than that prattle-chatter in the morning room? Was this how it would always be now? Pray not, or the morning room would be insufferable. School would be insufferable.

Thanks to Bede.

If only there had been some sort of wilderness or private garden. Strolling in full view of the house, where anyone looking out the window might see her, felt so exposed, so intrusive. But she dared not go into the woods on her own. Not with highwaymen about. The open fields would have to do.

She hugged her shoulders. None of this conflict with Bede was her fault. Would anyone, human or dragon, actually see that?

Bede kept singling her out for her unique brand of attentions that inevitably ended in Georgiana's humiliation or distress. And it kept getting worse. What would happen next? Did she have to fear for her own life at this point? She kicked a soft clod of dirt.

Surely not. That would violate the Pendragon Accords. No dragon was allowed to act in that fashion unless in direct fear for their life and even then, only as a last resort. So, no, that would not happen. But what short of that? How far could this go?

She needed advice, practical advice. Sympathetic advice. But from whom?

She dared ask neither Fitzwilliam nor Elizabeth. Despite their experience, they were too jaded against her. Who did that leave, though?

Miss Bennet!

Yes, perhaps Miss Bennet could be of assistance. She had written a rather encouraging letter recently and might be amenable to listening to Georgiana's side of things. If nothing else, she surely would not say "Think like a dragon and act accordingly," which was often the best Elizabeth had to offer.

How exactly did one think like a dragon when one did not understand how they thought in the first place?

Best get that letter written and posted before Bede could somehow interfere with that, too.

June 16, 1815

Georgiana cupped the porcelain pounce pot in her hand and leaned back in her chair, letting the pounce do its work on the third draft of her completed letter. The tone was wrong on the first and in the second, she had failed to actually ask the questions she hoped to find answers for. Finally, this time, with her head a little clearer and some distance from the initial shock, it felt like she had gotten it right.

The pounce pot had been Mother's, a gift from Father during their courtship. Pure white, with a raised lacy pattern wrapping the sides, the pot nestled in her hand, warm and heavy, a reminder of Pemberley and home. Perhaps when she returned, she would find Pemberley a place she could understand a bit better now.

Pax sneezed, blowing the fine pounce across the page. "I am sorry, I did not mean—"

"Not to worry, my Friend. The ink is nearly dry." She tucked the pounce pot into her portable writing desk. How lucky it was that Bede had not knocked it over and broken the contents. That would have been even worse than the damage to her gown.

"Are you all right?" Pax looked up at her, cocking her head nearly upside down.

"I am sure I will be, eventually."

"Are you angry at me?" Pax covered her face with her wing, barely peeking out from under it.

"Why would I ever be angry with you?" She stroked Pax's soft back between her wings.

"I did not guard our territory against Bede."

"You were in town with me. How could you have done that?"

"A dragon must guard her territory."

"You were guarding me, and that is entirely enough."

"You do not hate dragons now, do you?" Pax hunched her fluffy head against her shoulders, turning herself into a worried-looking little pouf.

"I hate that you should have to ask that of me. I think perhaps it once seemed that way, did it not?" She sighed and scratched under Pax's chin. "I am sorry. I have been angry for a long time, that is true. But I find, as I have been considering it, it is not really so much a dragon who has been the problem. In truth, I am angry at people, at my family, and have blamed the dragons because it was far easier to be angry at them than at the people that... that I love."

Pax flew to her shoulder and cuddled into her neck. "Will you stop being angry now?"

"With dragons, yes. At least I shall try very hard to do so. Except perhaps with Bede, who I am still not sure what to do with. With my family, though, that is going to take some time to sort out. But now I know what I am trying to sort out, so that is a start, I suppose."

Georgiana brushed away the pounce, carefully folded her letter, added a dab of sealing wax, and pressed her signet into the blue blob. "I have heard Cosette likes to press her feet into the warm wax. Would you like to try that sometime?"

Pax hopped from one foot to another, shaking her feet. "Oh no! I do not like the feel of anything between my toes."

Georgiana chuckled.

Talons scratched at her door.

Bother! "Come in."

Gale slipped inside, her grey hide nearly black in the door's shadow. She looked a like a widow in half-mourning that way. "Pray, Miss Darcy, Mrs. Fieldings has requested your presence in her office. If you will come with me?"

As much as it was phrased as a question, there was no option but to obey. "May Pax join us?"

"Yes, I think that is fitting."

Pax flitted to her shoulder and cuddled into the side of her neck as Gale preceded them downstairs. Happy chatter still filtered from the morning room, a place she had avoided the last several days. Too much potential for questions she did not want to answer, even with Miss Withington kindly attempting to redirect them.

Gale pushed the half-open office door and revealed Mrs. Fieldings sitting straight as a ramrod behind her imposing black desk, with Mica and Bede standing nearby. A tall, thin window, southwest-facing, so it offered little light at this time of day, backlit Bede. A fully laden, newly polished bookcase flanked the other side of the window, behind the desk. That explained the pervasive smell of books and furniture polish. Two black-lacquered bombe chests backed up against the adjacent wall, their tops covered with neat stacks of ledgers and correspondence. Mercail perched on the chest nearest the desk, hunched and pouffy. A simply framed, primitive portrait of a family, possibly Mrs. Fieldings', hung on the wall across from the desk.

Bede appeared to be studying it. The past few days had been quite pleasant without her. Now it seemed all that was about to change. Georgiana pressed her hands to her stomach. Maybe that would loosen the growing knot.

Mercail, her resplendent white feathers glistening with morning light, offered her a small smile and an encouraging—but not persuasive—coo.

"Thank you for joining us, Miss Darcy. Pray sit down." Mrs. Fieldings gestured at a plain wooden chair opposite the desk.

Gale shut the door behind them and slipped in next to Mrs. Fieldings as she shooed Bede away from Mica and to the other side of the desk. Mica ignored the whole proceeding and whispered something to Mrs. Fieldings.

"I am sure it comes as no surprise to you we are reviewing recent matters in some detail." Mrs. Fieldings tapped her desk.

"Yes, Mrs. Fieldings." Georgiana perched on the unforgiving, hard chair and bit her tongue firmly. This was one of those moments when it was far better to say too little rather than too much.

"It is time for us to hear your perspective on the matter. Please describe what you believe happened."

"What we believe!" Pax launched from Georgiana's shoulder and hovered in front of Mrs. Fieldings as though ready to nip an ear. "It is a matter of fact, not perspective or belief. That dragon trespassed on territory not her own."

"The school is Mrs. Fieldings' domain." Bede stared over Georgiana's head, toward the portrait.

"That is not under dispute." Pax twittered sour, angry notes. "But just as minor dragons on an estate may hold a parcel within the territory of an estate dragon—by permission and leave of that dragon, and ensuring the major dragon's dominance is always honored—so, too, might my Friend and I have space within the territory of another. By her leave and permission, which Mrs. Fieldings has given by assigning us chambers here."

"Well explained, Pax." Gale stared at Bede, who ignored the attempt at eye contact.

Mica snorted in Bede's direction as though trying to catch her attention. "She is entirely correct. In that fashion, each student, each staff member, has territory granted within the bounds of the school."

"There was clear trespass!" Pax zipped a circle over Bede's head.

"So there was." Mrs. Fieldings nodded somberly. "Miss Darcy, pray do answer my question."

"After Bede sought to share my quarters, I was under the impression that she had been specifically instructed that she was not to come into my chambers without an invitation." Georgiana measured her words softly, carefully. "I did not give her permission to enter, and I most certainly did not invite her to... to... handle my property, any of it."

Bede clapped her jaws and sputtered, clearly struggling to refrain from speaking.

Gale glanced at Mrs. Fieldings, who nodded. "You dispute this claim?"

"I assuredly do! Her claim is not accurate. Not accurate at all." Bede snapped.

Georgiana gripped the seat of her chair lest she jump to her feet. "I am quite certain about whom I have invited into my chambers, and you were not among those. I have given no one permission to handle that gown, not even the charwoman."

"Lies! Those are lies!" Bede leaned toward her and hissed.

"How dare you call me a liar! What proof do you have? What sort of invitation do you think I made? For I assure you I never invited you—"

"Did you not say 'I wish I didn't have to do all that sewing? I find it is not something I prefer'?" Bede tossed her head with a self-satisfied snort.

"I recall that conversation. And that you were not a part of it. It was spoken to Miss Sempil and Miss Withington. What had that to do with you?"

"I was present for that conversation. You say now that you were not speaking to me? How was I to know that?"

"Perhaps because you were standing with Mica, Coxcomb and Quicksilver, speaking with them, your back turned to me." Georgiana clenched her fist.

"But I heard you clearly."

"That does not mean I was speaking to you! Surely the circumstances would make that clear. Mica, is that not the case?"

"So, you claim that was not an invitation to come and do the work myself?"

Georgiana jumped to her feet. "How could you possibly think such a thing? I was making conversation with my... my friends."

"How could I not?"

"It was obvious! No one would mistake what I said for an invitation."

"I beg to differ. It was clearly a request for my assistance. A rather rude hinting for it, if you ask me, but I chose to ignore that lack of manners and respond more politely by doing as you asked."

Mica laid a paw over her snout and shook her head.

Georgiana turned to Mrs. Fieldings. "Surely this cannot be true? There is no dragon at Pemberley who would ever make such a mistake. No dragon working at the Blue Order offices who would consider such an argument. I resent the implication that this is somehow my fault. If the warm-blooded are not permitted—"

"Calm yourself, Miss Darcy. No one here is making that claim." Mrs. Fieldings looked from Gale to Mica to Mercail.

"Is it truly possible to mistake such a thing?" The pleading in her voice felt a bit more pathetic than she hoped she would be.

Mica chittered under her breath, still shaking her head as she looked at Bede. "Translation in any language is fraught with many difficulties. Moving from one culture to another is even more filled with misunderstanding and strife. It is a wonder we can get along at all."

Bede harrumphed softly, a touch of arrogance in her raised brow.

"However, I find it difficult to pass this misunderstanding off as a mere difficulty in translation." Mica turned a burning glower on Bede.

Mercail cheeped a sour note and opened her wings. "I think, perhaps, if, Bede, you truly believe what you are saying, that this was truly a misunderstanding—"

"Of course, I believe that. Why else would I have said it?" Bede's tail thumped the floor.

"If that is the case, then you are most definitely not prepared to interact with the warm-blooded students without direct supervision." Mercail fanned her tail for emphasis.

Bede hissed, forked tongue extended its full length. "What are you saying? You cannot possibly mean to suggest that—"

Mercail glided to the desk near Bede, raising open wings between Georgiana and Bede. "Yes, that is exactly what I mean. You cannot be trusted to conduct yourself properly among the warm-blooded."

"What of her? Is she not to blame for being so unclear?"

Mercail turned to Georgiana. "In no way is Miss Darcy at fault for this situation. The blame rests solely on you, Bede. Even if you did indeed misunderstand her meaning, you knew those chambers were her territory. All dragons know not to trespass."

"But Pax is only a—"

"Even a fairy dragon's territory is to be respected, or have you forgotten that?" Mica growled softly, exposing a row of sharp, pointy teeth.

"But I am the bigger dragon, therefore—"

"Enough!" Gale snarled, fangs exposed, her legs twitching as though restraining the urge to pounce. "Clearly, you need further tutoring and direct assistance to understand how to get along in a mixed community. Since Miss Darcy is no longer in need of a companion dragon's constant attention, I shall ask Auntie if she is willing to contribute to Bede's education."

Bede jumped back. "But there is no need. I am able—"

"No. If this has shown us anything, it is that you are not. If you are to continue with us, it will be under these terms or not at all. Pray, make your choice." Mrs. Fieldings slowly rose and towered over Bede.

Bede shifted her weight from left to right and back again, eyes to the floor. "I suppose... I suppose I will stay."

"Gale, please escort her to her lair. Mercail if you will stay with her there until I have spoken to Auntie? Mica, will you direct Auntie to my office? Thank you."

The dragons scurried out. Mrs. Fieldings shut the door behind them.

"I will, of course, see that you are properly compensated for the gown, Miss Darcy. I doubt there will be enough time before our dinner party for it to be suitably replaced, but since its loss was because of a lack of oversight by the staff here, I feel responsible to see you are not materially harmed by the incident."

"Thank you for that, Mrs. Fieldings. I appreciate it. Please do not think otherwise. This leaves me in a quandary, though, as I no longer have anything suitable to wear for the evening. I suppose it is rather arrogant, but pray do not make me attend if I cannot be properly attired. My pride can only bear so much." Georgiana bit her lip and stared at the desk. Pray let Mrs. Fieldings not be vexed with her for speaking out so.

"I am sorry you face such a situation. Your request is reasonable under the circumstances. I will see what can be done to find you a proper dress; in the meantime, continue to complete your assignments related to the dinner party. I am hopeful we can find some satisfactory outcome to this."

Chapter 12

AFTER SEVERAL DAYS IN the classroom, even with the upper students assisting, the ever-hopeful and positive Miss Bamber was forced to declare Georgiana's gown utterly unsalvageable. The next day had been spent in finding serviceable sections to be turned into whitework samplers. Many of the students might never have the opportunity to work on such a fine fabric again, so the chance to do so now was too excellent an opportunity to forgo.

Helping to cut apart the usable bits and seam them together into useful samplers had been difficult at first, but then became cathartic after a fashion. There was something poetic, even romantic about taking what had been destroyed and fitting it for use again.

Cross English teacher Mrs. Ramsbury had attempted to discuss the endeavor as some moral metaphor and likened it to one work of literature or another. But the attempt was so forced that not even the most dedicated of students appreciated it. So, Georgiana felt justified in giving it little credence as she crafted the essay that had been assigned as a result.

Still, it was nice to hear the little oohs and aahs of appreciation as the upper students stitched away on their whitework in the bright sunlight of the classroom. For all her faults, her former companion, Mrs. Younge, had taught her to sew beautiful whitework and other fancy work. Her use of praise, rather than constant criticism, as her primary teaching method, led Fitzwilliam to worry that Mrs. Younge was not strict enough. But Mrs. Younge was probably to credit for the comfort Georgiana found in creating handsome designs on fabric.

For utilitarian sewing and mending, she had less patience. Both Mama and Mrs. Reynolds were impatient and grumpy while instructing her in those arts. Perhaps that was why she always felt edgy and cross whilst sewing ordinary things.

Interesting thought, that.

June 21, 1815

In the morning room two days later, several of the upper students clustered close to the window to take advantage of the morning light to attend to their whitework samplers. Georgiana, though, had left her sampler in her room.

The fragrant platters of ham, potatoes, and fruit compote were far more appealing than any sort of sewing. No, today she was not in the mood to appreciate fine work. Today she resented everything about the project and that she would have to sit out the most interesting exercise of the school term because of Bede. All told, it was petty, and small, and not the way she wanted to feel.

But it was. So, she would make the best she could of it.

Mica burst into the morning room in a flurry of energy and enthusiasm that seemed her defining attitude, startling Berry and Pax from their sunny perch on the windowsill. "Excellent news, girls. The flower shop has sent over several baskets of cut flowers we might use to practice arrangements for our dinner party." A pink gillyflower was tucked behind her ear, rather like the trimming on a pretty mobcap.

"Flowers?" Berry hovered near Mica. "Have they any nectar?"

Miss Barton threw her sampler aside. "Flowers, yes! Colorful, lovely blossoms. Who cares about nectar? I am so dreadful tired of staring at white on white!"

That remark should not have felt so personal, but it did. With her whiny attitude and rather critical demeanor, Miss Barton was hardly Georgiana's favorite girl amongst the students.

"It is such a treat to work on this whitework, but playing with flowers sounds awfully nice, even if they are just the old ones that could not be sold before they would wilt." Miss Reed rose and stretched her long limbs. She had a lovely sense of when someone had said something prickly and was always quick to soothe nettled feelings.

Though occasionally she tried too hard.

"All who wish to participate may join me in the parlor. We shall roll up the carpet to keep it tidy, and then see what we might make of our unexpected windfall." Mica beckoned them to follow her.

"Will you join us, Miss Darcy?" Miss Withington paused at Georgiana's chair.

"I have not the patience for cut flowers today." Georgiana rose. "I think I shall go for a walk and see them in their natural state."

"I shall go with you, then." Pax landed on her shoulder.

Berry zipped out and Miss Withington followed.

"Cut blooms lose their flavor quickly. That was why the morning room always had the freshest flowers at Pemberley and Darcy House."

Pax flew ahead, toward the front door, a bright white spot in the dim corridor.

"I had no idea, but I suppose that makes a great deal of sense. I shall remember that. That makes a hothouse rather necessary, does it not?"

"I think so."

"Then I shall remember that, too." Georgiana opened the front door and warm sunbeams poured through. Oh, yes, that was just the thing to thaw the frost on her disposition.

"Where do you want to walk today?"

"There is that patch of wildflowers on the way to Ebbing and Flowing Well. It is quiet, and not too far from Bennetson Hall. I think there are coneflowers and yarrow blooming. I remember you saying how you liked those."

"Oh, I do, very much. And the little insects in that tract are deliciously sweet as well." Pax chirped happily as she zipped circles over Georgiana's head.

A crisp note in the fresh-smelling morning air made her wish for her spencer, or at least a light shawl, as they walked toward the well. But by the time they returned, it would probably be too warm for them, so it was just as well Georgiana had left them behind. Pax continued to buzz about in dizzying loops and circles, diving at tiny insects that swarmed up from the grass, swishing at Georgiana's skirts.

In moments like these, it was no wonder fairy dragons had the reputation for being carefree and fanciful. If one did not know better, one would think Pax had not a care in the world as she reveled in the bright sunshine.

But Georgiana knew better.

Troubled by Bede and the constant conflict among the dragon students, Pax's true state was closer to worn and weary than carefree. Her exuberance came from the momentary freedom she found here amidst sun and flowers. Would that Georgiana could shed her worries like Pax, even for just a few minutes.

Georgiana blew out a heavy breath and lifted her face to the sun, eyes closed against its brightness. If only she could remain in the soft, warm embrace of the sunbeams, bring it back to Bennetson Hall with her, hide it in her room and retreat to it whenever she wished.

"It sounds as though that breath has more words behind it than simply breathing." Mercail said. "Would you care to give voice to it?"

Georgiana jumped and turned toward the voice.

Mercail hovered mid-air in what should have been an utterly impossible feat for a creature her size, white feather scales all but glowing in the sun. Queen fairy dragons were indeed remarkable. "How do you do that?"

"In the same way you do many things that are natural to you. You just do them." Mercail laughed a sweet, musical note. "May I join you? It is a lovely morning for an outing."

"I cannot promise to be good company."

"I do not require 'good' company. I often find it quite dull and boring."

"You would rather know that I am tired of all the reminders of my ruined gown at every turn and relieved to have a little space from Bede?" Georgiana continued her walk toward the wildflowers.

"I should think it is quite natural, considering all that has transpired. How do you regard the situation now that you have had a little distance from it?"

"What distance? Would that I found any respite from it at all! With samplers made from my gown, it is impossible to escape. I fight with near-constant reminders of what Bede did, and what I have lost as a consequence."

"Have you encountered Bede in the last few days?"

"No, and I do not regret it, to be honest." Georgiana paused and squeezed her eyes tightly shut, pressing fingers to her temples. "It is so difficult to know what to make of her and the explanations she tried to offer. Her reasoning sounds remarkably much like excuses, and difficult-to-believe ones at that."

"I can see why you would think that. You are not the only one who does." How did Mercail make flight look so effortless?

"You are referring to the comments that Bede should simply be removed from the school and the matter be done with?"

"I have heard that said."

"Berry and Pax told you many of the upper students said that, no?"

"Even without their ready information, I had heard. There are few secrets in any house, really." Mercail flew a circle around Georgiana, then glided toward the flower patch. "I think few appreciate the complex and problematic situation Bede is in."

"I find it difficult to feel sorry for her." Georgiana sat on a fallen log just inside the wildflowers. Before them spread a carpet of tiny clusters of white, yellow, and even a few pink yarrow blossoms, with their pine-needle scent, punctuated with taller bunches of purple and pink coneflowers, their sweetness carried in occasional wafts of the soft breeze. Pax wove happily through the blossoms. "I suppose that does not speak well of me."

"Are you aware of why Bede is here with us?" Mercail landed on the log beside her.

"As I understand it, it is because her failure to understand dominance and get along with others has estranged her from her community."

"In essentials, that is correct."

"There is more to it than that?"

"Do you recognize the implications?" Mercail snatched up a tiny insect that had wandered too close, her frizzy white head feathers bobbing gracefully with the movement.

"The way you say that suggests you do not think that I do. Pray help me understand."

"If Bede does not succeed here and prove that she can get along in Blue Order society, she will have no place to go. Her community will not take her back; between her awkward manner and her remarkable coloration, she simply does not fit. She will have to make her way on her own, with no community, no job within the Blue Order by which to provide for herself, and no territory to live in. Where do you think she will go? What do you think she will do? There are no workhouses, no charity for dragons."

"I suppose I never really considered it. Surely, she will find some territory in which to establish herself."

Mercail clucked softly. "That may be true, but for a drake raised in community, living in isolation is difficult at best. If she can do it at all. With her inability to recognize dominance, one must wonder what the state of her other instincts must be."

"Are you suggesting that Bede's survival depends on a favorable outcome with Mrs. Fieldings?"

Berry dove at them, flying frantic circles around her head. "Mercail, Mercail! You are needed back at the house! Immediately!"

"What is wrong?"

"They are fighting! It could come to bloodshed!"

"Who is fighting?"

"Bede. Everyone, I think; all the dragon students are fighting with her."

"Pray forgive me, Miss Darcy, I must go," Mercail zipped away with the speed and grace of a hunting cockatrix, which should have been impossible but clearly was not.

"Why are they fighting?" Georgiana lifted a hand for Berry to perch.

Berry landed and curled her toes tightly around Georgiana's finger. "I do not really understand. I was just asked to find Mercail. She is exceptionally good at calming such situations."

Pax suddenly appeared and told Georgiana, "We should return. If there are upset students, we will be helpful in calming them."

She hurried along behind the fairy dragons. Best not be alone so far from the house.

Highwaymen, angry dragons, exasperated teachers. How surprised Fitzwilliam would be about the reality of her experiences here.

"Do these sorts of conflicts between dragons happen often?" Georgiana asked.

"The peaceful coexistence at Pemberley is the exception rather than the rule, as I understand it," Pax said.

"But the Dragons at the Blue Order offices seem to get along tolerably well. When we were in London, I saw more conflict between the warm-blooded members than the dragons there."

Pax landed on her shoulder. "When a strong, dominant dragon, like Dug Matlock, is present, fewer conflicts take place. Barwines Chudleigh and Barwin Dunbrook are also dominant dragons. They accept Dug Matlock's role, setting the example for the other dragons to follow. That makes a significant difference. The Council dragons are all committed to the Order and willing to set their dominance instincts aside for the greater good. It is a mark of wise, accomplished dragons. The Order would never survive without wise dragons at the helm."

"I am confused. I know fairy dragons live in harems, drakes often live in communities, wyrms live in clusters. Do you mean those dragons do not coexist together peacefully in those groups?"

"Certainly not." Berry laughed outright, hovering near Georgiana's shoulders.

"I do not understand."

"A pair of dragons may sometimes live together peacefully, but few live together for life, as pairs of wyrms do. For the rest of us, there are always squabbles for dominance going on—someone invariably claims they have sufficient reason for a challenge When larger groups reside in proximity, tensions increase accordingly."

"I never suspected that."

"It is quite true." Pax warbled. "I am not a particularly dominant dragon. I am content to allow the vying for position to go on around me as I mind my own business. Few would bother much with me. But I am the exception, not the rule."

"I had no idea you were so exceptional. I suppose I have taken you for granted."

"Staying out of conflict is your nature, too. I knew that from the moment I hatched. That is why I chose you as my Friend," Pax said so matter-of-factly that it seemed like nothing at all.

But to be known so well, so quickly, so easily, was absolutely everything.

Bennetson Hall's front door stood open, allowing the growling and hissing to pour out. Exactly the sort of thing she wanted most to avoid. But no, if this was how dragons were, it was something she needed to better understand. She slipped through the doorway and into the corridor leading to the dragon tower.

Miss Grant and Miss Withington stood near the tower door. The angry dragon voices of their training partners rose from within.

"Oh, Miss Darcy!" Miss Grant rushed to her side. "I am sure you do not want to be here! I know Bede was your partner, but you have no part in this ruckus."

"She is right; pray go upstairs. You can help Miss Dunn calm the lower-form girls." Miss Withington appeared at her other side.

She might do just that, but not yet. Georgiana shouldered past them to peek into the open tower door.

Bede stood in the corner, with Coxcomb and Quicksilver facing her, all three as large as they could make themselves. The three dragon-governess students stood in behind them, effectively cornering Bede—a position in which anyone—let alone a desperate dragon—would have felt threatened.

Bede hissed and waved her front paws widely. "I have recognized your dominance; what more do you want from me?"

Coxcomb and Quicksilver edged back. "You recognize it in name only. You have spoken the words, but you do nothing to make us believe it."

"What do you want from me? What would convince you?"

"Any appropriate show of submission." Quicksilver's throat pouch flushed bright red as it expanded.

"And what does that look like?"

Coxcomb growled and exposed her fangs. "Every dragon understands what it looks like. Just do it."

"Pretend I do not. Tell me like you would explain to one of our training partners. How does a non-dominant dragon behave?" Bede's red eyes cast about, as though searching for escape.

"Even your tone in the question is challenging, is daring us to prove dominance over you yet again." Coxcomb pressed in closer.

"How? What sort of tone should I use?"

"You insolent lizard! You well know the answer to that question. How dare you demand further explanations when you simply argue with anything that is said!" Coxcomb swiped at her.

Bede barely avoided her talons. "I do not know! I do not know. Tell me what you want."

Quicksilver growled and stepped closer.

Mercail dove between the angry dragons, wings spread wide, forcing all to step back several paces. "That is enough. You might be dominant over Bede, but not over me. You will stand down."

"I cannot do what I do not know how to do, no matter how much you tell me I should already know." Bede turned her back and raised her tail.

Did Bede have an acid or a smell defense? One book or another Elizabeth had made Georgiana read mentioned some minor drakes possessed one or the other to protect themselves.

"No! There is no need to expend your defenses here. It will be intolerable to the warm-bloods and will do nothing to further your case." Mercail pecked the back of Bede's head. "You must stand down as well."

"Do you realize what she did?" Coxcomb puffed her chest and stepped toward Mercail.

Now who was challenging dominance?

"She does not fit here. She does not belong. If she cannot get along with her own kind, she will never manage among the warm-blooded. Send her away and be done with it." Quicksilver's entire body had turned bright red, a most intimidating, even threatening color.

"I will not have my territory challenged every time I walk into my lair. Do you consider that acceptable behavior?" Coxcomb snarled, tail lashing.

The other three dragon-governess student muttered similar complaints and pleas.

"I issued no challenge! Those were honest questions. How can I otherwise understand?" Bede shrieked.

"Can Bede be so ignorant?" Georgiana whispered.

"I met a wild fairy dragon like that once." Pax nestled into the crook of her neck, shuddering. "I met her in London. No harem would take her and she had no desire to find a Friend. Some of the other fairy dragons told me what had finally happened to her. I do not want to repeat the details." Pax squeaked miserably and trembled.

Georgiana pressed her cheek to her shoulder, cradling her Friend. Was it possible Bede could face such a fate?

"How can I be expected to know what is not taught? Will no one help me?" Bede's plaintive tones were those of a criminal condemned to the noose.

As bad as she was, did Bede deserve such a fate?

Pax wriggled from Georgiana's embrace and launched into the midst of the angry dragons. "Maybe I can help."

"You? How can you be of help?" Quicksilver's scorn dripped from her voice. "You are a fairy dragon!"

How dare she! Miss Withington gasped and Berry squawked. Did Coxcomb share Quicksilver's attitude? Would Miss Withington remain paired with her if she did? Hopefully not, for Bede's sake.

"I am well aware of my own species, thank you. And I also understand more about submissive dragons than any of you." Pax zipped a quick circle over Coxcomb and Quicksilver. "I have lived in the community at Pemberley and at Darcy House, as well as having spent time in the London offices of the Blue Order. I have more experience than any of you with real-life groups of dragons living together, and with warm-bloods as well. More than any of you more dominant dragons, I am qualified to help instruct Bede. Mercail, allow me to assist Bede."

Fairy dragon feathers! What had just possessed Pax?

Mercail twittered something none but the fairy dragons seemed to understand and gestured for Pax to follow. They flew upstairs, probably to the dragon common room on the highest floor. Berry darted back into the main house and, a few moments later, led Gale and Mica upstairs to join them.

Hushed conversations filled the tense air between the stone walls, now grown heavy and stifling.

Mercail fluttered back down to the crowd of girls and dragons, Pax in her wake. Mica and Gale trailed behind them.

Mercail sang a sharp, sour note, quelling all conversations. "After due consideration, we accept Pax's offer. Bede, would you accept Pax as your tutor in these matters?"

Bede shrank and seemed to struggle not to cower. "A fairy dragon as my tutor?"

"She has convinced me she is an excellent choice for the task."

"But her Friend is so highly ranked. How can she understand so much about being a subordinate dragon?"

"I have offered you an option to stay, not an invitation to challenge my judgment. You have two options. Which will you choose?"

Of course, Mercail had never named the other option, but it seemed all the dragons understood. It probably meant her being turned out.

"I, I will accept."

Quicksilver and Coxcomb snorted something that sounded less than pleased.

Gale pushed her way to Bede's side. "Understand, this is your last chance, Bede. And Pax's tutelage does not imply you are again partnered with Miss Darcy. You must leave her well alone. Is that understood?"

"Yes, Gale."

"Good. Then we will see you in my office immediately. The rest of you, clean up the tower and return to your own lairs. There will be no gathering in the common room tonight. Girls, to your own territories. Now go, all of you."

Mercail swooped through the doorway and Bede scrabbled after her.

13
Chapter

June 26, 1815

GEORGIANA TUCKED THE EXTENSIVE list Mrs. Fieldings had entrusted her with into her basket and tied the strings of her poke bonnet. A trip into Chapel-en-le-Frith would be just the thing to soothe her nerves. Though the school's tension had diminished somewhat since the student dragons' fracas, an air of uneasy anticipation that something might erupt again hung with the dragon musk in every room.

Over the last several days, Pax had spent a great deal of time with Bede, returning to Georgiana each evening to express her frustration in the privacy of their chambers. Bede's cluelessness was no affectation. Those things she insisted she did not understand were, in fact, actual points of ignorance and difficult to explain.

Apparently, dragons, even little, peaceful fairy dragons who rarely became flustered, did not excel at patience with members of their own species who were, as Quicksilver put it during a rather unguarded moment, "defective". Between Pax and Auntie, Bede had been kept under good enough regulation that this morning she had been allowed out of the dragon tower and into the company of the other students—with both Pax and Auntie close at hand.

The warm-blooded students seemed to accept the change well enough, at least restraining their comments whilst Bede was present. They understood sufficient basic etiquette to behave like ladies, even under such duress, which earned Mica's and Mrs. Fieldings' praise.

The dragon students were less than discreet about their disapproval. Far less. To the point of cutting Bede whenever she was nearby. They refused to eat with her. Some had even taken to sleeping in the girls' common room and the parlor to avoid her presence. No one could accuse the dragon students of subtlety.

Why was Mrs. Fieldings so determined to make Bede fit for something—anything? Miss Withington suggested it was because it had become a life-or-death matter for Bede. Was it really possible, though? It seemed an overly emotional exaggeration that Bede would not survive if Mrs. Fieldings did not make something of her. But Mrs. Fieldings did not seem prone to hyperbole; nor did Pax, who now seemed to share that belief.

Perhaps this was the sort of thing she should write to Elizabeth about. If anyone would understand the situation, it would be the Dragon Sage. She might even identify a solution.

"Are you ready to go?" Miss Withington—Neville, as she had recently invited Georgiana to call her—settled her straw capote into place over her blonde curls and glanced around the front hall. "There it is!" She retrieved her basket and another list from the table, near the large vase filled with drooping pink gillyflowers in need of being changed.

The front door stood partly open, allowing sunshine and honey-suckle-tinged air to flood the otherwise rather dark space.

"I am. I even tucked a few of Cook's lovely hand pies into the basket to tide us over when our errands run overlong." Georgiana winked as she tucked a napkin over her treasures.

The late-morning air promised an exceedingly warm afternoon. Even if it did, though, a long walk in the fresh air and sunshine, with the grasses whispering at their skirts and the soft breeze kissing their faces, could not be a bad thing. Ewe-Minder trotted behind them at a respectful distance, so much less intrusive than the guard drakes that often traveled with Elizabeth.

"Mrs. Fieldings' list is rather extensive, is it not?" Neville giggled.

"Delightfully so. I am quite ready to be away for a bit. Poor Pax is at her wit's end."

"I cannot fathom why Auntie and Pax have taken to tutoring Bede with such vigor."

"Fairy dragons are so accustomed to being dismissed as twitter-pated fluffy-tufts that they are overjoyed when someone takes them seriously. They apply great energy to anything of a serious nature they are asked to do. At least that is what I saw in London when—oh, I am sorry, I am not sure if I should speak of it. I can say they were given an important task and approached it with all the seriousness of Auntie on assignment."

"Auntie is a remarkably focused individual, is she not?"

"If there is anyone who can rein in Bede, it is certainly she." Indeed, Auntie had a particular way about her. But even that had seemed to mellow a bit recently, at least when Auntie was with Georgiana.

"I am not sure where Berry has gotten to this morning." Neville glanced about, probably looking for her Friend.

"I think she is with Mercail. Pax mentioned something about that before she went for her morning nectar. Berry reminds me of the Sage's Friend, Pax's brood mother, April, who is quite the spirited fairy dragon."

"That is one way to describe it. At least she is much easier to tolerate than Bede." Miss Withington rolled her eyes in a manner slightly different than the Fitzwilliam family's eye roll, but it conveyed the same annoyance.

"Have you any idea why Mrs. Fieldings has not chosen to cancel the dinner party? It seems so inopportune now."

"The mood has been rather dampened, has it not? I am glad she has not called it off, though. And I am entertaining some suspicions as to why." Neville whispered and drew a little closer.

Georgiana gasped. Did Neville have actual gossip to share? The head girl would stoop to the level of the ordinary student? How delightful! "Do not keep it to yourself! We must indulge ourselves in some conversation! We risk walking all the way to town in utter silence. Besides, since we are without our Friends to listen in, we should not waste the opportunity."

"The virtuous Miss Darcy longs for gossip now? I never expected."

"Do not be such a tease. It is cruel and you know I cannot tolerate it. We can go back to discussing the weather and never mention it again, if that is how you will be about it." Georgiana turned up her nose.

"Do not be offended. I am only teasing. I do not dare share this with anyone else. I cannot say for certain. These are simply my suppositions, not facts." Neville cupped a hand near her mouth.

"Of course, of course."

"I have overheard a few conversations, as has Berry. And putting together what the servants have said with what Mrs. Fieldings has said, and keeping track of notes sent from some of the surrounding estates..."

"Gracious! Is there anything that you are not aware of?"

"Your Friend is a fairy dragon, too. What do you think?"

Georgiana snickered.

"Having put all that together, it is my belief that Mrs. Fieldings is dipping her toes into the matrimonial waters of the Blue Order."

"You mean she has a suitor?"

"I do not think that likely." Neville glanced back toward Bennetson Hall, shaking her head. "But, if you watch carefully at church on Sunday, there is a particular gentleman who goes out of his way to speak with her."

"The one who escorted us to the school the last two weeks?"

"One and the same. Mr. Nicholson. He is a widower and the master of a local dragon estate, Wilde Boar Clough."

"Then he would be a suitable suitor for—"

"No, not her. I think the matter is that he has a son, a marriageable son. I believe he has asked Mrs. Fieldings for assistance in finding a wife for his son of whom Buxton, the estate dragon, will approve. As I understand, he is a cranky wyvern and will require a firm hand to manage, so a properly trained, Blue Order wife will be essential."

"I can see how that might be the case." It sounded rather like Mrs. Collins and Longbourn in some respects. "And Mrs. Fieldings is trying to train up her young charges for such purposes. But I must ask how there can be matchmaking, as it has been made abundantly clear there will be no young men at the dinner? Considering that none of us are actually out, it is remarkable enough that we are allowed any guests at all."

"No young men, but—" Neville leaned in close. "—there will be dragons. I have it on good information that the young man's Friend, a drake called Wild Boar, will attend and pass judgment on the eligible young ladies."

"Is this young man of interest to you?"

With a most coquettish look, Neville batted her eyes and looked aside. "I am saying nothing in that respect. Absolutely nothing."

"Is that not the young man we saw at church, back from his grand tour? He seemed a pleasant-looking fellow." Pleasant and well-mannered, though not as genteel as the company Fitzwilliam preferred to keep. A bit like Mr. Bingley, who had always been rather an anomaly amongst her brother's friends. "Wait, do you mean that the estate dragon's approval is necessary to obtain an introduction?"

"I know nothing about that myself, but Berry says that Buxton is extremely particular about who might be connected to his Keeper. I understand he did not like the late Mrs. Nicholson and does not want to repeat that experience. So, he has deputized Wild Boar to screen potential candidates."

"And are you pleased with this arrangement?"

"Mr. Nicholson is not the only one who will screen candidates for a son. Merchants and farmers will be there with their Friends and their sons' Friends as well."

"Then we are to meet dragons instead of young men?"

"Did you give any thought to the fact that the event is being held at a new moon, when travel is the most difficult for the warm-blooded, but the easiest for dragons? Mrs. Fieldings would not arrange for such an inconvenient date by chance. You realize the cottage and the carriage house are being prepared for guests, did you not?"

"No, I did not. How like the Blue Order to host a dinner party specifically for dragon acquaintance." Such an exceedingly strange notion indeed.

"I suppose that is one way to look at it." Neville lifted an open hand and shrugged. "But it does seem practical, all things considered. Dragons can screen potential candidates and prevent unfruitful introductions before they happen. Then Keepers and Friends might contact other Keepers and Friends and arrange approved introductions themselves, thus leaving Mrs. Fieldings free of any accusations of matchmaking."

"I was not aware matrimonial introductions—I am not sure what else to call them—were among the services offered at the school." Dragon's bones! Miss Bennet had never intimated such a thing. Surely Fitzwilliam and Elizabeth were not aware. They would never approve of introductions made in such a way. Would they?

"Heaven forfend! Never say that about Mrs. Fieldings! She wrote to all the parents of the upper-form students. I did not see the letters myself but the maid's puck, who, oddly enough, is able to read, said that Mrs. Fieldings sought parents' and guardians' permission for the event, with all the details and guests disclosed. And that all responded before she announced the dinner. I can only imagine that all agreed to the plans before she moved forward with them."

"But why would parents agree to introductions with those they have never met? It seems rather ill-advised to me." After Mrs. Younge had permitted Wickham access to her at Ramsgate, why would Fitzwilliam permit any sort of introduction at all? "It does not seem like my brother to agree to such a thing."

"I doubt he did. I mean, I do not think he will accept any suggestions that introductions be made. But for you to meet dragons? That seems the very reason that you were sent here. And yes, I am aware of more about why you are here with us than you would probably like me to. I am sorry. You know what fairy dragons are like."

Oh, merciful heavens! Georgiana pressed cooling hands to painfully flushing cheeks.

"All I will say is that there is not one of us upper-form students without some less-than-proud moments in our history, and leave it at that." Neville patted her shoulder. "In any case, you are the only one among us with a dowry that might make her of interest to men of good fortune. For you, the marriage mart is different. Plus, you have extraordinary connections in the Order. You will have little difficulty finding a husband. When you decide you are ready, mark my words, only tell your uncle, your aunt, and your brother, and there will be no fewer than half a dozen, perhaps a full baker's dozen, suitors knocking at your door."

"So, you mean to say that there will be no one in attendance who might be seriously interested in me—that the reason is not personal, but entirely due to matters of fortune. But I should not be disappointed because I will enjoy plenty of other opportunities in the marriage mart."

"Do not make it sound so cold. That was not what I meant. You ought to know me better than that. I have asked you to call me by my given name, after all."

"Well, Neville," Georgiana cocked her eyebrow, "I do not think it will be so easy as you suggest."

"No, of course not; your brother and his wife will be particular about who they admit into your company. But it will be far easier for you than the rest of us. You really do not understand how difficult it is to meet a suitable dragon-hearing man, nor how much many of us wish to avoid the trials of a half-Blue family."

"The Sage's family is half-Blue. I have come to see why that would be worth avoiding."

"Then you understand the motivation! I, for one, am grateful that Mrs. Fieldings would undertake such a complicated effort on our behalf. One in my position cannot afford to be romantical. Finding a young man of appropriate situation and a member of the Order is doubly complicated. I must be practical about these matters." How like Mrs. Collins, she sounded.

"I am not sure if any of us can risk a dragon-deaf husband. Were you aware that the Order compelled my brother and his wife to marry, but had that not happened, I think they would eventually have chosen that path for themselves."

"What a novel that would make! Certainly, for Blue Order eyes only, but if you possess any inclination to write, you should try your hand at it. You would have to cleverly conceal their identities. Even so, it would be a lovely story."

"I never considered that. I will give it some thought." What a great laugh that would be. Putting a Blue Order novel alongside all the serious and important works the Sage and the Historian had written.

Incomprehensible.

Half an hour later, the quaint buildings of Chapel-en-le-Frith welcomed them with the quiet bustle of village traffic. The gentle pace was easy to join, even pleasant, making one feel rather welcome and at home.

"Should we stop at the haberdashery first?" Neville glanced at her list. "Or would you prefer I go to that shop alone?"

"You think it will remind me of the fate of my favorite gown more than the constant presence of samplers made of its scraps?"

"I have always felt a mite awkward about working on that, even when you are not around. It seems so wrong that we should benefit from something so unpleasant for you."

Georgiana drew her basket a little closer. "I think I have resigned myself to it. And given

what you said, I shall not be missing very much by sitting out the event, after all."

Neville gasped. "That was not at all what I meant for you to understand in any of that conversation."

"Yes, yes, I know. I do not mean to be disagreeable about it, truly I do not. And yes, I shall be far more content in missing out now than I was before." Georgiana forced a small smile that was hopefully reassuring. "Does it help to hear that I am by no means ready to make a match myself? So, I can happily ponder what good will come out of this for you and Miss Sempil and the others?"

"Truly, you are not put out?" Neville looked a little relieved.

"Absolutely. I actually think it is a good thing. I do not like to perform for others, except of course on the pianoforte." And even then, not so much, but that did not need to be said now. "Still, if you do not object, I should like to stop at the post office first. That will give me something useful to do whilst you browse through Mr. Felton's new wares."

"I am only going to pick up the things Mrs. Fieldings has ordered."

"So you say, but I can see from here there are new pretties in the shop window. I know your fondness for gloves."

"New gloves? Gracious, then I am indeed lost. Hurry, then, to the post office we must go!" Neville turned toward the post office. "Could you tell the colors? Perhaps of what they were made? My purse is rather light at the moment, but enough for a new pair of gloves, especially if they are lovely and different from what I already have."

"You see, I know your weakness!" Georgiana laughed as she pushed open the post office door and a trio of little brass bells rang.

The cramped little post office was nothing to the spacious, efficient one near Darcy House in London. With only a single long desk and one row of pigeonholes behind, it might have been dreary and gloomy. But it was warm and friendly and everyone who entered was greeted by name.

A bored-looking clerk with a shock of dark hair falling into his eyes looked up from his desk. "Miss Withington? You are here for Mrs. Fieldings?"

"Indeed, we are." Neville approached the desk.

"Just a moment." He disappeared into the back room and reappeared with a bundle of letters and a package. "This is addressed to Miss Darcy, in care of Mrs. Fieldings."

"Oh, that is for me!" Georgiana took the lightweight, brown-paper wrapped bundle of intrigue. The direction was written in Miss Bennet's handwriting.

"Who is it from?" Neville looked over her shoulder.

"Miss Bennet. But I have no idea what she might send me."

"Then you must open it."

"Here? Now?"

"No, let us go to Mr. Felton's, and you can open it there whilst I make a fool of myself admiring the gloves." Neville looped her arm in Georgiana's and half guided, half dragged her out.

A package from Miss Bennet! It was not heavy enough for a large book. A monograph would never have been sent in such a large parcel. She shook it and the weight shifted with a soft sound.

"What do you think it is? Were you expecting something?"

"Expecting? No, not at all. But... Mrs. Fieldings said something about trying to find me something suitable to wear at the dinner party..."

"Perhaps your family sent you something! Oh, that would be delightful! And if so, Mr. Felton's is exactly the place to open it and see if there is anything needed!" Neville all but ran across the street and into the haberdashery.

The large pewter bell on Mr. Felton's door rang as they burst in. The fragrance of fresh flowers in all the vases and the yapping of Biggles the puck on the squat golden-yellow couch near the front window greeted them. Mr. Felton must have recently gotten new stock in. Drawers were open along the wall and in the dressers that flanked the couch, with tantalizing bits of the wares within peeking out. Somehow, he made all those deliberate enticements appear accidental, increasing their appeal. What a shrewd shop owner he was.

"Good afternoon, ladies. I imagine you are here to pick up the package for Mrs. Fieldings?" Mr. Felton, his long, waxed mustache arranged in graceful curls that ended near his nose, removed a bundle from under his counter.

"Indeed, we are, but we might need a few more things once she opens her package." Neville pointed at Georgiana's box.

"Well, do sit down and make yourself quite at home. Let me know if I might be of assistance." Mr. Felton pointed at the worn couch.

Biggles rolled belly-up on the couch and wiggled his legs at them.

"I have never known a... pug... more in love with belly scratches than Biggles." Neville leaned down to scratch the little dragon's round belly.

"He always knows who to ask, Miss." Mr. Felton chuckled. "So full of himself he is. If he is a bother—"

"Clearly, I am not." Biggles writhed and groaned as Neville continued to scratch.

"Sit down and open that package. I can hardly contain my curiosity." Neville patted a couch cushion.

Truth be told, neither could she. Mr. Felton came to stand near and handed her a pair of scissors, probably to hide his own curiosity. She cut the string and carefully opened the wrapping and the box. Atop the tissue paper was a note in Miss Bennet's hand.

As you and I are of similar build, I hope this will not require much fitting. It is nothing to your white muslin, but perhaps you will find it useful.

~LB

Georgiana's hand trembled, and she swallowed hard as she moved the tissue aside, revealing pink sprigged lawn with pintucks. She shook out the folds, and a gown appeared. Embroidered with scattered leaves and flowers along the skirt, the bodice boasted a fashionable neckline, trimmed with more embroidery. Short sleeves with a delicate puff finished the gown. Not comparable to what she had lost, but entirely appropriate for the dinner party at the school.

"It is beautiful! Just lovely! And it looks like it will fit!" Neville clapped softly.

Georgiana held it against herself. "I think so. I cannot believe it. Miss Bennet sent this."

"I am not surprised; that sounds just like her. I am so glad for you. Now you do not have to sit out! What shall we do with this gown, then? It seems a shame not to make it uniquely your own. There is time." Neville spread out the skirt to get a better look at it.

"If I might make a few suggestions?" Mr. Felton pointed out possible improvements to the gown.

Georgiana barely heard, though, blinking back the blurriness in her eyes and gulping past a lump in her throat. Such thoughtfulness and kindness! No doubt Elizabeth had been party to this as well. With so many fairy dragons about, there would be little that she did not know. All of which meant she approved.

Feather dust! That should not make her cry, but it was certainly difficult not to.

Half an hour later, with dainty buttons, pink ribbon roses, and a small length of lace for Georgiana and a new pair of gloves for Neville, they gave Biggles a final belly scratch, tucked their packages into their baskets alongside Mrs. Fieldings' order, and left Mr. Felton's.

"You might want to stop smiling." Neville whispered with a giggle. "All the conduct books recommend that a young lady be cautious about smiling too much."

"Since neither Auntie nor Mrs. Fieldings is here to disapprove right now, I shall take my chances, for I am quite certain I cannot stop." Georgiana turned her face aside, just to see if it were possible to return her face to a more decorous arrangement. It was not.

"I can hardly wait for you to try on your new gown! You will let me help you with those ribbon roses, yes? They will be so perfect on the pintucks—"

"Look there, does that look like Quicksilver?" Georgiana gestured with her chin toward an alley near the butcher shop. "There with Bones, the butcher's Friend."

Neville pulled up short and stared. "She is the only drake of that color in the region, I am sure of it. And who is that other drake, the one with the odd knob on his head? I am quite sure I have never seen him before."

"Nor have I." He was a memorable sort of creature and not likely to be mistaken for another. He stood tall, chin raised high and chest puffed out. "Look at their postures. Something strange is going on."

"That strange one seems rather dominant, does he not?"

"Exactly what I was thinking, with his frill extended now, and tail high. Quicksilver and Bones seem like they are accepting that, too. What is their connection to that dragon?"

"Perhaps there is a wider community of drakes in the region? Major dragons are supposed to keep a record of all the minor dragons in the territory they oversee. Could this be related?" Neville chewed her bottom lip.

"But why now? Quicksilver and the other student dragons have been at Bennetson Hall for months. If a major dragon were interested in keeping track of them, it would have happened much sooner."

"Perhaps it has something to do with the dinner party? There will be minor dragons attending from other major dragons' territories. It would make sense that the local major dragons would need to be informed of the plans. If several strange dragons pass through the territory at once, I would imagine that needs some preparation?"

"That makes sense, I suppose." Georgiana dragged her knuckles along her chin. It made sense. "But should not Gale or one of the other staff dragons be managing that sort of thing? As important as dominance is, why would that sort of task be shifted to a student dragon?"

14
Chapter

June 29, 1815

IT SEEMED LIKE THE entire school shared in the joys of Georgiana's new gown. A bit of jealousy that she should have a family so well able to provide for her subsided when Neville let it be known it was Miss Bennet, a former student at Mrs. Fieldings', who provided the garment. An excellent example of how regular Blue Order members should look after their own. After that, everyone was eager to assist Georgiana in fitting and trimming the dress. Miss Bamber, the needle-work teacher, though, insisted she should manage the fitting to ensure that no more disasters befell Miss Darcy before the dinner party.

Three days later, Miss Bamber handed Georgiana the pink lawn gown and gestured to the dressing screen set up in the corner of her office. "There now. Why not try this on and see how those adjustments fit you?"

Georgiana took the dress and headed toward the embroidered dressing screen in the far corner. Though rather crowded, Miss Bamber's office somehow was as light and gay as its occupant. With sewing projects in various stages of completion strewn about the large work-table that took up most of the small room, hanging off hooks on the walls, and draped over the tall, well-used dresser in the corner, the room radiated a constant sense of busy energy, a touch chaotic, but entirely good-natured. Much like pretty, bird-like Miss Bamber herself, whose hands were always occupied with some sort of useful employment.

"It was kind of you to do the work on this yourself. Thank you." Georgiana slipped the gown on.

Miss Bamber chuckled. "Ordinarily it is the sort of thing that would be better for you and your fellows to do yourself, but considering the lack of time and the highly unusual circumstances under which things have occurred—"

"It is hardly your fault that Bede took it upon herself to be so helpful."

"While the responsibility remains with her, it is also true that she might have gotten the idea sewing was not difficult and that she was equipped to do the task from listening to my admonitions to some of your fellow students. And yes, I well know she was not part of that particular sewing lesson, but when dragon students are involved, it behooves teachers to be careful of their words and attentive to how they might be misunderstood."

Georgiana peeked around the screen.

Miss Bamber beckoned her out. "Besides, working on such a lovely fabric is a rare treat, so there may have been a mite of selfishness attached to the offer as well. Now come here and let me see how the adjustments have worked."

Georgiana paused at the cheval mirror shoehorned in near the dressing screen. It was certainly not her white muslin. She swallowed hard. Nothing would ever change that fact. However, the pink lawn fit beautifully now. Almost as if made for her. It was truly a lovely garment and an incredibly thoughtful gesture from someone who owed her no such courtesy. An expression of warmth and regard she would have never known had things not happened the way they did.

That was what she would focus on.

Miss Bamber tugged the right puffed sleeve. "Very nice. I do say, one might think it was made for you. The color suits you well and the fit is nearly perfect. I suppose we could still make a slight adjustment on the sleeve if you prefer—"

"No, I think it is excellent as it is."

"Then to the classroom we shall go, where a room full of students is ready and excited to help you trim this lovely little confection." Miss Bamber led the way out.

The pink lawn rustled and whispered in the particular way linen had when skirts swished. Not like the soft voice of muslin, but like a breeze with just a touch of crispness. Rather like a cluster of pink Michaelmas daisies rustling together in the wind. Pax loved Michaelmas daisies, and she had loved the dress at first sight, although she could not hide as well against the pink as she could the white. Dear, sweet, little Friend.

"How lovely you look!" Miss Reed exclaimed as they walked into the upstairs classroom.

The upper students flocked to Georgiana in a rush of appreciative murmurs.

"The pink suits you well indeed." Miss Sempil circled her. "It is my favorite color. We shall look very well together when we play and sing after dinner."

"The trims are in the box on the desk." Miss Bamber waved in the general direction. "Miss Sweet, pray bring them and we shall see how we might gild this lily."

The girls crowded around her, their excitement tingling against her skin. Not long ago, this sort of attention would have terrified her and sent her scurrying for cover. But in the warm light of sunshine and friendship, the dread melted into something soft and comforting. She lifted her arms and closed her eyes, allowing it to wash over her.

"What is she doing here?" That was Miss Barton's whiny voice.

Georgiana opened her eyes a fraction. Dragon's bones! Bede? She was not supposed to be anywhere near her or her gowns.

Pax hovered nearby, twittering something soothing. Was that for Georgiana's benefit or the other students'?

"We are here under Gale's direction." Auntie peeked over Bede's shoulder, her blue-green such a contrast above Bede's black-and-white speckles.

"Surely you are not here for needlework lessons. I have not the time for that now. You should have—" Miss Bamber pointed toward the door.

"No. Handwriting practice, which is best done at the tables in this room. We shall bother no one over there, you shall see." Auntie nudged Bede toward the far corner, nearest the windows.

Auntie and Miss Bamber locked eyes in what seemed to be some sort of dominance contest. Both took a small step back.

"We shall bother no one." Auntie elbowed Bede, who nodded vigorously.

"Focus on your task, girls, lest you apply those ribbons unevenly. There is no time to do this over." Miss Bamber clapped her hands sharply, and the girls returned to their ribbons and pins.

Pax continued to sing from her station near Bede. Perhaps because Georgiana could see through Pax's intentions, or maybe because she knew Pax's song too well, she found little soothing in the fairy dragon's song. The friendly tone of the surrounding whispers, though, eased into the comfortable comradery as the girls settled back to placing the trims on the pink lawn.

Georgiana tried to focus on the ribbons and flowers and lace appearing and disappearing on her skirt. But Bede's restlessness overwhelmed all the other activity in the room.

Bede turned to Auntie as though asking a question.

Perhaps, if she concentrated, Georgiana might hear it. She closed her eyes and focused.

"I do not understand why you insisted on dragging me to the classroom when I am unwelcome here. My standing desk in the dragon tower is entirely sufficient to the task," Bede muttered.

"Not the task I had in mind." Auntie murmured.

"Might I know what I am to be learning now?"

"I actually have several lessons in mind, each important in its own right." A note of finality in Auntie's voice should have curtailed all further questions.

"Tell me that I might understand to what I am to be attending."

Did Auntie just sigh? "First, I want you to attend to the hand motions the girls are using in their sewing. Do you see how your paw is ill-suited to those movements? You have difficulty in bringing opposing digits together, limiting the size of what you can grasp with any measure of control."

"What of it?"

"If you are aware of this limitation you possess, you then should use it to identify those tasks for which you are well-suited and those you are not. No amount of practice will enable you to hold a needle and command it properly. Thus, it is foolish of you to attempt tasks which require that skill."

"How, then, am I to improve myself if I do not undertake things I cannot do?"

"There is a difference between what you are unpracticed at and what you are incapable of doing. Or will you jump from the dragon tower in the effort to learn to fly? Only a fool is unwilling to recognize the difference. For your handwriting practice, I want you to make a list of no fewer than twenty skills which you possess, twenty you might yet learn, and twenty that are clearly outside your capacity to do so."

"To what purpose?" Bede harrumphed. Such cheek!

"So that you better understand yourself. Self-awareness is a vital step in self-control, which you might make the first item on the list of skills to master."

"Yes, Auntie. You said there were several lessons."

"Indeed I did. After you finish the required lists, you should also take the opportunity to write the essay Gale assigned you to compare and contrast dominant and subordinate behaviors in dragons and warm-bloods."

Bede groaned softly—just like Miss Barton did when Mrs. Ramsbury assigned them an essay.

"All of which will help you practice your handwriting, which, though it is best you limit yourself to the use of a pencil since you use your left paw, is a skill you are far better suited for than you claimed. You are only in want of practice to become reasonably proficient at it."

"But I do not like it." Now Bede sounded like some of the younger girls after an assignment from Mrs. Ramsbury.

"You dislike it because you find it challenging. As soon as you become better practiced, you will appreciate the utility it provides and see how you might use that to advantage."

Bede grumbled again. "Yes, Auntie."

"Ouch!" Georgiana yelped and jumped. She opened her eyes. Who had just stabbed her?

"Pray forgive me, I did not mean to catch you with the pin." Miss Grant squealed, wincing as she spoke.

"What do you think, Miss Darcy?" Miss Bamber gestured at the dress.

Granted, it was a little difficult to sort it out whilst wearing it, but Georgiana craned her neck and tried. "Gilding the lily indeed! Delightful, utterly delightful!"

"And in excellent taste, I would say. I think some of you have been studying the newest fashion plates that arrived in the last post."

Miss Barton blushed. "I am glad it shows."

"All right, I think it is ready to sew. Time to take it off and submit it to the needle." Miss Bamber pointed toward the door. "Just pop off to your chambers now and get changed, then bring it back to us, and we shall get started."

When Georgiana returned, Miss Reed took charge of the gown, with Miss Barton at her elbow, suggesting that Georgiana looked pale and in need of fresh air. They were right; after all that attention—and exposure to even a well-behaved Bede—she felt rather desperate for a bit of quiet and solitude. Auntie herself suggested that she take a walk immediately, as it looked like there would be rain coming soon. She should avail herself before the opportunity was lost.

How could one refuse such a suggestion? Georgiana hurried for her shawl and bonnet and shut the front door behind her less than five minutes later.

Auntie was right, as she usually was; the scent of rain hung in the air, bounced about on a bumpy little breeze, stammering and stuttering, unable to decide what it was saying: fair weather or foul?

What an eloquent little thought. Perhaps Mrs. Fieldings' literature lessons were finally taking hold. Georgiana laughed. Fitzwilliam would probably suggest she should give up the novel she was reading in favor of more serious tomes.

Perhaps Shakespeare would suit. The bard was known for interesting turns of phrase. And it was just possible he was a Hearer as well. No official record existed of him as part of the Order, but it was well known that old records were often incomplete, so it was possible. Why else would his works include references to dragons?

Such odd and fanciful thoughts today—a visit to an odd and fanciful place would be just the thing. She turned toward the road that ran past Ebbing and Flowing Well. Such a peculiar spot—called a wonder of the Peak District by some. Others said it was a sacred place of the old religion. In either case, the hillside spring that flowed at unpredictable times and stopped at others was an intriguing spot.

Some said it flowed more after a rain upstream, that the water would flow down and feed the well. Others claimed it was not nearly so predictable. That might be so, but one could always assume it would be boggy and muddy near the stones in the hillside where the spring issued forth when the mood struck it.

It was the sort of place Elizabeth would appreciate. She should include that in the next letter she wrote.

The grey limestone banking the hillside from which the well sprang came into view. Behind it, stone walls lined either side of a path that snaked back to the dairy farm about half a mile from the well. A cow lowed in the distance, as though to prove that cows, not sheep, had possession of those fields. Silly creature.

The cow and the odd songbird were the only sounds near the well. Apparently, it chose not to flow today, capricious spring. But perhaps she could get a closer look at the limestone wall and the spot from which the water flowed. That would help her describe it better in her letter.

Georgiana stepped off the road into the grass that sloped down into the muddy basin that held the waters when they flowed. Boggy green and muddy smells enveloped her, stirred up by a suddenly active breeze that forced dark clouds across the wan sun. Tiny insects rose around her and several grasshoppers careened off her skirts and back into the tall grasses.

A few more steps brought her to the edge of the mud, perhaps ten feet from the spring itself. An odd spitting sound presaged a splash of water that landed with a lazy plop not far from the hill. Perhaps she could see the start of a flow. That would be interesting—the old charwoman who did the school laundry said it was good luck to be privy to that sight.

Georgiana gathered her skirts away from the mud and crouched down to watch as the spring spat again. A startled frog leapt out of the way, right past her ear. Heavens, they could jump so far!

Wait, what was that sound?

That was no frog. Those footfalls—talons, that was the scratch of talons! She rose slightly to peer over the stone-banked hillside. Strong, unfamiliar dragon musk assailed her. Three heads, one blue, which had to be Quicksilver, another with Coxcomb's profile, and a third, with a large knob on its head that seemed vaguely familiar, bobbed behind the path's wall.

Would it be right to announce herself? She hardly wanted company, but it seemed polite. Yet...

Something did not feel right. She dragged in another dragon-musky breath, her heart racing, pulse pounding in her ears. Something about that scent felt wrong.

What should she do?

Think like a dragon and act accordingly—that was what Elizabeth always said.

What would a dragon—what would Pax do?

She would hide and determine who was approaching. Fairy dragons always hid and then determined what to do next. That might not be what a major dragon would do, but it was what her dragon Friend would do. Good enough.

Where to hide?

Bless it all, there was nowhere to hide! No shed, no trees, nothing but the well's basin. Full of mud and biting insects, it was no place for a young lady. No, she would—

"What do you mean, this torment cannot go on?" a gruff, unfamiliar dragon voice said.

"Exactly what I said. It is intolerable and must stop." That was Coxcomb.

"And you agree?"

"I do." Quicksilver, no mistaking her mercurial tone.

Clearly, this was a conversation they did not intend for warm-blooded ears! If it had just been the two dragons she knew, she would have announced herself, offered apologies, and been on her way. But the strange dragon, his voice sent shivers right into her bones. How would he react to being surprised?

Surprising a strange dragon was always a bad thing.

Gulping in a breath that went down like a rock in her throat, she stooped down, pulled her skirts up as far as she could, and picked her way toward the stone wall in the hillside. There was a space in the wall, just large enough to press into and be out of sight from the path. If they came this direction, though—

No, not the time to think of that. The boggy ground collapsed underneath her until she was ankle deep in the mud. She nearly stumbled. Bother and dragon's bones! Cold, squishy mud!

The distinct odor of wet limestone coated the back of her tongue with a weird metallic taste. She wedged herself between the stones, into the shadows, the mud reaching to her calves now. She clutched her arms to her waist to stop the shaking—cold or fear? Difficult to tell.

"It is a serious accusation you are making." That had to be the knob-headed dragon.

"You have heard what she has done. Do you think we are wrong?" Quicksilver always turned red when using that tone of voice.

"How have the warm-bloods responded?"

"With their typical hemming and hawing and dithering about." A tail lashed across gravel—maybe Coxcomb's?

"They have counseled patience and further efforts to train, to educate, to ensure she knows the proper ways to behave," Quicksilver said. "Somehow they think she can learn what she should already know by instinct."

"They do not understand the danger of a dragon with undeveloped instincts," Coxcomb said.

"Undeveloped instincts, you say? That is a serious accusation. She is quite old for such a case. Usually, such creatures are dispatched quite young. How has she made it this far?" The footfalls stopped. Was the larger dragon staring down at the two females?

"I do not know how she made it to maturity, but the dominant of her community owed her a favor, which is why she is here," Coxcomb said.

"And you would cross the will of that dominant?" The strange dragon's voice had a bit of a growl.

"He sent her away to be rid of the problem, with no invitation to return. That is a powerful statement." Coxcomb snorted.

"He intimated she would not have a place if she returned," Quicksilver added. "That is important, to be sure."

That grating sound must be Coxcomb rubbing her scaly front paws together. "You will help us, then? Present our petition and see that its importance is understood?"

"It is not for you to decide what is important enough to be heard. Much less to recommend a remedy. I am in no position to speak for—"

Cold spring water spat from the stone wall in a thick, burbling stream. Georgiana slapped her hands to her mouth to contain her startled scream.

"What was that?" Coxcomb asked.

"The well has decided to flow—"

Another splash of water spewed from above, landing directly on her head. Pendragon's bones! That was cold! What were they saying?

Overhead, the spring flowed in earnest, spitting and sputtering and splashing, drowning out all the sounds around her. Capricious thing spewed water for at least a quarter of an hour, drenching her to the skin, then it slowed to a trickle. She jammed her fist into her mouth to silence her chattering teeth.

A final watery plop and the spring stopped.

Songbirds, a cow lowing, buzzing insects, but no voices. Perhaps they were gone.

Lightning streaked the ominous grey sky. How much darker it had grown whilst the well flowed!

Crack!

Thunder shook the ground and rippled the water lapping at her calves. Not now! Pray, not now!

She held her breath and listened again. No more dragon voices. No scratchy talon steps. She leaned away from the stone wall and peered up toward the walled path.

No sign of dragons as more lightning flashed across the darkening sky.

Thunder, so close her skull rumbled.

Shelter. She needed to get back to Bennetson Hall.

Slick mud refused to allow her to scrabble back onto the grassy slope, forcing her to slog through the newly formed pond to make her way out as the water shallowed, and from there, back up to the road.

Sudden wind whipped her skirts against her legs. She shivered, teeth chattering, and hurried toward the school as heavy splots of rain spluttered around her.

15
Chapter

Georgiana staggered through Bennetson Hall's front door. Arms piled with thick towels and hot blankets greeted her. After plying her with steaming tea in front of a warm fire, Mrs. Fieldings trundled her off to her room with instructions to sleep as long as she needed. With Pax nestled against her neck, she did just that.

The next morning, she woke feverish, with a thundering headache pulsing with each breath. Although Mrs. Fieldings scolded her for being caught out in the rain and catching cold, it was a half-hearted effort at best. The prompt visit from the apothecary made it clear that Mrs. Fieldings was well and truly concerned.

Chest plasters and multiple noxious compounds were dutifully administered over the course of the next several days until, at last, her breathing eased and her fever broke.

July 6, 1815

A soft rap and the door opened just enough for Neville to peer in. "Are you awake? Are you accepting visitors?"

"Most gladly." Georgiana's voice rattled in her throat, still painful from fever and disuse. She pushed herself up with her elbows and pulled pillows underneath her shoulders. "I think this is the first morning since getting caught in the rain that I feel strong enough for conversation."

"May I?" Neville skirted the bed to the still drawn curtains. At Georgiana's nod, she pulled them back, permitting painful brightness to fill the small room. She took the chair from the dressing table and dragged it close to the bed. "That was dreadful bad luck, was it not? I am surprised Coxcomb and Quicksilver did not see you whilst they were out. They returned to the house not a quarter of an hour before you did, just before the rain became so heavy. If only they had been able to help you, you might not have gotten so ill."

Dragon scales! What was she going to do about those two? Georgiana pushed herself up a little farther to lean against the headboard. "I am sure I would only have slowed them down and then all of us would have suffered. You know how bad it is when the dragons get chilled."

"I do indeed. Quicksilver and Coxcomb spent the rest of the day on the kitchen hearth trying to prevent a deep chill." Neville sat heavily on the small wooden chair. "Pax became quite frantic when you fell ill. I had to promise her I would sit with you and I sent Berry off with her to get her to eat."

"It was dear of Berry to be so attentive to both of us. I cannot thank you enough. There is something especially soothing about such a faithful Friend." Georgiana smoothed unruly locks back from her face. "Do tell me, what did I miss whilst indisposed?"

"You realize it was not just Berry who sat with you? Yes? Auntie and Mercail both took their turns."

"I thought I remembered their presence. I suppose I was not dreaming after all."

"You might be amused to know that Bede earnestly offered to sit with you as well."

"She did? I am astonished. I would not have thought her one to favor the sickroom." The back of Georgiana's neck twitched. She owed a debt of gratitude to whoever had refused that request.

"Bede has been rather a changed creature since that argument with Quicksilver and Coxcomb. She has been... different. Less provoking and more..., is 'diffident' the right way to describe it? Perhaps it is Pax's tutoring."

"If that is so, I can imagine it has soothed the other dragons in the house not to be constantly challenged."

"Maybe so. In any case, it has seen a decided reduction in tensions, which, with the dinner party approaching so quickly, has been welcome." Neville patted the plain counterpane beside Georgiana. "I am so glad you are feeling better now, and that you might attend."

"After all the work on the pink gown, it would be rather insensitive of me to absent myself, would it not?"

"Most insensitive!" Neville chuckled. "You ought to know your presence has been sorely missed during music lessons. Mr. Elkins has suffered deeply in your absence. Your excellent playing seems the balm that makes the rest of our muddling through tolerable."

"That is kind of you to say, but you are hardly a fumble-fingered muddler yourself."

"But no one here is as accomplished as you on the pianoforte, and Mr. Elkins has made that absolutely clear this week."

"I am sorry for that. That is no way to teach or to be taught."

"Never fear. We have forgiven you for your accomplishments by insisting that you are to be the last to play during evening entertainment, saving us the mortification of playing, all the while knowing we are being compared to you."

"Then I shall suffer in silence, as waiting to get the performance over with is no small torment. Hopefully that will be sufficient penance for my sins." They laughed together. "What about learning the cotillion?"

"It is difficult to do the cotillion properly with only seven dancing. Nonetheless, we have improved dramatically. Miss Barton can now reliably tell the difference between right and left." Neville winked.

"Is she wearing a ring or a bracelet?"

"Both. She has a mourning ring for the small finger on her right hand and a bracelet of blue glass beads to match the trim on her gown for her right wrist. She says your suggestion has made all the difference in the world for her. And I agree, we are all much better for her newfound directional clarity."

Georgiana tried to hide her laugh behind her hand but there was little point.

"We missed you. It will be good for you to be back amongst us..."

How nice to be so wanted.

"Especially as there is so much to do in the next two days! Oh, I almost forgot to tell you. The most exciting news of all! It came in the post the day after you fell ill."

"Do not keep me in suspense." Georgiana pressed a hand to her chest and coughed. "In my frail condition, you might send me into a swoon and leave me unable to do anything today but lie in bed."

"Such a tease you are! I have half a mind to let you languish in suspense, but I cannot keep it to myself. But the news must not go beyond you. I saw the letter with my own eyes, so it is not fairy dragon gossip. And I happened to see Mrs. Fieldings' response as she was writing it, so I am certain of what that letter said."

"Oh, such intrigue. I must know."

"The letter was from a Mr. Bowles, or rather Sir Horace, an actual baronet from the Blue Order. He has requested an invitation to our dinner party! I can only imagine it is because of you he is paying us any attention at all, but it is rather thrilling. Even if he has no interest in the rest of us for his son, the acquaintance must certainly be a good thing, yes?"

"Bowles? That name reminds me of something, but I cannot recall what." Was it someone that Fitzwilliam knew?

"Perhaps—and I looked it up in the Blue Order edition of Debrett's to confirm the matter—it is because his patent is rather unusual. Although a baronet is a hereditary knight, Sir Horace is a knight of the Pendragon Order, and by decree of the Pendragon Accords, that title must be earned, not inherited. So, his heir must earn his knighthood before the title and estate can pass to him."

"I recall something of that sort. Baronetcies of that nature are rare, or at least I think that the case."

"Yes, it is most unusual, and rather romantic, like a novel, do you not agree?"

Another interesting Gothic or maybe romantic plot that might be written for Blue Order audiences alone. A young man who has to prove his worth to receive his inheritance, while his brothers wait in the wings for the opportunity to prove themselves first. "The baronet has more than one son?"

"Twins, as I understand. And Berry said—and of course you must consider the source first—that he has never named which of the twins is actually the eldest. Instead, he has told them that the first one amongst them to earn his knighthood will be declared the eldest and made his heir. I imagine there will be Blue Order assistance to suddenly discover the necessary documentation to agree with his declaration."

Pendragon's bones, what a particularly odd situation, especially considering what it took to earn a knighthood of the Pendragon Order.

"Is it not a delicious notion? So much potential as a tragic hero! Such young men are far too much of a risk to entertain a connection with." Neville pressed the back of her hand against her forehead.

A sharp rap on the door made them both jump.

The door opened to reveal Mrs. Fieldings, dark furrows etching her brow. "Good morning, Miss Darcy, Miss Withington. I am glad to see you returned to health after a most unpleasant several days. I need to speak to Miss Darcy rather urgently. Come to my office in, say, a quarter of an hour?"

Georgiana gulped. "Yes, Mrs. Fieldings."

She closed the door firmly behind her.

Pendragon's bones! What now?

"Pray, come in and shut the door behind you. And do sit down." Mrs. Fieldings waved her in and gestured to a cup of tea and a plate of jam and toast on her desk near a single wooden chair. "Partake. Some things should not be discussed on an empty stomach."

"That thought is not exactly one which stimulates the appetite." Georgiana sat down slowly and stared out the window at a lone sheep that had wandered behind the house.

"I suppose not, and yet I insist." Mrs. Fieldings stood over her until she had choked down the toast, washing it down with the rather cold, flavorless tea.

One might have expected Mrs. Fieldings to waste no time launching into her concerns immediately, but she walked silently to the window, stuck her head out, looked around, and pulled it firmly shut.

The thud left Georgiana's stomach a troubled little puddle in her chest. "Forgive me if I am speaking out of turn, but you seem distraught, madam."

"I am afraid I am, Miss Darcy. Things have taken a rather more complicated turn than I expected, and it will have some bearing upon you." Her shoulders stiffened and her head sank as she leaned on her hands against the windowsill.

"Have I done something wrong?"

"Not at all; in fact, you are doing very well. I am most satisfied with your progress." Mrs. Fieldings pushed back and stood straight. "I am pleased that your family has seen fit to provide you with a new gown so that you might take part in our dinner party."

"But there is a problem with that?"

"Not a problem, not exactly, but a complication, I would say." Mrs. Fieldings returned to her desk. "Truthfully, it is not of your doing. In retrospect, I should have anticipated it, but I did not. How can I put this delicately?"

"Perhaps you should not. There are times, as I understand, that it is better to be forthright and put things the way a dragon might."

Mrs. Fieldings screwed her eyes shut, shook her head, and then chuckled a bit. "Well said, Miss Darcy. Well said. In that case, I shall come directly to the point. You have, no doubt, surmised that this dinner party is intended as a way for some of the local dragon Keepers and Friends—individuals without the social rank, connections, and standing that you and your family enjoy—might identify potential connections for their families. Connections within the Blue Order. I hope you appreciate how difficult it can be for minor members of the Order to make suitable matches for their children."

"Miss Sempil and Nev—Miss Withington—have helped me to see that rather clearly, I think." So clearly that a letter to Elizabeth really was in order over the matter.

"Good. Then you will understand just how important such an event might be to them."

"It has been an animated topic of conversation in the evenings after dinner."

"Then you might appreciate the difficulty you present to the situation."

"I, madam?" Georgiana pressed her hand to her throat. "No, I do not understand."

"I have been working to make this dinner party happen for some time and did not anticipate the possibility of a girl of your rank and connections as part of my plans. I have never had a student both fortune and connections like yours before, and that presents some unique challenges. Ones which, I am ashamed to say, I did not adequately think through."

Mrs. Fieldings unprepared? Had that ever happened?

"You see, every aspect about you makes you the brightest prize among my students."

Georgiana pulled her shawl more tightly around her shoulders.

"There will always be one girl who, by her fortune or her family, will outshine the rest. That is inevitable. But the degree to which you do so is a serious problem. There is not a single family among my invited guests who is—to put it in rather crass terms—up to your level.

The few dragon-Keeping families who will attend possess only minor estates and dragons of little or no influence in the Order."

Except for the baronet that Neville had just discovered. But then again, with the vagaries of that inheritance, perhaps not. How did one judge one's worth under such unusual conditions? Not easily, for certain, and that would make the marriage mart exceptionally difficult for those sons.

"Your family has consented for you to be introduced to dragons, but not for liaisons to be made with the Friends of those dragons. While I well understand what your family wants, I fear our guests will not and will take offense. Moreover, so much attention will be focused on forcing their way into your acquaintance that they will ignore the girls who would be far more appropriate."

Heavens, what a situation! "I hardly know what to say, madam. What you suggest is most uncomfortable."

"I mean to cast no shade on your character, Miss Darcy. But people are what they are, and I well know how they act when there is a possibility of gaining a prize that would ordinarily be entirely out of their reach. While this runs counter to many romantic notions—"

Georgiana raised an open hand. "A girl like me cannot afford romantic notions." Wickham had proven that beyond any doubt.

"I am glad you said that. The question is what is to be done for it."

"I believe you just implied, rather strongly, that I could not in good conscience participate in the event."

"That would be the simplest alternative, but it is hardly fair to you. I should have thought this through far more clearly at the start. But only today has it become clear how determined our guests are to become connected with you." Mrs. Fieldings tapped the desk sharply several times. "Ordinarily, I consider correspondence confidential, but I think it would be helpful for you to see some of what has brought me to this point." She unlocked a drawer and placed a pile of letters on her desk.

Georgiana glanced down at the topmost letter at the point Mrs. Fieldings indicated.

We are pleased to attend and thank you most graciously for your invitation. Wild Boar will join us, of course, as a representative for Buxton, the estate dragon. We learned from one of the local fairy dragons that you have a particularly well-connected student with you this term. Might we inquire as to the family's expectations for this young lady?

Georgiana gasped. This was Mr. Nicholson, the dragon Keeper that Neville hoped to become acquainted with. How revolting. Had Neville any idea of his rather mercenary attitudes?

"And that is the mildest of the inquiries. I know it will be upsetting, but pray continue to read." Mrs. Fieldings pulled away the top sheet to reveal another, though she carefully hid the signature.

Is it true that you have a student with a dowry of 50,000 pounds? What do you understand about her family's intentions for her? What sort of estate will they require to make a connection?

Georgiana shuddered and ran her hands over her shoulders to smooth the shivers away.

"I see you are grasping the difficulties this presents. And so you see, this is not an uncommon sentiment." Mrs. Fieldings pulled away the letter and gestured to a paragraph on the next one in the stack.

Is her family open to connections from families of good fortune who are not landed? If so, what sort of fortune would be required for consideration?

The audacity! As though she were some prize horse to be purchased at auction. Maybe not even that, but merely a cow.

"Not all inquiries are so crass; some are much better mannered. Like this one." Mrs. Fieldings revealed yet another letter.

Georgiana skimmed the neatly penned, polite version of what had already been asked. A few more words of some sort of politeness and...

Dragon's blood! No, it could not be!

Georgiana picked up the letter and studied the bottom corner in direct light. The signature—it came from the dairy farmer down the road. A watermark on the bottom corner of the paper...

She fell against the back of her chair.

A snapdragon.

"You are as white as your ruined gown. What is wrong?"

Georgiana gingerly placed the letter on the desk, pointing to the signature. "How well do you know these people?"

"They are fairly new to my circle of acquaintance. They took possession of the farm on Michaelmas last year."

"Then I should understand that you do not know them personally?"

Creases formed between Mrs. Fieldings' eyebrows. "I have not sat in their parlor and taken tea with them, no."

"What are their dragon connections?"

"They are respectable farmers; they have a Friend. A drake, Nob, I believe they call him."

"Does he have a bony knob on the top of his head?" Georgiana gulped back bile.

"As I understand, that is what he is named for. Why do you ask? Is there something amiss?"

"I am not sure, but I feel there is something I must discuss with you and the dragon staff."

Mica closed the door with her tail as she brought in a tea tray complete with two plates of sweets; on one was biscuits favored by dragons, on the other, clear cakes of various colors and flavors. They might all need to be fortified by the time this conversation was over.

Georgiana chewed her upper lip. How much should she say? What should she say? It was all conjecture and based on conversations that she had overheard, so what did she really, actually know? This might be worse than a fairy dragon spreading gossip.

But it might not, and that was the problem.

Berry and Pax tapped on the window and Gale let them in. They perched on the bombe chest beside Mercail, who extended her wings and drew them close. Gracious, the little dears were so anxious!

Auntie slipped in and closed the door. "I believe we have as much privacy as possible. The student dragons are meeting with the household dragons regarding preparing a retiring room for the dragon guests at the dinner party."

"I did not know one was necessary." Mrs. Fieldings' forehead furrowed into something just short of a scowl.

"I do not know that it is. But considering it is done at Darcy House, it seems a useful exercise for the students to consider." Auntie sat on a stool Gale had pulled into the room to accommodate the additional guests.

"An excellent assignment." Mica stood near Mercail and the fairy dragons. "It would also make an interesting addition to our discussions in the salon—what sort of consideration is appreciated by dragons when socializing? Very interesting."

"Yes, it is, but perhaps we should focus on what concerns Miss Darcy." Gale cocked her head.

All eyes turned toward her. Georgiana stared at her hands. "I am not sure. I fear perhaps I am overreacting and all this is foolishness."

"Let us determine that." Mercail pulled the fairy dragons a little closer, like a hen with chicks under her wings. "Under the circumstances, an abundance of caution is not foolish, even if it all comes to naught."

"I agree," Auntie said. "And I am entirely certain the Darcys would agree. They have always insisted upon knowing every detail, no matter how insignificant it might seem."

That sounded just like Elizabeth. "Very well. There are two things, one which is merely uncomfortable, but considering the second, which is absolutely troubling, may be truly dangerous indeed."

"Out with it, please." Gale drummed her talons on the desktop.

"The day I was caught in the rain, I was walking near Ebbing and Flowing Well. I heard the voice of an unfamiliar dragon and, I am rather ashamed of it now, I hid."

Mrs. Fieldings' eyes widened. "Why did you hide?"

"I was afraid. I do not know why, but—"

"Instinct, it was instinct." Mercail bobbed her head.

"The Dragon Sage says: when in doubt, think like a dragon and act accordingly. Hiding seemed exactly what Pax would have done. So, I hid against the stones in the hillside where the spring flows from. I heard, and later saw, Coxcomb and Quicksilver with the strange drake with a large knob on his head. I think he must be the Friend of the dairy farmers near the school. Their conversation was... uncomfortable."

"In what way?" Gale's words were slow and deliberate.

"They were talking about Bede, about the problem she had become."

"With a dragon outside the school? That is most irregular." Gale snapped her jaws in a hard clap.

"Not just irregular, but outside the order of dominance." Mica flexed her front paws to reveal her talons. "They well understand such things. That is quite troubling."

"When a dragon goes outside the normal lines of dominance, it is a powerful statement about their attitude toward those in the recognized line of dominance." A soft growl edged Gale's voice. "What did they want from the strange dragon?"

"They said something about presenting a petition and making sure it was understood, but I do not know to whom the petition would be directed."

Gale's tail lashed hard as Mica shifted from foot to foot.

"Surely not!" Auntie barely kept to her seat.

"I am certain of what I heard. I wish I could have learned more, but the well began flowing at just that moment, and by the time it stopped, they were gone." She hugged her shoulders.

"Most troubling. You were absolutely right to bring that to us." Mrs. Fieldings drummed her pencil on the open journal before her. "Berry, Pax, can you offer any insight into who those two have been speaking with?"

Berry and Pax twittered to one another and to Mercail, who seemed to encourage them with nods and coos.

"Quicksilver asked Bones, the butcher's Friend, for an introduction to the new drake at the dairy farm. His name is Nob. Bones made the introduction in town the day you received your gown from Pemberley," Berry said. "He was not especially impressed by Quicksilver and it was not until Coxcomb was mentioned that he expressed any willingness to continue the conversation with her. Coxcomb has connections which interest him."

"Coxcomb? Interesting," Gale said.

"I thought it was odd for them to converse like that with a dragon outside the school. But it was not until you showed me that correspondence that I became concerned." Georgiana gestured at the locked drawer. "Pray, would you bring out the letter from the dairy farmer so I might show you?"

Mrs. Fieldings seemed to consider it briefly, then presented the letter in question.

"At the bottom right-hand corner of the paper—hold it up in the light to see the watermark. What do you see in the mark?"

Mrs. Fieldings held it up.

"It is a flower." Mica peered at it.

"What of a flower? It is an unusual watermark, to be sure, but I do not understand the significance." Mrs. Fieldings stared at it as well.

Mercail, Berry, and Pax launched from the bombe chest. "It is not just a flower." Mercail hovered closer to the paper in Mrs. Fieldings' hand. "It is a specific flower, not abstract, at all. It is a snapdragon."

Pax screeched. "It is! It is! She is right! This is dreadful!" She flew three anxious circuits around the room and dove under Georgiana's shawl.

Mrs. Fieldings jumped back and dropped the letter to her desk. "Clearly, I do not understand the significance of the mark. Would one of you be good enough to clarify?"

Auntie extended her paw and Gale handed her the paper. "I am afraid you are right. It is that mark." She adjusted her glasses. "This is a snapdragon flower, and it is the same mark that has been seen in London, identified with those who are enemies of the Order, involved with poaching and smuggling of dragons and their parts."

"Pendragon's bones!" Gale's jaw dropped. "Is this true? Is there such a thing?"

Pax peeked out from beneath Georgiana's shawl. "Yes. Yes, it is. There were those whom we knew in London who were exposed as members of the group. Dreadful! Terrible! The mark was also connected to the Sage's kidnapping."

Cold chills ran down Georgiana's spine.

"Let me see if I understand this correctly. The stationery from the dairy farmers is marked with the symbol of a known criminal group, and Quicksilver and Coxcomb were seen secretly meeting with a dragon from this farm?" Mrs. Fieldings pinched her temples.

"Yes, madam. I hardly know what it means—"

"You were right to bring it to my attention. What is to be done?"

Pax flittered to the desk. "In London, we were to watch for those with the mark and find out as much as we could about them. We relayed that information to a team, who gathered it and made a plan."

"It would seem wise to do something similar under these circumstances." Auntie removed her glasses. "Obviously, we should write to Sir Fitzwilliam for further instruction, but even if carried directly to Pemberley by one of our dragons, I cannot imagine getting word back in time for the dinner party."

"We should cancel the dinner. The risks—" A shiver started at Mercail's elegant head feathers and coursed all the way to her tail.

"Unfortunately, the future of the school is riding on the event." Mrs. Fieldings covered her face with her hands.

"Excuse me?" Gale all but snarled.

"Other Blue Order Girls' Seminaries offer introductions as part of their menu of services. If we do not do so, we will lose most of our students within the next year or so. Or at least so I have been told. If we cancel this dinner party, I fear it will only hasten our demise."

"But the danger—" Mercail hovered in front of Mrs. Fieldings' face.

"To whom? Who do we expect is in danger?" Auntie asked. "Forgive me for observing that the only girl here with any fortune or connections of real note is Miss Darcy. None of the others is worth more than a few hundred pounds and none of them have connections with any real property or power within the Order or outside. They are essentially worthless. Similarly, the only dragon Friends here are small and common and not likely to be considered valuable. The dragon students are all common drakes like me—if one wanted to take one of us captive, there are far easier targets, like the shepherding drakes in the field. Bede is the only one who might be at risk, given the conversation you overheard."

"A cold, if accurate, assessment." Mrs. Fieldings stared at the ceiling.

"So, then, the question is how best to protect Miss Darcy whilst carrying on in the best interest of the other students," Gale said.

Auntie resettled her glasses. "Clearly, I shall return my focus to Miss Darcy. Gale, Bede must become your responsibility."

"Of course."

"Miss Darcy, I will write to your brother immediately and ask for his guidance on how to proceed, if you are to continue your studies here or not. I would take you back to Pemberley myself this very moment, except for the threat of the highwaymen in the area." Auntie chittered under her breath.

"Since the Blue Order cotillion was not canceled because of the snapdragons, I do not think the dinner party should be, either." Georgiana wrung her hands as she stared at them. "The school needs it. But I do not think I should attend."

"That seems best." Mrs. Fieldings said. "Of course, close watch will be kept on the contingent from the dairy farm. Pax and Berry, can you recruit the local fairy dragon harem to help us keep watch on them?"

"The fairy dragons can report to me," Mercail said. "I will prepare a report on what they hear."

"The question is how best to protect Miss Darcy whilst the house is full of unfamiliar people and dragons?" Mica asked.

"Without question, the safest place in the house is the Dragon Tower. There is only one way in, through the main door, and there is a bolt across the door from the inside. All the windows are fitted with iron grates that only a fairy dragon could fit through," Gale said.

"And neither of them is likely to be any threat." Georgiana glanced at Pax, who twittered in agreement. Fairy dragons were never taken seriously enough to be invited into anything nefarious.

It was a sound plan, even if it meant that she would indeed become the princess locked in a tower because of a dragon.

Far too tired a concept to even make a good story.

16
Chapter

July 8, 1815

WITH THE STOICISM OF a tragic heroine, Georgiana helped Neville and Miss Sempil prepare for the dinner party. Helping them dress and do their hair was a poor substitute for actually attending the event herself, but it was hardly their fault that the nearby dairy farmer might somehow be connected to the snapdragons—or they might not, there was really no way to tell. Nor did they have anything to do with many of the guests viewing Georgiana as no better than a prize for their hoard. Maybe there was something to Bede's assertion that people hoarded wealth like dragons.

Georgiana had enough of the Darcy pride to find that attitude revolting. That made knowing she would be ensconced in the dragon tower a little easier. At least it gave her the illusion of having chosen that fate, and that was worth something.

"I had no idea you would be so clever arranging hair!" Miss Sempil patted the delicate braids Georgiana had pinned up with rose-headed pins, accenting the lush blond curls around her face.

"Should I take that as a compliment?" Georgiana asked.

"Absolutely!" Neville laughed, handing Georgiana a ribbon to match her yellow dress. "She never jokes about her hair. If there is one vanity I would ascribe to her, it would be those envy-inducing curls."

She was right. Miss Sempil's curls were straight from a fashion plate. "Each of us has that one thing that we are especially proud of. I do not see it as a flaw. Not if kept under good regulation." Miss Sempil stood and twirled, the skirts of her gown flaring as she did. "I still think it a shame that you cannot play for us all and indulge your vanity, Miss Darcy."

So, she could increase her novelty as prize livestock? Georgiana shuddered. "I appreciate the thought, but it really is best if no one pays attention to me."

"I am not sure how to feel about it all, to be quite honest. I hate you are being left out." Miss Sempil patted her curls. "But to wonder if a new acquaintance I am making is resigned to meeting me instead of you would be a troublesome thing."

Neville smoothed the ribbons Georgiana had added to her hair. "The important point to remember here is that it is the dragons we are to become acquainted with, and they did not pen those disagreeable letters. I have heard that there are plans for you to make one of those dragon acquaintances yet tonight."

"Indeed, no one has spoken to me of such things."

"Berry brought that information." Neville glanced toward the window.

"Well, then, good. It will not be a total waste for you then." Miss Sempil urged Neville to stand and straightened a bit of trim that had turned up. "I, for one, am glad that it is out in the open. And I appreciate the way it is being dealt with, even if it is uncomfortable for the moment. It really is for the best for all of us."

Neville looped her arm in Georgiana's. "I will be happy for a friend with good connections, draconic or otherwise. One never knows when she will need good connections, no? It is time. We should go downstairs to be ready to greet our guests."

Mrs. Fieldings intercepted them at the base of the stairs. "Excellent. I am glad to have caught you now. Miss Withington, Miss Sempil, go on to the drawing room. Miss Darcy, if you will come with me, please. There is a guest awaiting you in the parlor."

It would have been nice to have had some warning that this had been the plan. A little time to prepare herself for cold-blooded introductions would have been fitting. But then it would have only led to wondering what sort of dragon she would meet and how cross they would be. At least she could be sure no angry firedrake would be waiting in the parlor. Anyone else she could probably manage with sufficient equanimity.

Mrs. Fieldings opened the parlor door and ushered her in.

With the help of faded burgundy curtains, the white and gold paper hangings, though tired and dusty, captured the rays of sunset, and held them in a honeysuckle-scented glow that warmed the room just barely not too hot. A white rose-embroidered screen, the work of previous students, perhaps, shielded the fireplace as it brought the flowers peeking in the window all the way across the room. With the extra chairs from the salon now removed, a double-wide wrought iron dragon perch stood in front of the screen. The perch presided over a conversational grouping of dark burgundy chairs and walnut settee, neither of which looked particularly inviting—though that perception was probably the lingering effects of the ill-fated salon with Bede.

The practical wooden chairs, with plain lines and simple cushions, that circled an old oak table near the window, seemed far less stiff and formal.

"Ah, Miss Darcy!" Mercail sat on a dragon perch near the fireplace beside another, somewhat larger, bird-type dragon.

The strange dragon looked remarkably like Mercail, though her feather-scales were silver and blue rather than white. Shaped like a large, fancy pigeon, with resplendent head crest and opulent, draping, tail-feathers, the stranger was even more... well, just more than Mercail, who somehow paled in comparison.

"Thank you, Mrs. Fieldings. I am sure you are quite busy. Do not feel obligated to stay," Mercail said.

The strange dragon chirruped, low and throaty. "Indeed. My Friend shall be here soon, and he will require a bit of fuss and bother as his kind are wont to receive."

"I will make sure everything is ready for his arrival." Mrs. Fieldings nodded and slipped out.

Something about the deference with which she spoke. Was this strange dragon's Friend the mysterious baronet?

"His kind?" Georgiana tried not to stare out the window through which she could make out several carriages approaching the house.

"He's the titled sort of warm-blood. They require special management." Could bird-type dragons wink?

Georgiana struggled to hide a chuckle behind her hand. "You remind me of my aunt's Friend, Cait."

"Cait of Rosings Park?" The strange dragon warbled and gave a little wing flap. "I am acquainted with her and consider any similarity to her a compliment."

"You are acquainted with Cait?"

"She is the sort of cockatrix all of us know." The strange dragon's chirrup suggested she was cut from a very different cloth than Cait.

Mercail cleared her throat and extended her wing. "Miss Darcy, may I present Janae, a roost-mate of my youth."

"Roost-mate? Pray excuse my ignorance, but I am not familiar with the connection."

"Few are." Mercail glanced at Janae, head cocked as if to invite comment. "Queen fairy dragons strongly resemble the Petite Crowned Cockatrix. We both bear enough resemblance to certain exotic, fancy pigeons that we often share a dovecote with them, and with each other."

Cockatrix and fairy dragons sharing a roost? Predator and prey lying down together. Gracious, how like a sermon that sounded.

Janae bobbed her head rather vigorously for a cockatrix. "We hatched on the same day. Our brood mothers shared a dovecote."

"So, you were raised together?"

Both dragons cooed.

"I had no idea. Even the Sage's writings include nothing about cockatrix and fairy dragons living together in such a way."

"That is precisely why I asked Mercail to arrange for me to meet you. When I learned of your dinner, I pressed my Friend, Sir Horace, to seek an invitation. I could not pass up the opportunity to make your acquaintance."

"I am pleased to meet you, Janae." Georgiana curtsied, but not all the way to the floor like Cait would have required. "Would I be too forward to suggest you would like for me to introduce you to the Dragon Sage?"

"While that would be an absolutely lovely notion, I could hardly ask such a thing. That would be far too much of an imposition on you and on her. As I understand, she is overwhelmed by demands on her attention, especially now with a new hatchling to be expected."

"A new hatchling? I had no idea! Pray forgive me for asking, but how is it you are in possession of such very personal information?"

"When Cownt Matlock announces something in the hearing of fairy dragons in the morning, by evening, dragon wings have spread the news afar." Janae chuckled. "As I understand, the Cownt's declaration came as rather a shock to the Sage herself."

"She is with child? How very wonderful!" And what a fitting way, if entirely unconventional, for the Dragon Sage to learn of it. "If you are not looking for an introduction to the Sage, pray, tell me, what am I able to do for you?"

"Mercail and I have been working on a monograph of sorts on the unique nature of the connection between our species. I... we hoped that you might present a copy to her for her input, approval, consideration. I am not quite certain of the correct terms here, but I hope you understand."

"We believe it would be a valuable resource to the Blue Order community," Mercail added.

"I imagine a monograph authored by a fairy dragon would also be helpful to demonstrate that fairy dragons are more than mere flutter-tufts and flitter-bits, no?" Georgiana said.

"It would not hurt, I am sure."

"The same holds true for cockatrix. We are considered vain, aloof creatures, and to be honest, there is little in the way of factual information available about us. Usually, we are a single line or maybe two in a bestiary."

"Now that you say that, I have read very little about cockatrix." Georgiana stroked her chin with the back of her hand. "I learned more in Mica's salon about your type than I had anywhere else."

"And it is high time to remedy that." Janae clapped her beak sharply.

"I shall be honored to present your work to the Sage when next I see her. Though I do not know when that might actually be."

"Thank you—"

"Oh heavens, what is that?" Georgiana strode to the window and peered out through the blooming honeysuckle vines.

Janae flew to the window sill, Mercail just behind her. "Oh that?" She snorted. "He does rather enjoy making an entrance. I fear he might have learned that from me."

"I do not recognize the crest on the carriage."

"It is the Bowles family crest. The baronet likes to use it as a reminder of rank wherever he can."

Georgiana stepped back from the window. "Forgive me for asking, but is he a pleasant fellow?"

"I find him so, but I suppose you should consider the source. I am a dragon, after all, and that influences my tastes."

"But he affords you every courtesy and deference appropriate to your standing." Mercail said. "There is much to be appreciated in that kind of warm-blood."

"Indeed, he does, and he expects the same courtesy, so I suppose you can say we understand each other. His hatchlings, on the other hand! They could still use a lesson or three in manners."

"When will you believe me, that they are quite normal for warm-blooded young? They will settle down to be more to your taste soon enough." Mercail twittered. "Trust me, of the two of us, I know far more about young warm-bloods than you."

"I concede to the latter point. But as for the other, only time will tell."

The man himself stepped out of the carriage, looking every bit as a baronet might be expected to. Broad shoulders with something of a paunch, a strong jaw, eyes that seemed to take in every detail, and a posture that could only be called 'dominant.' He was a man who knew his place in society as much as his dragon Friend knew hers.

"What sort of dragon does he Keep?" Georgiana asked.

Mercail tittered.

"Do not laugh at Burleigh. She has no tolerance for such things."

"Her pride is utterly ridiculous," Mercail said.

"But not at all atypical for a basilisk."

Those were frightful creatures, even more so than firedrakes! "He Keeps a basilisk? I have never met one, but it is said—"

"I am sure you have heard a great deal, but you know how gossip is. A hefty dose of fluff and nonsense surrounding what may or may not be a grain of truth." Janae fluttered her feathers like a woman flipping a wrinkle out of her skirts.

"Is it true they are not personable?"

"After a fashion. She has little tolerance for chatter and idle talk. She prefers conversations of substance, or nothing at all. Just as some people are sociable, the same is true of dragons. Burleigh is not one who is open to a great deal of company. Not that she is taciturn or unkind, she just wanders away when she is bored with a conversation, and one may not realize she is gone for quite some time."

Georgiana giggled. "I have wished for that skill myself at times."

"You might get on with her, then." Janae said.

The baronet's carriage pulled off toward the carriage house. A far more modest hooded gig pulled to the front door in its place. Though handsome and well-kept in its own right, the little vehicle seemed poor and underdressed, following a crest-bearing carriage.

"Have you any idea who that might be?" Georgiana asked.

"Certainly no one of any note." Janae snuffed and returned to her perch.

"I am not familiar with it." Mercail peered through the window beside Georgiana.

"I recognize that drake! The one running beside the gig." Georgiana caught herself before she tapped the glass. "I know him. That bony knob on his head!"

"The dairy farmer's drake Friend?" Mercail asked.

"A dairy farmer? What sort of dairy farmer has been invited here?" Janae squawked.

"I told you there would be girls of many backgrounds here." Mercail returned to the perch beside Janae. "You came to meet Miss Darcy. That is the only acquaintance I thought you to be interested in."

"Of course. But how am I to trust the intentions of Mrs. Fieldings? Despite what some say, his sons are quite marriageable and one can never be too careful where connections are involved—"

"Pray stop!" Georgiana hissed and held up an open hand. "Where is he going?"

"He is not going to the front door?" Mercail craned her neck to get a better view out the window. "That is strange. It looks as though he is going around to the back of the house. But why would he go to the kitchen now?"

"Who is ever to know the intentions of that sort?" Janae snuffed.

"No, this is not right. It does not feel right at all." Georgiana rubbed her hands along her upper arms.

"It seems very odd and uncomfortable." Mercail cooed softly.

"More than that, it feels... dangerous. I cannot explain it, but it feels dangerous."

"Shall I..." Mercail asked.

"No, there is no need to disturb everyone because an odd sensation rumbles in my belly. I will take a peek and see that all is well, and that will be that."

"But you are supposed to go to the dragon tower when you leave here." Mercail protested.

"I will, after a brief detour to the kitchen to make up a tray to tide me over for the evening."

Chapter 17

Georgiana slipped into the dark hallway. To her right, the dragon tower awaited. To the left, the front hall, brightened with candles and flowers, still receiving guests, and the drawing room just beyond.

Maybe Mercail was right. She should just go to the dragon tower and bolt the door behind her, just as Mrs. Fieldings had decided. Pax could fit through the window bars, so she would not be alone. The dinner party would pass, and all would be well.

After all, the last time she had been forbidden to take part in company, she had been willful. When she had accepted Mr. Oakley's call, everything turned into a nightmare. She had lost Fitzwilliam's trust, and possibly his regard. Her life turned inside out.

Did she dare act willfully now?

But this was different. Was it not? Surely it was. It had to be.

Did not Elizabeth say, "*When in doubt, think like a dragon and act accordingly.*"? But what would a dragon do?

Pax and Berry zipped toward her from the dragon tower door.

"Why are you still out here? Are you not supposed to be in the tower?" Berry sounded so much like April, it was amazing she had not turned bright blue to match.

"I was called to the parlor to meet Mercail's roost-mate. I am on the way to the tower now, though." She screwed her eyes closed and held her breath. It actually helped her think at times. "I do not know what to do. I saw Nob through the window. He was heading to the back of the house. I know I am supposed to go to the tower, but something does not feel right. I want to go to the kitchen and see what he is doing. What would you do, Pax?" If one was to think like a dragon and did not know what a dragon would think, it made sense to ask, did it not?

Pax cheeped and flew several circles over Georgiana's head. "I am small and hard to see. I would go to the kitchen and determine what sort of threat he poses. Hiding now might be the most dangerous thing. Better understand the danger first, then hide if necessary."

"But not by going out in the open. One must make oneself quite inconspicuous to obtain that information," Berry added.

"How would I do that? There are no servant's' corridors here, and I cannot hide like a fairy dragon."

"No one is in the back part of the house right now. The housekeeper is not in her office either. She is overseeing the dining room. Her office is very cluttered. There are many places even you could hide that would afford you a view through the door to the kitchen." Berry buzzed back and forth near her face, so close the brush of her wings past Georgiana's cheek tickled.

"Is that what you would do, Pax?"

"I would go outside and listen through an open window, but I do not think you can do the same. So, what Berry says makes sense."

Now she knew what a dragon thought and would do. But should she?

"What does your instinct tell you?" Pax landed on her shoulder.

"Warm-bloods do not have instincts like dragons."

"Yes, you do. What does your instinct tell you?"

"That there is something not right. Something dangerous, but I am not sure to whom."

"What does your instinct tell you to do about danger?"

"To run from it. But I do not know from what I am running. I need to, lest I run the wrong direction."

"We will go with you," Berry said.

Georgiana sucked in a slow breath, steeling herself. "Then to the housekeeper's office." She glanced down the left-hand corridor. No one remained in the front hall, but there were one or two guests still lingering outside the drawing room door.

"You are not dressed for dinner. They will not notice you, especially if you are not going toward them," Pax whispered.

Berry flew toward the ceiling and disappeared into the shadows there. "Come."

Georgiana turned towards the dragon tower, then down the hall of teachers' offices. The sounds from the drawing room faded away until only her footsteps and the buzz of fairy dragon wings remained in the shadowy corridor. Since no one was to be in this part of the house, no candles had been lit; only the dying rays of sunset, filtering through the single window beside the dragon tower door, offered any relief from the gloom.

"Just keep going. There is nothing to trip over, and no one else here." Berry called from above.

"Trust me, I can see in the dark better than you. Keep going." Pax whispered in her ear.

Georgiana pressed onward, following the corridor as it turned left at the library door. Mrs. Fieldings' office and Gale's lay ahead.

"No one is in those rooms. I would hear them breathing if there were." Pax pressed close to her neck.

Georgiana strained to listen, but her pounding heart drowned out all else. "Your hearing is that acute?"

"That is one way we stay alive in the wild."

"So, you really cannot help but overhear everything?"

"It is in our nature." Pax nudged her to continue on.

"Come, come, the housekeeper is away." Berry buzzed down the corridor toward the housekeeper's office.

Georgiana met the closed green baize door with her open hand, a clear indication this was the territory of the servants and not to be meddled with.

"I cannot open it," Berry said. "You must."

Berry was right. Georgiana could not simply follow the dragons now. She had to take the lead. If she were caught, there would be so much trouble. Fitzwilliam would be so disappointed in her...

But Elizabeth would not. Not if Georgiana was thinking like a dragon and acting accordingly. The Sage would always support that—and she would explain it to Fitzwilliam.

Georgiana inched the door open and slipped inside.

Even with curtainless windows open wide, the moonless night, now devoid of any glow from sunset, bathed the room in the darkest shadow. A few large dark figures proved Berry's assessment correct. The room was indeed cluttered. How could she navigate it?

Pax launched from her shoulder. "Follow close behind me. You can hear my wings."

Yes, barely, just a tiny hum ahead of her. She crept along behind it, sliding one foot forward, then the other.

"Listen. Can you hear?" The buzz of her wings nearly masked Pax's voice. "The kitchen door is open ever so slightly."

Voices, angry dragon voices.

"Get back! Someone is coming!" Berry cried.

Pax dropped near to the floor. Georgiana followed. They scurried under a table that smelt heavily of drying herbs.

The kitchen door flung open and taloned feet burst in. "What are you doing here, fairy dragon?" Quicksilver? What was she doing in the kitchen?

"Sweet. I want sweet. I am hungry." Berry snipped, her voice heading toward the now open door. "What are you doing here? You were invited to the dinner party."

The rustle of scales suggested Quicksilver tried to block her path. "None of your business, flutterbit." Flutterbit! How dare she address Berry that way! "You do not belong here. Go join your Friend or go to the Tower. Sweets for Pax have been put there, and she always shares with you."

"I do not want flowers, I want—"

Quicksilver growled, probably baring her teeth. "I said go. Do I need to make myself clearer?"

Berry squawked and darted out the open window.

"Do not go around to the kitchen or you will regret it." Quicksilver snarled and shut the window behind Berry. The footfalls stopped and Quicksilver sniffed, long, deep breaths, like Pax did when trying to identify an unfamiliar scent. Finally, she sneezed. "Chervil and rosemary! Dreadful stuff." She stalked back through the kitchen door, leaving it open behind her.

"She cannot smell us for the herbs. Her hearing is not as good as mine. If we remain silent, she will not detect us." Pax's beak was nearly in Georgiana's ear.

If only she could see what was going on, but she dare not move. Listen. She still had that.

"Bloody fairy dragons! Nuisances every one of them." Quicksilver muttered.

"She is gone now?" A deep male dragon's voice rumbled. That had to be Nob.

"As much as one can be sure of vermin. Send the cockatrice after her. Serves her right for flying out at night if she turns up missing. I will tell her Friend that I saw her dart out a window and fear the worst."

Georgiana stuffed her fist in her mouth. Pax shuddered.

"Go!" Nob barked and large wings flapped. "You have what we agreed upon?"

"You are going to handle the matter as agreed? Without the Order's interference?"

"The Blue Order has no right to interfere in the way we govern ourselves." Nob hissed, tail lashing.

"Absolutely." Quicksilver clapped her jaws. "She is in the pantry."

She? No! That could not mean—

Taloned feet scraped their way across the kitchen and a door squealed open. Writhing and thumping and a desperately foul smell followed. Georgiana pressed her arm against her face. Pray, let her not retch and be discovered!

"How are you going to explain the stench in the larder?" Nob asked, huffing as though he were lifting something heavy.

"Bede was caught stealing from the pantry, used her defense, and ran off. They will be so busy trying to clean up the damage, no one will ask questions. They will be so relieved she is gone. That will be the end of it."

"You are certain no one will be sent to look for her?"

"No one wants her here. There may be a search made to preserve appearances, but nothing more. What are you so concerned about?

Your connections are not so incompetent that they cannot hide from a pack of loud, smelly warm-bloods, are they?"

"They want her for her hide, but the buyer wants to inspect the wares 'on the hoof,' so to speak. The transaction will not go through if the hide is not in good condition. It takes more to conceal livestock on the hoof than it does a carcass."

"See that this does not come back to me, whatever happens. I have done you a favor by getting you what you needed."

"And I have done one for you, getting rid of the thorn in your side that stood in the way of your ambitions."

"What do you understand of my ambitions?"

"Do not think yourself so clever, little blue. You are not the only designing little drake I have dealt with. Scuttle on away and let me be about my business. Be glad that I did not ask for more than an exchange of favors."

Quicksilver huffed and shut the backdoor rather too loudly, muttering under her breath. She stalked toward the housekeeper's office. "Arrogant, self-serving, bone-headed cur. See if I ever provide him with any more goods once I am connected with a dominant Blue Order family."

Pendragon's bones! Was Quicksilver connected to the snapdragons? Surely dragons could not turn on their own like that, could they?

Cold flowed across her, like the waters of Ebbing and Flowing Well.

Who had been placed in Nob's hands?

Bede—it had to have been Bede—had just been hauled off like a pig to slaughter by that brute Nob to be handed off to some sort of poacher in want of her hide. Cold or warm-blooded, who knew? But none could mistake their intention.

Her heart pounded so hard in her ears. Surely, they would burst.

Quicksilver stalked through the housekeeper's office and out into the hall, quietly closing the door behind her.

Help, they needed help. She glanced over her shoulder.

"Who do we tell?" Pax asked. "Who can you trust?"

"Mrs. Fieldings? Gale? Mercail? Mica? Surely, they must not be aware."

"I do not know. They all have an interest in saving the school. With that motive, will they be willing to listen to accusations against the dairy farmer's Friend? That farmer has already contributed significantly to the school, providing the milk and butter and cheese for the kitchens without charge. The impact on the budget would be substantial."

"Mrs. Fieldings might be bought for so little?"

"I doubt it, but I fear it might make her slow to act. Too slow for Bede, I fear."

But if she did not do something, Bede would certainly die.

Think like a dragon, think like a dragon.... "What would the boldest dragon do? What would Walker do?"

"Walker is brave and strong and dedicated to the Order and dragonkind. He would find Bede and rescue her. We are not strong enough for that."

"What are we strong enough for?" Georgiana chewed her lip. "Perhaps we might find them and send for help? It is so dark, though..."

"I can guide you in the dark like we did here. Yes, we are enough for that. If we find them... I could go for help."

"But where? Is there anyone here we can trust for that?" Dragon's bones! Could any of the staff here be trusted?

"Not here. I can fly. I can go to Pemberley very fast. There is help there." Pax leaned into the side of her neck, as if to draw strength.

"And you can lead them back? In the dark? I hardly think that possible."

"The horses who are trained to be ridden near the cockatrice. I am sure I can get them to follow me."

"Are you absolutely certain you want to do this?"

"Bede will be sold for her hide if we do not."

"Not even she deserves that fate." Georgiana crept out from under the table. "We will go, then."

"There are hand pies on a tray just there. Tie some up in your shawl. I may need to eat in order to make it to Pemberley."

"But you dislike meats and vegetables."

"It will do." Pax launched from her shoulder and flew toward the window. "Can you get through the window? I can make sure it is safe first."

Safe? Dragon's bones! The cockatrice. "Nob sent..."

"Yes, I know. The fairy dragons in London talked a lot about how to evade cockatrice and hawks. And there is no choice."

Georgiana opened the window.

Berry darted in. "I know what direction Nob went."

Pax twittered and launched through the window.

Berry followed. "Hurry, Nob is moving quickly. Stay with me and we can follow without being detected."

Chapter 18

CLIMBING FROM A WINDOW into the deepest dark of night, following a fairy dragon in search of a dragon who had done her nothing but harm. What sort of bedlam-worthy notion was this?

Foolish. Impulsive. Utterly ludicrous. And exactly the kind of thing Elizabeth would do.

That meant it would be at least defensible to Fitzwilliam, when he found out about this—and he most certainly would. Assuming they did not get themselves captured, or worse.

Oh, this really was a terrible idea.

"Which way do we go?" Georgiana pushed herself off the ground and shook her skirts straight. That windowsill had been higher than she expected.

Did darkness have a smell? It certainly seemed to this night. Cloying warmth and damp, with lingering traces of Bede's scent defense. Still ghastly.

So profoundly dark.

"They are traveling at a steady clip. They may have already made it into the woods behind the house. We must hurry." How did Berry expect her to hurry under these conditions?

Those were the woods thought to conceal highwaymen. Lovely. Heaven forfend, that might be exactly the company that Nob was in search of.

How could she possibly think like a dragon when it violated all good sense?

"That means we can cross the fields without worrying about finding cover. Come." Berry rushed ahead.

"We will never catch up if they are already in the woods." Georgiana struggled to keep up. Nothing about running when one could not see was natural or even sensible.

"She is right." Pax's soft voice nearly disappeared in the surrounding rush.

"They cannot keep up the pace once they get into the woods." Berry called back. "A drake's vision at night is not nearly as good as ours. He will have to slow down. And he will tire from carrying Bede. That will give us an opportunity to catch up."

Berry made sense. Unfortunately.

Running across the field was bad enough, but how were they going to get through the woods? Nob would not be the only one having a hard time. Perhaps she should go back, get help.

But who would help? Who had the means? Who could be trusted?

If she went back, all she could do would be to lock herself in the tower and leave Bede to her fate. After all Bede had done, it was tempting, but no, it was neither right, nor the person she wanted to be.

This was the only way.

Pax and Berry slowed their flight as the field gave way to sparse trees that grew denser and more determined.

Georgiana stumbled over something long and rugged. Perhaps a tree root? Or a fallen branch? "I can hardly see my hand in front of my face. I do not think I can do this."

"I will fly low to the ground and Berry can fly at your shoulder. Follow us and you will be well." Pax's voice followed the hum of her wings toward the loamy forest floor.

"Trust us, it will work." Berry twittered.

That was highly unlikely, but at least she could say she had tried, and that must count for something. Unless she fell into the hands of highwaymen herself...

No, that was not helpful. Focus, she had to focus. Find Bede, send for help. That was all she dare think about.

The fairy dragons paused. "Which way?" Berry asked.

In the stillness, the sounds of night creatures, scurrying, wings slicing the air, a squeal of fear. Something, maybe an owl, maybe a dragon, must be having its meal now. What other secrets hovered just out of reach in the thick smothering cloak of darkness?

Pax flew slightly ahead, sniffed, and snorted. "I smell Bede. This direction. They seem to have crossed the stream."

"It is shallow, do not worry. It poses you no danger." Berry flew into the black velvet that threatened to smother Georgiana's soul.

No danger, perhaps. But wet shoes led to blisters at the very least, which would hardly help their cause. Denying her every sensible instinct to stay where she was, she forced step after blind step behind the fairy dragons. Placing her fate on the wings of fluttertufts that none took seriously...

"There is a particularly shallow place to cross just to the right." With Pax's help, she picked her way across the stream, barely more than a puddle at the point of crossing, so her shoes remained reasonably dry.

"This way now, though, the scent is getting muddled with others. There are warm-bloods—"

A flurry of wings. Both fairy dragons screeched.

An arm snaked around Georgiana's throat, yanking her into a strong shoulder. "Who are you? What are you doing here?"

Georgiana kicked back like a horse into hard shins and drove her elbow into something softer. The arm released.

She turned and staggered back.

"Stop! Stop! She's from the school!" A dragon voice called from the tree. That sounded like a cockatrice. "I recognize the fairy dragons."

"Let go, you leather bound chicken!" Pax squawked.

"Not between the toes! All right, enough!" The cockatrice flapped hard, and the voice moved, probably to another tree.

Pax and Berry landed on her shoulders and pressed hard into her neck. Poor little dears trembled—but who would not, having been manhandled by a creature ten times their size? "Who are you? What are you doing here?"

"What is it to you?" A different male voice spoke from the opposite direction of the first.

"Considering you—one of you—had your arm around my throat just moments ago, I would say I have the right to ask such a question."

The cockatrice swooped down to land near her feet in a great rustling of deadfall. By its sound, it was not a large cockatrice. "They are both boys playing at being men hoping to be made knights."

"Stuff your beak!" the voice to her right said.

"Sir Horace's sons?" Berry and Pax twittered in unison.

"You have met our father?" The left-hand voice was slightly deeper, rounder than the other.

"Not yet. His Friend, Janae, asked to make my acquaintance this evening."

"Naturally." Right-hand snuffed. "Did she approve of you to make our acquaintance?"

The gall of the brute! "I did not ask for your acquaintance, or even hers. She asked to make mine."

"Indeed?" The cockatrice made a whistling sound. "I have never heard of such a thing. She has little time for the warm-blooded."

Left-hand stepped closer. "Who are you that Janae would be interested?"

"It does not matter. Pax, Berry, are you well enough to continue? We must hurry."

Right-hand shuffled as though crossing arms over his chest. He smelt of shaving oil, but not the nice sort like Richard and Fitzwilliam used. Something brash and sharp. "What business do you have in the woods, in the dark of the darkest night? Surely it cannot be any manner of good work."

"What business is it of yours?"

"When you are seeking a knighthood, you find everything is part of your business." The cockatrice said.

"Pendragon's bones, Blisters! That is enough!" Left-hand seemed to wave his arms.

"Blisters? What kind of name is that?" How bold Berry was to take such a mocking tone.

"She had a terrible case of tail blisters when she was a hatchling. Never quite got over them." Right-hand coughed, but it was probably to cover a chuckle.

A cockatrix?

She must be a lesser cockatrix. That explained some of Berry's boldness. "I have an excellent recipe for a salve for tail blisters. If you are interested in it, Blisters, I will be happy to share it with you."

"You understand tail blisters?"

"I know of many things. But detain me no further. I am on urgent business."

Georgiana tried to step forward, but Blisters' open wings around her knees barred her way. "What are you seeking in these woods on a night like this?"

There was something in Blisters' voice... "We are seeking a... a... dragon."

"At this time of night? What sort of fool are you? Do you know nothing about approaching dragons?" Right-hand really needed to moderate his scoffing tone if he actually expected an answer.

Georgiana resisted the urge to slap her forehead, rolling her eyes in a most Fitzwilliam family way instead. "I do not need to explain myself to you."

"Is this a call you are paying to a dragon, or are you actually looking for one whose location you do not know?" Unlike her Friend, or at least companion, Blisters seemed to understand how to be polite.

"The latter."

"You must tell her why you are here." Blisters flapped in the way bird-types did for emphasis.

"To what end?" Left-hand said.

"We do not need to explain ourselves to anyone."

"Then you are both fools, and I disavow myself of your company." Blisters hopped backwards. "May I join you and the fairy dragons in your quest, Miss? I think we may be on similar errands."

"The dragon you seek has been taken away?" Right-hand said.

"What would you know of that?" Pax leaned toward Right-hand's voice.

"Tell us what you know."

"You are a fool, Eli! Stop playing at dominance and act the gentleman," Blisters snapped.

"We are in search—" Left-hand said.

"Stop. We don't know if we can trust her. Do not tell her anything." Eli planted a foot hard.

"Trust me? This is pointless. Be out of my way now. We cannot waste any more time."

"But I think they can help us." Pax's sharp little toes squeezed her shoulder.

"Why should we help you? You need to go back to that school of yours and play the respectable young lady," Eli said.

"Do you know who you are talking to?" Pax launched and buzzed towards Eli.

"If she is familiar with tail blisters, she is the daughter of a Keeper, no doubt. An important one, I expect." Blisters said.

"So what? She can hardly be above us. She is a Keeper's daughter. We are the sons of a Keeper. So far, we are equal." Did Eli really want to get into a contest of rank?

"But who is your estate Dragon?" Blisters hissed. "A cranky basilisk who has little to do with her own kind, and little standing in the Order... Who is your estate dragon, Miss?"

"Pemberley." Why could Pax not keep quiet?

"Pendragon's Bones!" Left-hand gasped. "You are Miss Darcy? Sister of Sir Fitzwilliam Darcy and the Dragon Sage?"

"She is." Pax cut off Georgiana's tart remark.

"Pray accept our deepest apologies, Miss Darcy. We had no idea with whom we were dealing. I am Ambrose Bowles, and that is my brother Eli."

"If you were intent on behaving like gentlemen, not bickering school boys, our connections should not have mattered at all. Now pray, allow me to be on my way." Georgiana tried to step around Eli, but Blisters barred her way again.

"Our Friend disappeared from our Keep a week ago. A few days ago, we learned he might not be traveling of his own free will," Ambrose said. It was nice to have a name to put with the left-hand voice.

"We have been following a trail of sorts that has led us here. What has brought you here?" Eli asked.

"I saw a dragon taken, bound and muzzled, from our school this evening by a larger minor drake. Berry saw them going off in this direction."

"There is a dragon involved as well? That is deeply troubling." Ambrose's tone turned quite dark.

"This is far worse than I had imagined." Blisters said.

"You should not be caught up in this, Miss Darcy. This is far more dangerous than you realize." At least Eli's tone had become polite.

"Unfortunately, I understand far more than you would imagine. That is why we cannot waste any more time talking, lest they get too far from us for Berry and Pax to scent them."

"Fairy dragons have a far better sense of smell than I." Blisters sounded a little downcast. "I can, though, offer to keep guard over them, as they are far more vulnerable than I."

"We should go, then." Was Ambrose the leader of the two brothers?

"Let the fairy dragons lead us and leave her here." Eli muttered something under his breath.

He really should realize that such insults could easily be heard by the dragon-hearers nearby. "I will choose to ignore that statement. Pax, Berry, will you lead us on?"

Pax twittered and buzzed on ahead.

One slow step at a time, they followed the fairy dragons deeper into the woods.

This must be what it was like to be blind. The entire world swathed in the deepest black. Branches slapped at her face; she stumbled over roots and fallen limbs that, during daylight, would never have been an issue. Strange, alarming sounds filled the woods, sounds she had never noticed before.

Not the least of which were the sounds of breathing, heavy steps, and simply the movement of bodies much larger than her own. Each foreboding, menacing in this lightless world.

If she had her way, she would never be without a candle again.

Were these truly the sons of Sir Horace? Everything pointed to that as true. Even if it were, though, how very inappropriate that she would travel in the depths of night virtually alone with them. Except for the companionship of the dragons, of course. At least they would vouch for her honor, and her reputation need not be besmirched for this adventure.

As if that were the only danger she faced.

What would they do if they did not find Bede and the twins' Friend?

What would they do if they did?

Chapter 19

HOW LONG HAD THEY been walking? How far had they gone? Time and distance lost all meaning in the black velvet cloak enveloping them. Every stone under her foot, every leaf brushing her face assaulted her senses. Each one sent her heart racing and her breath catching in her throat.

"Do you smell that?" Eli sniffed and snuffled.

"I definitely smell Bede," Berry said.

"And there is smoke from a fire, too," Pax said. "Dragons do not use wood fires. There are warm-bloods with Bede."

"I smell Bede, and possibly another dragon." Berry said. "I hear several warm-blooded voices, too."

"I had no idea fairy dragons' hearing was so acute. No wonder your kind has stayed alive for so long." Had Blisters no fairy dragons in her acquaintance?

"We need to get a closer look." Ambrose took a step nearer to Georgiana. "Pray, Miss Darcy, would you stay behind whilst the dragons help us approach?"

"Do as he asks." Pax landed on her shoulder. "It is enough that you have come this far. You must know when to allow another dragon, sometimes larger, sometimes smaller, to handle matters."

But was it cowardice to stay behind when she was asked? Was it failure to go no further? What would a dragon do? Pax had just told her. "I will stay."

Eli and Ambrose huddled with the dragons, discussing their plans. Georgiana leaned against a nearby tree and closed her eyes to listen to their plans. Had they forgotten about the preternatural hearing they all shared? Probably. It was easy to when you lived among the dragon-deaf. Not everyone existed in a world like Pemberley. But for now, it was to her advantage.

A fairy dragon would go with each of the twins as they approached from opposite directions. Blisters would assist them in communicating with each other and keep watch over the fairy dragons. It seemed a simple and sound enough plan, although any number of things could go catastrophically wrong.

And if they did...

Dragon's bones and feather dust! What had she done? Even if she stayed safe here, what would she do when the sun rose? Would she even be able to find her way out of the woods when she could move freely again? Stupid, stupid girl! Impulsive, short-sighted, and perhaps she needed to add cowardly as well!

Surely Elizabeth did not feel fear when she behaved like a dragon? She always seemed confident, sure of what she was doing. Maybe it was because of her connection to major dragons who always seemed sure of themselves. Georgiana had no such bond. Only fairy dragons, little flutter-tufts and flitter-bits, made any sense to her. Following their lead could hardly have been what Elizabeth meant by thinking like a dragon, could it?

The twins and the dragons set off, slowly, led by the dragons who could see through the darkness. Without so much as a 'by your leave.'

Their footsteps faded into the other sounds of night and the darkness tucked in around her, a cool, vaguely smothering blanket.

She sank down to the ground, back against the tree. Blind and helpless. Shivering despite the still warm night air, she clutched her shoulders to still herself, rough bark biting through the thin fabric of her gown. Surely, there was an angry dragon waiting to come out of the darkness and pounce like Old Pemberley…

No! Not helpful! She pressed her fists to her temples. There was no major dragon in these woods. It was not reasonable to fear one now. Plenty of other things, but not that. And those things she could listen for and possibly evade. Yes, that was what she could do. Listen. Closely, carefully.

She closed her eyes. Deep breaths slowed her heart to more normal rhythms. Her ears adjusted to the sounds of the woods, like her eyes would have adapted to light. Other sounds came into focus, sharpening, becoming clearer as she attended to them.

Oh heavens! The fire and the camp were far closer than she had expected! That was the only reason that she should be able to hear the creaking of cart wheels with a poor horse still attached.

"You sure they ain't getting' out o' dem cages?" That was a man's voice, coarse as his grammar.

"Tied and caged? Both of them are quite secure." That was Nob. If there were a dragon in the woods to fear right now, it was him.

"I don't trust what dem lizard ken do, ya know? Some of dem has some powers—"

"Do not be an idiot, Sanford." That was a woman's voice! Well bred, elegant. "They are animals, not supernatural creatures. Dragons do not have 'powers' of any kind."

"Dem things talk, Miss Marie, and that ain't natural."

"You talk and it seems quite unnatural to hear it from a warm-blood." Nob snarled.

"I ain't gonna take that from a cold scaley, I ain't. You gonna let 'im talk to me dat way?"

"Just do your job. What does it matter what he says about you?"

"That lizard don't got no—"

"Who are you calling a lizard?" Were those Nob's footsteps approaching Sanford?

"If da describin' fit."

"Enough, both of you."

"I have half a mind—"

"The first accurate thing you have said yet." Nob snarled.

Georgiana pressed a hand to her throat. Not the time to retch now.

"I'll just load up my cargo and go me own way. Yours ain't the only buyer, ya know. I 'ad two other apothecaries approach me for me wares."

"An' yet you have ended up here with us. Waiting on the highest bidder. You really want to give up that price over a few measly insults from one you will never see again? That seems a very short-sighted way to do business. I had thought much more of you." Was there a beautiful woman behind those honeyed tones?

"You sure da' buyer will come? I seen many o' dem never come to claim dere orders."

"One can never be entirely certain of the behavior of another. But he has been reliable in the past."

"'ow many times?"

"You do not need to know. He was clever enough to bring in highwaymen to keep meddlers out of the woods for us. That should say enough about his commitment—"

"Quiet, both of you—" Nob's tail thumped. "I hear something."

"The buyer?"

"No, he is not due until morning—"

A cockatrice screamed in a flurry of wings.

Georgiana jammed her fist in her mouth. No! No! No!

Was that a fairy dragon scream? Or was that Blisters? Oh, Pax! Pray she had not been… no, she could not even think that now!

"Warm-bloods!" Nob growled. "Go now!"

Who was he sending off? Probably smaller dragons, but of what sort? Wings, she heard wings, but were those taloned feet as well?

Were they coming her direction? Yes, yes, something was. Surely, they would scent her, find her quickly.

Hide, how could she hide? How did one hide when one already could not be seen? Her smell, she had to hide her scent. How? How did one do that?

How did dragons do that? Did dragons do that?

She squeezed her eyes shut and pressed her temples with the heels of her hands.

Tatzelwurms! The barn wyrms at Pemberley. They rolled about in dung heaps and refuse piles. Fitzwilliam said it was to disguise their dragon scent from the vermin they hunted.

What would cover her scent?

No dung heaps or refuse piles in the middle of the woods.

Piles. Piles! There had been a pile of fallen leaves, blown against a stand of small trees. The fairy dragons guided them around that just before they had stopped. It did not stink like dung, but they had said its odor confused them somehow.

Where was it? Just behind her. Maybe a dozen steps. Steps in the deep dark.

Talons scrabbling along the ground, coming nearer.

No choice! She forced herself to her feet, hands extended. One step, two steps!

Faster, faster. Talons were coming.

Six steps, seven.

It must be close now! Pray she had gone the right direction. Ten, eleven, twelve. Nothing! What now?

Wait. She closed her eyes and breathed deep. The smell of rotting leaves nearby. To the left. She turned. Three steps, four.

Crunch.

Leaves.

Bending low, she reached out into a pile of leaves and other deadfall.

Scraping, snorting. Closer still!

She burrowed beneath the leaves. Deeper and deeper until she reached loamy ground beneath. Cold, damp, slimy in spots. Heavens, what was that under her hand? No, she did not want to know.

Still, quiet, she needed to be quiet, lest she give herself away.

"They were here." A raspy dragon said.

"I smell them, too."

Feet and tails scraped the ground. Nearer and nearer.

Georgiana held her breath and bit her lip. Closing her eyes probably didn't help, but it felt like the right thing to do.

A muzzle—or at least it sounded like one—snuffled at the leaves.

"Wyrms, I smell wyrms."

"Don't bother them. They have a temper when their nest's disturbed. There's no one else about. We go back."

Wyrms! She'd crawled into a nest of forest wyrms. Stupid, ugly, nasty-tempered creatures! Out! She had to get out!

But not until the others were gone.

How long should she wait?

Too long, it was taking too long! But she still heard feet and tails close.

Still, she must be still.

Muscles screamed in protest as she held her breath and clenched herself in a tight ball.

There, yes, it was quiet. Silent. They must be gone. But no, do not hurry. Wait, just in case.

Long enough. Yes, it was long enough. She swam through the leafy ocean, surfacing as one drowning, finally breaking through the surface of a pond, sucking in fresh air. Feather dust and dragon's blood! That pile smelt far more foul than she realized. It must be the wyrms. She rubbed at her nose, wiping debris from her face.

Now what? She wrapped her arms around herself, waited, and listened.

"Are they securely tied? What are we to do with them?" Miss Marie asked.

"Held fast as those dragons." Nob said. "No one's getting free."

"Too bad we don't 'ave another cage. We should kill 'em and be done with them."

"I did not sign up for murder."

"But you will deliver dragons to their death?" Nob snarled.

"These dragons have a bounty on their heads."

"And that makes it different?"

"If they had a bounty, I'd turn the men over to get the bounty." Miss Marie said.

"Ya know who dey are, don't ya?"

"You know them?"

"Da heirs to da estate where dat lizard come from."

So, they had the twins' Friend!

"Pendragon's bloody bones!" Miss Marie was a member of the Order? Only Order members used that particular invective—no one else understood what it meant.

"I say we just kill 'em and be done with it."

"You idiot! These are not the sort of men you can just kill and leave to rot in the woods." Miss Marie's voice turned shrill.

"An' why precisely might dat be?"

"You know who their father is?"

"A bloody baronet, which make dis a cryin' shame we canna take dem for ransom."

"The baronet is a knight."

"Meh, we all bloody well know dat."

"A very particular kind of knight, you imbecile. A knight of the Pendragon Order."

"By my brood mother's bones! You did not tell me there was a Pendragon knight involved in there." Nob actually sounded alarmed.

"The father were not supposed to be. What in the bloody hell is this Pindragoon knight?"

"Pendragon! Pendragon! You fool. They are not a ceremonial knighthood, like the governors who are knighted for making speeches. These knights are made for the valor and service to the Order. They are knights in the oldest sense of the word." Miss Marie definitely had to be affiliated with the Order.

"What do dat mean ta us?"

"It means that their remains will be found and found quickly, and the resources of the Order, warm- and cold-blooded, will be put to bear on the case. Even wild dragons may be pressed for assistance. We will be caught and hanged by the end of the week."

"And poaching the lizards won't put us there?"

"The Order has shown little interest in the matter. No resources applied to the matter. As long as no warm-bloods are injured, they are not likely to even search for the missing dragons. Much less be bothered to prosecute."

"Wat are dem two doing, then?"

"I imagine the dragon you took was Friend to one of them. Did you not think to check for that?"

"Friend? What? Like that Nob fellow?"

"Nob is my employee, not my Friend. If you are going to be in this business, then you really ought to know the distinction."

"Hungry!"

20
Chapter

"Hungry!"

Georgiana opened her eyes, though it made little difference. Something, some things writhed at her feet.

"Foxes, hungry foxes. You has foods. You want to feeds them." Those were wyrm voices. Raspy, persuasive wyrm voices.

Of all dragon types, she really, really disliked wyrms.

She pressed wrists to her temples against the rising headache that always accompanied hearing persuasive dragon voices. "Stop that. I can hear you. You are not foxes, you are wyrms. Stop trying to persuade."

"She knows! She hears!" Slithery sounds retreated.

"Hungry!" a persistent, plaintive voice drew nearer. It sounded smaller than the others, younger, perhaps? Less dominant? "You have food. You give it?"

"Yes, you give?" The persistent wyrm must have a mate.

Two wyrm bodies looped around her ankles, rubbing against her a little like cats.

Wyrms, it was said, were ruled by their stomachs. But why... oh, the hand pies! She felt for the shawl tied around her waist. Broken, crushed, but they were certainly still there.

Should she feed them? What did Elizabeth say about feeding wyrms?

The azure forest wyrms, the ones who had assisted in her capture—Elizabeth had won them over with food. Even gained their help. Perhaps.

But no, Georgiana was no Dragon Sage. That was a foolish notion.

"Hungry!" The writhing around her ankles grew more insistent.

Still though, just maybe... what else was there to do?

"I have food. I can share." She fumbled with the shawl and retrieved several morsels from her waist. "I will put it down for you. Do not take it from my hands. I do not want to be bitten."

"Yes! Yes! Hungry." The pair of young wryms circled her ankles again.

She dropped the bits slightly away from her feet and the wyrms pounced on it. More slithering sounds approached.

Their bellies getting the better of the rest of the cluster, no doubt.

"Good! Good!"

"More! Give more!"

Georgiana tossed out a few more nuggets, one for each of the slithery bodies she thought she had heard.

More wyrms pressed close, slinking around her. "More, we smell more."

"Yes. I have more." No, that was a stupid idea. But what else did she have at her disposal? "I gave you something. Now you must give me."

"Give you? No! No! Not hoarding dragons! No! Have nothing!" The wyrms slithered away as a group, the scraping sounds of their long bodies disappearing into the darkness.

Bless it all!

She swallowed hard as she clutched her sides. Though the wyrms had hardly been Friends, or even actual acquaintances, somehow the night felt so much bigger now. And she was smaller, more alone than ever.

Where was her tree? At least there was some comfort there. Five steps, and her hand smacked into something hard and long and rough. It might not have been her tree, but it was enough. She huddled at the base of the trunk.

Now what? Was there anything else to do but wait until morning?

Listen, there was always that. She closed her eyes again. Bede's faint odor and smoke still hung in the air. The smell of wyrms, of the forest, of the night. But the arguing voices had stopped, as if the paltry camp and its captives had disappeared.

Alone.

An owl in the distance. Frogs. Other small things that roamed the night.

"Hungry?" A rumbly, familiar voice, six, possibly ten feet away.

She fumbled for a tidbit and tossed it in the voice's direction. Slithering and gobbling and grunting.

"Good."

"Hungry."

"More? Yes?"

She reached for the hand pies, but wait, perhaps... "I gave you. You help me. I give more, yes?" Good heavens, now she was sounding like them! Had the night stolen the King's English from her, too?

"Help? How help?"

"You smell the fire?"

"We smell fire. We stay away. Fire not safe. Bigger dragons there. Bad warm-bloods." They knew something about what was going on!

"I know it is not safe. But I need your help. There are dragons and warm-bloods tied up there. They are my... my friends."

"Small dragons. We are small dragon. Cannot help. Not big and strong."

"Not can help. But still hungry."

"I am not asking you to rescue them. I am not big enough, not strong enough for that, either."

"What help you want, then?"

"You have sharp teeth. You can chew, yes?"

"Can chew."

"We want to chew food."

"First, I want you to chew something for me."

"Chew what?"

"Chew ropes. My friends, two men and two dragons, are bound by the bad warm-bloods. With ropes, I expect. Sneak in. Chew the ropes that bind them. If the cages for the dragons are wood, not metal, chew through them, too, so they can free themselves."

"Too dangerous! No. No!" The wyrms slithered away.

Terrible little creatures.

Terrible, but they were hungry.

Georgiana took out a larger piece of hand pie and nibbled it slowly, sighing and moaning a little over the wonderful tastes and textures. Definitely overdone, but who would laugh at her here?

Wriggly sound approached, again. "Hungry!"

"I will give you more if you help."

"Two of us. Not enough to chew so much."

"I have enough to share with your whole cluster."

"Not enough for what you are asking."

"I can get you more. Much more. There is a whole kitchen of food, and they will give it to me. I will give you all I have when you are done and then give you as much as your bellies can hold back where I live."

"You live in the house with the dragon tower?"

"Yes."

"Dragons are welcome there." It was a statement, not a question.

"Most welcome."

"They are the kinds to feed hungry dragons." Further away, that voice sounded older, maybe wiser than the rest.

"But warm-bloods lie. So much risk."

"Hungry. We are hungry. So much food."

"I have a dragon Friend, a fairy dragon. She is often hungry. I will not let a dragon go hungry."

"Which fairy dragon?"

"Pax. The white fairy dragon."

"The white fairy dragon is well-fed. She has shared the garden with wyrms." The wyrms drew closer together, voices lost in the cluster's writhing.

"Yes!" "No!" "Trust warm-bloods." "Plump fairy dragons..."

The cluster broke apart and wyrms surrounded her. "We will go, we will chew. Then you feed? Then you take us to house and feed more? Yes?"

"Come to me after, and I will do exactly that."

The wyrms left again. Somehow, their slithers sounded determined, purposeful as they disappeared into the darkness.

Georgiana huddled into her tree once again.

Would they actually do as she had asked them? Wyrms were not terribly reliable. What if they lied to her and demanded food? Could she hold her own against a cluster of hungry, angry wyrms?

Who knew? But now was not the time to consider that. It was time to wait again. Wait and listen.

Cockatrice screeches and the sound of a launch. A wyrm shrieked, but it did not sound injured. Was it possible? Could they have sent one to draw off the watching cockatrice? Were they that smart?

How many winged watchers were there? What had happened to Blisters, Berry, and Pax? She would not have been able to hear fairy dragon wings at this distance, and they could be keeping silent. But what if—no, that would wait until later.

Listen.

Blast and botheration! Nothing.

The stupid wyrms had failed her. At least they had not come back begging for food. Cold comfort, that.

21
Chapter

"DAMN IT ALL! NO!" A meaty fist slapped an open palm—or at least it sounded that way.

She jerked her head up and stared into the darkness, heart lodged so hard in her throat she could barely breathe.

"I ain't standing for it." Sanford snarled.

"What are you talking about?" Nob's gravelly voice had taken on an impatient note that Sanford would be wise to pay attention to.

"Thems boys is too dangerous to keep alive. I'm gonna be done with them."

No! No! No! Her hands trembled. She hugged her knees harder, but even that did not make it stop.

"No, you are not. Sit back down or—"

"Or else what, Lady?" He made the word sound like a curse. "What ya think ya a'gonna do ta me?"

Lady? Wait. Was Miss Marie really an actual lady? Were there any titled ladies in the region?

"Nob will readily stop you."

"I know how to handle the scaley-type. Done in my fair share of them already. Come at me, lizard, if ya thinks ya can."

Yes. Yes, let the two do each other in. Perhaps if it were only a lady alone—

"Do not be provoked, Nob. He is not worth it—wait, what is that?" It was easy to imagine a faceless Lady Miss Marie raising an open hand. "Do you hear it?"

What did she hear? Georgiana squeezed her eyes shut. Focus, focus. Perhaps she could hear it, too.

Confusion, commotion, yips and barks. Were those the wyrms? Scuffling of bodies.

Louder. Men approached? It had to be men from the sounds of the boots.

Highwaymen? Were they coming to fetch the dragons? Perhaps she should return to the pile of leaves.

Breath caught fast in her lungs, as though it would stop anything bad from happening.

Voices, so many voices. Men! Dragons!

Cockatrice screeched and screamed with the sounds of attack and injury.

Cries and shrieks of pain. Definitely from Miss Marie.

Fists, were those the sounds of fists? Perhaps clubs. Wood against flesh. A man—or was that men?—screamed. It might have been a dragon...

Voices. Those voices. A tight tenor and a round baritone.

Oh, merciful heavens, it was the twins! They were freed! Had the wyrms really come through?

She stood and hugged herself! Yes, it was their voices! Another familiar one?

Feather dust, it was! That was a voice she would never mistake. Tears sprang to her eyes. Relief and the pungent scent of Bede's defense.

What must it be like up close? Coughing and gagging and retching. Truly awful, no doubt.

Still more voices? When had they become a part of this?

Familiar! They were entirely familiar! But that was not possible, was it? How? Fitzwilliam! Richard! They were here?

Tears cascaded down her cheeks, and she sobbed into her hands. It was them. There was no mistaking those commanding tones. They were here!

Pax, it must have been Pax! So quickly! How had she done it?

A familiar buzzing on either side and two fluffy bodies pressed against her neck. She cupped her hands around them and pressed them close. They were shaking as hard as she.

"You are safe! You are well!" Pax trilled.

"I told you she was!" Berry said. "And so clever! You sent the wyrms? It had to be you. How did you manage that? Wyrms are never cooperative."

"The hand pies. They like hand pies. I imagine they will be here soon for them."

"We will take you back to them. Your brother told them not to leave. He sent us to find you." Pax wriggled free of her hand for a triumphant wing flap and warble.

"Yes, yes. Take me to them!" Her knees nearly buckled, but her tree kept her steady.

Painstaking step by painstaking step, the fairy dragons guided her to the small camp around a fire that still smelt strongly of Bede. Oh mercy! Light, there was light now! Enough to see by. No more drowning in the darkness.

As her eyes adjusted, she could make out the cages, one of which now contained Nob. A man and woman, Miss Marie and Sanford, no doubt, were bound at opposite sides to the other. Sanford looked exactly like his voice implied. Scruffy, unshaven, and angry.

Miss Marie wore a dark gown, fit for the mistress of a fine house. Dark purple or black, it might even be a mourning gown. Maybe she was a lady, that was more difficult to discern, though it was obvious she was used to a far easier life than Sanford.

Two young men sat near the fire. So that was what Eli and Ambrose looked like. One, a lanky, unfinished ginger who matched Eli's voice, rubbed his wrists. The other, broader and more genteel looking, with dark hair and a bruise on his face, nursed what were probably bruised ribs. So, they were not the identical sort of twins. All things considered, it would have been far more surprising if they had been.

A brown drake with pronounced spinal ridges and four stubby horns around its head lay at their feet. Rope burns around his muzzle and ankles would need attention soon. A lesser cockatrix that could only be Blisters paced along the ground from the twins to the drake and back. She had the face, chest, and wings of a raven, and a thick, rather stubby tail more lizardy than serpentine. Ugly as she was, no wonder Janae tolerated her presence. Blisters had proven herself a sensible creature, and there was much to be said for good sense.

Walker and Earl, in all their dangerous glory of razor-sharp beaks, impressive wings, glistening feather scales, and powerful serpentine tails, perched atop the cages. They followed Blisters' pacing with menacing watchfulness.

"Look there!" Walker launched toward her.

Fitzwilliam, weary and disheveled, ran to her and swept her off her feet a moment later. Face buried in his shoulder, she gulped in the smell of home.

"I feared the worst," he whispered, voice so ragged it rasped across her skin. "I never would have put you in such danger had I known. How did you come to be out here?"

"I did not know what else to do! I tried to think like a dragon, like Elizabeth always says. But I don't know how. I'm so sorry."

Fitzwilliam set her feet on the ground only for Richard to catch her up and hold her so tight she could hardly breathe. "You have no idea what we have been through this night."

"I can imagine far more than you think." Her laugh was a little weak, but they seemed to appreciate it.

"Come, sit near the fire." They each took one of her arms, escorting her to the light and warmth.

"Miss Darcy!" The ginger twin, Eli, stood. He clasped his hands before him, a little less sure of himself than his voice had suggested in their past encounter. "It was you who sent the wyrms?"

"Her! Her!" A cluster of ragged, forest wyrms, with their shaggy leonine faces and rough scaly bodies, poured in from the darkness just beyond the firelight. "Hungry! Hungry! We did. Now you do!"

"Yes, yes, of course." She untied the shawl at her waist and tossed out the crushed remains of the hand pies for the wyrms.

They dove on the bounty, like creatures starving. Although they ensured that each got some share of it. Somehow, she had not expected that from mere wyrms.

"That was brilliant." The other twin—Ambrose—stood, arm pressed tight to his ribs. "That one was ready to slit our throats." He pointed at Sanford, who growled back and pulled against his bonds. "I have no doubt you saved us."

"I think the wyrms may have had something to do with it." The drake at his feet muttered, barely moving his lips.

"Indeed, they did." Georgiana crouched and addressed a cluster of attentive, hungry faces. "Thank you very much. Come morning, you will come to the house, and I will see the rest of what was promised to you is delivered."

"What did you promise them?" The corner of Fitzwilliam's lips quirked.

"Full bellies."

Richard laughed long and hard. Oh, the wonder of that sound! "I expect we will have to restock the larder to make good on your promise."

"It is exactly what Elizabeth would have done and clearly the right thing." Fitzwilliam found a crumb near his feet and tossed it to the waiting wyrms.

"Pray, may I introduce our Friend Trotters, Miss Darcy?" The genteel-looking twin asked.

"You are Master Ambrose Bowles? I think I have matched voice to man, but it is best to be certain," Georgiana said.

"Pray forgive my brother," the ginger man spoke. "I am Eli, and he is Ambrose Bowles, sons of Sir Horace Bowles."

Trotters lumbered to his feet. Gracious! He was quite round and, well, pig-shaped. "Pleased to make your acquaintance, Miss Darcy. It is good to see my young Friends have not entirely forgotten their manners."

"Pleased to make your acquaintance." She tried to curtsey, but only managed the barest dip before her knees threatened to give way. "Pray allow me to introduce my brother, Sir Fitzwilliam Darcy, and my cousin Sir Richard Fitzwilliam."

"I think that is enough of the pleasantries for now. You ought to sit down right away." Trotters snuffled like a pig. "You've been through quite the ordeal. I do not imagine you can make it back through the dark again tonight."

Fitzwilliam caught her arm as her knees well and truly gave way. "We will remain until first light, then return to Mrs. Fieldings' and send into town for the—"

"You will need the regional undersecretary!" Berry hopped off Georgiana's shoulder and into the air. "I will go now to fetch him. My Friend is his daughter!"

"That would be most helpful. Pray ask him to meet us at the school." Richard addressed the fairy dragon with the same courtesy he extended to all the other dragons. Considering she was a heretofore unknown and certainly unproven fairy dragon, the respect was note-worthy, and not lost on Berry. She twittered happily and zipped away into the darkness.

"Should Blisters send word back to the school?" Ambrose asked.

"It would be best if they are prepared for us when we arrive in the morning. There is a carriage house there. Perhaps it may be pressed into housing this lot," Richard jerked his thumb back toward the cap-tives, "until we can bring the proper authorities to bear on the matter. If you would present that request, Blisters, we would be grateful."

Blisters squawked and bobbed her head. "It will be a pleasure to bring some good news, since all has been an uproar in the wake of Trotters' leaving us."

"I did not leave you! Is that clear enough?" Trotters snuffled and grumbled, the sounds of good-natured banter between old friends.

"If you did not have the habit of disappearing for days at a time, we would have looked for you sooner, and you would not have been trussed up like a boar awaiting the spit." Blisters flapped her wings.

Trotters growled and shuffled until his back was toward her. Blisters snorted and flew off.

Darcy sat on an old log and encouraged Georgiana to sit beside him. He took her hand, nearly crushing it in his grasp. "It would be helpful to understand how Burleigh's Keep came to be involved in this matter."

"After nearly a seven-day passed, we started asking about after Trotters. One of the garden wyrms offered a confusing little story that suggested Trotters had been taken. So, we began to look for him. Father, a knight of the Pendragon Order, sent out cockatrice to search for traces of our Friend. Their information led us to Chapel-en-le-Frith. He sent us to search while he was occupied at the school."

"He should have notified the Order." Richard huffed. "Bringing Miss Darcy into this affair was simply unconscionable."

"What point to involving the Order? Minor dragons are not important enough to get their urgent attention—at least not yet, for all the talk of the Sage trying to change things." Ambrose sat on the ground beside Trotters. "We could not have imagined that Miss Darcy would have become involved in this. Do not accuse us of that."

"With Blisters' help, we were searching the woods for Trotters when we came across Miss Darcy." Eli patted Trotters' hindquarters. "She was here of her own accord. Do not blame us for that."

"I think I am to blame for that." Bede stepped into the firelight, bearing the marks of her ordeal. How was it possible she had stayed so quiet, so unnoticeable for so long? Had she ever been so silent before? "Did you really come after me?"

"Yes, she did." Pax scolded, sharp little toes driving into Georgiana's shoulder. "It is your fault we are out here."

"I am grateful, to be sure." Bede worried her front paws together. "But I do not understand. You see, Sir Fitzwilliam, Sir Richard, Miss Darcy and I have not been on excellent terms as of late."

Pendragon's bones! "No, we have not. But now is not the time to discuss those matters."

"But I do not understand. I must understand. Coxcomb and Quicksilver…"

"Wait," Georgiana threw up an open hand, "Coxcomb was also involved in this?"

"Most certainly. She obtained what I think were dried poppies and a few other herbs and brewed a tincture that she used to render me senseless."

"I have never heard of such a thing," Fitzwilliam turned to Richard. "Have you?"

"No. Are you certain it was dried poppies and herbs only?"

"I believe so. She called me to the still room to show me what she was crafting. I think she showed me all the ingredients, but I suppose it is possible that was a lie. I am not very good at discerning falsehoods." Bede's tail lashed over the dry ground.

Richard scrubbed his palms over his face. "We will have to search the still room. Do you think you can show us what herbs she claimed to have used? Would you be able to identify the substance if we find it?"

"It had some unique properties. I am sure I could. As I understand, the annals of dragon medicine do not list such an elixir. It appears to be an unknown formulation."

"Annals of dragon medicine?" Georgiana asked.

"Yes, I am well-versed in that and a number of other subjects. You will find my memory is excellent." Bede worried her front paws as she turned to Richard. "You are concerned that if such a formula became known, it would be a threat to dragonkind?"

"I may not discuss that sort of business—" Richard crossed his arms over his chest and jerked his head toward the captives. "Later. I will want to hear all of that later."

They were so quiet. It was difficult to remember they were there. But he was right.

"Of course," Ambrose said. "We should find something more appropriate to discuss."

"My cousin has had rather a colorful career. I am sure he has some diverting stories to tell." Georgiana suggested.

Richard relaxed a bit. "Indeed, I do."

Beside her, Fitzwilliam did not relax, but he put his arm around her shoulder and, in his warmth, the fire melted into the fuzzy haze of sleep.

22
Chapter

FITZWILLIAM ROUSED HER AS soon as golden-rose rays of dawn drove enough darkness back from the landscape for them to walk without the aid of fairy dragons. Under Earl and Walker's watchful eyes, they set out for the school. Auntie, shortly followed by Sir Horace and the Bowles' winged-dragon Friends, intercepted them in the woods.

Auntie insisted on taking Georgiana into her care and urged Fitzwilliam and Sir Horace back to the woods to deal with 'unsavory matters.' With a gentleness Georgiana would not have attributed to her character, Auntie escorted her back to the school and helped her into bed. Perhaps once she had some sleep, the scolding would begin, but for now, she would relish the sun's light and the warmth and softness that surrounded her in her own little room.

July 10, 1815

"Miss Darcy?"

Georgiana pulled the blanket over her head. "Not yet. I am not prepared to face anyone. I have only slept a few hours."

"I am afraid not. You slept all day and night. It is well into the next morning now." Auntie—yes, that blue-green dragon at the window was Auntie pulling open the curtains.

Georgiana forced herself up on her elbows, the blanket slipping aside. Late morning sun assaulted her eyes. "How could I have slept so long?"

"No doubt your escapades in the woods left you spent. I imagine you are more rested now. Sir Fitzwilliam has asked me to see to your needs." Auntie opened the closet and removed her traveling dress.

"No, pray not now. I need sleep. That is the only thing I want." Her stomach rumbled.

"That may be the case, but you need to eat. I am sure you will be able to sleep in the carriage on the way back to Pemberley."

"Back to Pemberley?" Georgiana sat all the way up and put her feet on the floor. "What do you mean, back to Pemberley?"

"Sir Fitzwilliam has asked that you be taken to Pemberley today as soon as you are ready. Pax has made a good recovery from her injuries, which were more superficial than we first feared. She has already gone out to the garden to enjoy the honeysuckle vines one last time before you depart. Several guard drakes arrived yesterday to accompany your journey. After what has happened, you surely cannot imagine your brother wanting you to remain here?"

"Is he very upset with me?" She bit her lip and squeezed her already burning and blurry eyes shut.

"I do not consider myself an expert on warm-blooded feelings." Auntie laid a bony paw on Georgiana's shoulder. "He is angry, to be sure, but not at all with you."

She gasped as the tension sloughed away, clutching the edge of the bed lest she fall back into the mattress, and Auntie declare her too dramatic.

"It is my inexpert opinion that both your guardians approve of your intentions that night, if not all of your methods. I know the same is true for Mrs. Fieldings, Gale, Mica, and Mercail. Bede is most... profoundly grateful. For her protection, she is being sent to Pemberley, too."

Georgiana grimaced.

"Gale and Mica have already taken her on ahead. The Dragon Sage was impatient to become more acquainted with her and the matters concerning her."

"I am certain Bede can provide her with material for many monographs. She seems rather encyclopedic."

"Quite." Auntie wrinkled her nose, lifting her glasses in an exasperated expression. "Get yourself dressed now, and I shall attend to your packing. Best be ready to leave in an hour."

"So quickly?"

"Your brother has already left, with Sir Richard and Undersecretary Withington, to Bantry Park. It is a more appropriate venue to deal with matters than a girls' school. He would have told you himself, but he did not wish to disturb your sleep."

"I see." She stood and hugged her shoulders. "I am sure he is busy with serious matters."

"Extremely serious matters, to which you have made an extraordinary contribution." Auntie caught her gaze held tightly.

"He said that?"

"In exactly those words."

An hour later, Georgiana and Pax made their goodbyes to the upper students gathered in the front hall. Miss Sempil led the group in asking permission to write to her at Pemberley, which was, of course, granted. The thought of receiving letters from friends of her own was rather thrilling. Only Neville's presence and the promise of correspondence would have made it better. But her father, Regional Undersecretary of the Peaks District, had probably whisked her away when he returned to Bantry Park with Fitzwilliam and Richard.

But that did not mean they could not correspond. In fact, Neville's would be the first letter she would write from Pemberley.

Still, she would miss Mrs. Fieldings and her school. How she would have to eat her words, though! No doubt Aunt Matlock and Aunt Catherine would happily lord that over her when she confessed that calling the school a place of medieval torture was a bit of an exaggeration. She would just have to maintain her sense of humor in the matter. Being laughed at, a little, was certainly not the worst thing to ever happen to her.

After Georgiana took her leave of Mrs. Fieldings and Mercail, Auntie escorted her to one of the Darcy coaches that waited near the front door. Fitzwilliam had sent the oldest, plainest of the family vehicles to convey her home. All things considered, that was probably a wise and considerate choice. As were the large and suitably formidable-looking guard drakes that flanked either side.

They yipped a polite, "Good day, Miss," as she walked past.

The driver opened the door and handed her inside.

"Good morning, Georgiana!"

"Neville?"

Berry met Pax midair and flew circles around each other, twittering their pleasure.

"As you see." Circles under Neville's eyes belied her somewhat forced smile.

The driver mounted the box, and the horses began to walk.

"Auntie said nothing about you traveling to Pemberley, as well." Georgiana pressed her shoulder to Neville's. "I thought you had already gone back to Bantry Park."

"That was discussed, in the animated way that things in the Blue Order tend to go." Neville admired her new gloves.

"What would become spirited about that?"

"Neither of our guardians were pleased with poachers and who knows what other sort of blackguards coming within arm's reach of a premier Blue Order girl's school."

"I suppose when you put it that way, it does sound rather dramatic."

"Father invited you to Bantry Park, but Sir Fitzwilliam insisted Pemberley was far safer and would not settle for any other option."

"That sounds like him." Dear, considerate, and protective were exactly like Fitzwilliam. She leaned back and closed her eyes as his warmth and security embraced her, even without his presence.

"It has been an interesting way to leave Mrs. Fieldings' for certain. Not how I expected to spend my final term at school." Neville cocked her head and raised one eyebrow in a look particularly her own. "You know, for a girl who does not like attention drawn to herself, you create quite a stir."

"Imagine what might have happened if I had played pianoforte for the dinner party?" Georgiana giggled behind her hand.

"I cannot fathom that! The dinner party itself was quite interesting, to be entirely honest. I have never interacted with dragons in that way before. They make memorable party guests, to be sure."

"And you are now planning to host such parties in the future?"

"Honestly, I think it is the sort of thing that one might become accustomed to. I am sorry that you missed that experience."

"I expect I will have that opportunity in the future, at least I hope to. Elizabeth—the Dragon Sage—seems intent on making such events more common. How was the time in the drawing room? Were you all able to display your accomplishments credibly for the guests?"

"I am uncertain how the dragons enjoyed our musical displays. Their expressions suggested they were far more sensitive to missed notes and fudged timing than our warm-blooded guests, despite their polite responses. Dancing was a little better. At least Miss Barton continued to tell her right from left during the cotillion. Thanks in no small part to your help to her. We could perform that credibly. I may imagine it, but it felt like the dancing made more sense to our cold-blooded guests."

"We might have to ask Elizabeth about that. I am certain she will have some insight on the matter. What did you think of the dragons to whom you were introduced?"

"To be honest, I am still reeling from trying to keep straight the different greeting each requires!"

"Forgive me if I say that those are nothing to what is required to learn for presentation at the Cotillion. Major dragons. They are ever so much more particular about such things!"

Why did Neville smile so broadly? "I am sure you do not know, but the story has been told that the Dragon Sage has summoned us both to Pemberley to be prepared for next year's Cotillion. That she has taken us under her wing and will sponsor us herself to come out to the Order next year! Poor Miss Sempil was so jealous. I should feel sorry for her, but I cannot until I stop pinching myself to believe it is true."

"Neither she nor my brother would allow such a story to be bandied about lightly."

"So then, I am right to believe it? I could hardly allow myself to, but my father is convinced that it would do a great deal of harm to the Darcy reputation if word got out that they did not follow through. So, amid all the disagreeable circumstances, he is utterly delighted. I, on the other hand, am equal parts delight and terror."

Fitzwilliam and Elizabeth had already decided that she would be presented? She blinked rapidly and looked away, every inch of her skin tingling. "It will be better because we can do it together."

"Oh, so much better! It is what I have always wanted, especially after meeting Mr. Nicholson's Friend, Wild Boar. His son may be in want of a wife, but that will definitely not be me! Oh gracious, he was a disagreeable, demanding sort, wanting to know if I intended to continue dressing in the fashion which I currently displayed, as that might put too much of a strain on the estate's budget. Can you imagine saying such a thing to a new acquaintance?"

"It sounds quite draconic. Janae, Sir Horace's Friend, only wanted to meet me in hopes of having her writing presented to the Dragon Sage." Bother, there was that Fitzwilliam family eye roll she had been trying to get under control. Then again, Janae deserved it.

"She did not deign to be introduced to the rest of us, I will have you know. In fact, she did not even appear in company until Blisters arrived, shrieking and shouting everyone into a great uproar. She went straight to her Friend, Sir Horace, who, in true Blue Order fashion, took control of the situation and began barking out orders to everyone."

"I can well imagine."

"He and Mrs. Fieldings exchanged some heated words. As headmistress of the school, she resented his heavy-handedness, and he resented her failure to grasp the gravity of the matter. It was quite the to-do. When it was finally determined that the school itself was not in immediate danger, we were all hustled to our rooms with Janae and Mercail standing guard at either end of the corridor. More to ensure we did not go wandering about than to actually protect us, I think."

"What do you think happened to the dinner party guests?"

"The maid's puck was watching and said that the dairy farmer and his wife tried to slip out unnoticed. That same puck, having overheard a certain conversation you had with Mrs. Fieldings, set Sir Horace into motion to detain them, which led to no small to-do, one that we could hear upstairs. As I understand, Mr. Nicholson assisted in apprehending them and sat guard over them in the cottage to which they were removed. I am under the impression that they have since been taken away, probably under my father's authority, to Bantry Park."

"I have never quite understood how the lines of authority in the Order work in matters like this."

"That hardly makes you unique, I am afraid." Neville shook her head and pressed her temples. "Father had a terrible row with the three Pendragon knights, who had insisted in taking matters into their own hands. I am still not certain that has been settled entirely to anyone's satisfaction. Which, upon reflection, is probably why the three of them went to Bantry Park, instead of leaving matters in Father's hands."

"What a terrible way for our families to meet!"

"I had thought the same, but Blisters—who is, by the way, the first lesser cockatrix that I have met—assured me it is part and parcel of Order officers to clash like dragons whilst they are sorting out dominance in a situation."

"Dominance, it always reverts to dominance." Who knew she could sound so like Elizabeth?

"Quite. But Blisters assured me they would sort it out and our families would enjoy a beneficial connection after this. They agreed, though, that a full investigation would have to be conducted of the school and all its connections."

Georgiana gasped. "You do not think that Mrs. Fieldings is involved in anything unsavory?"

"I am quite sure my opinion counts for very little. But I cannot believe that she would be engaged in anything that would put dragons or the Order at risk. That is simply not in her character. Still, though, it will not look well upon her when you and I have been so suddenly removed whilst these matters are investigated."

"And the rest of the students? What do you think their families will do?"

"I tried to persuade Papa that there was no need to inform all the students' families until they actually knew the truth of the matter. No doubt, word of the investigation will get out, though. Hopefully, by that time, it will be known that there were no nefarious activities and the school will not suffer unduly."

"Who knows, it could even become a mark of notoriety for Mrs. Fieldings, to have been proven true under such intense scrutiny." Hopefully, that would be exactly what happened.

Epilogue

GEORGIANA CLOSED HER EYES and drew in a deep breath. There was no place like Pemberley's morning room. Peachy-colored walls reflected light from the east-facing windows, making the room as inviting as the smells of fresh sweet buns. The windows had been opened, just enough to fill the space with crisp morning air and the perfume of the abundant cut flowers on the table and sideboard. It was almost like being in Mama's little flower garden.

Berry and Pax buzzed back and forth from a vase of sweet honeysuckle to another filled with larkspur and chrysanthemum. They had told April about the bower at Mrs. Fieldings' school and plans were already in the works to dedicate a section of one of the hothouses for the use of resident fairy dragons. Though Elizabeth had been quite fond of the idea, it was April who had insisted on wasting no time before implementing the plan.

Neville sipped her tea. "Gracious, I wonder they have not grown big as a house with all the nectar they have been drinking."

"I have never heard of a fairy dragon growing fat. I do not know if they can." Or at least Elizabeth had strongly suggested that in the monograph she had written for fairy dragon Friends.

"I know you are tired of hearing me gush, but truly, Pemberley is a remarkable place. I have met more dragons in the few weeks I have been here than I have in my entire life. And they are all so warm and friendly. Ring, especially, with his refined sense of the ridiculous! Who could have imagined!"

"I warned you what to expect." Neville was right, though. Ring was delightful company. It was sad not to have learned that earlier in her life, but Georgiana was determined to make up for lost time.

"Yes, you did, but that paled in comparison to the actual experience."

Cosette zipped in to join Pax and Berry. Cosette had taken to Berry as quickly as Pax had, and the three were most often found in company together, like a little harem of their own.

"Pemberley is quite the place, is it not?" Miss Bennet sashayed in and sat near the window. How did one be so jolly and yet exude an air of sensibility at the same time? "It took me ages to sort out my place here. It is nothing like Longbourn, where Lizzy and I grew up. The only household dragon there was April, who resented being thought of as a bird by the dragon-deaf in the family. I think it is all much better here. Someday I should like to manage my house as Lizzy does."

"Indeed?" The word slipped out before Georgiana could censor it.

"Well, perhaps not entirely like she does. She is rather draconic in her style, is she not?" Miss Bennet laughed heartily as she filled her plate.

Neville gasped.

"She is my sister. I get to say things like that about her. Things everyone thinks, but no one dares say. And no, Mrs. Fieldings did not cure me of that. No one will, I think. Was I much missed at school after I left?"

It was rather strange to recall how many of the same experiences Georgiana shared with Miss Bennet now.

"Most definitely, though there were only a few of us left that knew you by the time Miss Darcy joined us," Neville said.

"Really? So much change in the students so quickly? I suppose it is the way of things. It is a little sad knowing that the place I recall does not exist anymore, though." Miss Bennet poured herself a cup of coffee—horrid bitter stuff that Georgiana still could not abide.

"I wonder what the Blue Order will find in their investigations of the school." Georgiana added a splash of milk to her sweetened tea.

"I am sure they will find nothing untoward. I am convinced of Mrs. Fieldings' excellent character," Neville said.

"Of her, I am certain." Miss Bennet leaned her elbows on the table. "But that does not mean that there are not others who are, perhaps, a little less virtuous in her midst."

Neville nearly dropped her teacup. "You think some of the teachers might have ill intentions? The warm-blooded or the cold-blooded?"

"I really do not know. But something went awfully wrong. What else could explain Bede's unfortunate experiences?"

Georgiana swallowed hard and set down the sticky bun she had been about to eat. "Are you suggesting that Bede was not at fault?"

"Hardly!" Miss Bennet laughed, again. "I had only been introduced to her for five minutes before I found myself at loggerheads with her. I do not know how you managed as long as you did. I am in awe of your tolerance, Miss Darcy—and I mean that most sincerely. And I know Lizzy feels the same."

"Truly? I had no idea. She has said nothing to me either way. I had counted that as a good thing, since I do not expect she could easily refrain from remark if she thought I was much at fault." Georgiana winced. Perhaps she had just said too much.

"Lizzy does not excel at those niceties, and probably never will." Miss Bennet lifted open hands and shrugged. "It is the way of things with her, I fear. Cosette heard her mumbling about Bede in a rather unguarded moment, something rather like 'I do not know how Georgiana managed'. I would most definitely count that as approval, sideways though it might be."

Miss Bennet was right, if one thought about it in a draconic sort of way. And where the Dragon Sage was concerned, that was generally the right way to understand things.

Things like the amount of time Elizabeth and Fitzwilliam had spent dealing with all things related to the school crisis, making them effectively unavailable for the long discussion Georgiana needed to have with them. Bothersome, to be sure, but, at least for now, it did not feel quite as personal as it once had. Maybe she was finally moving on as Mercail had suggested.

"What will become of Bede? Clearly, she does not seem to get along with anyone, warm- or cold-blooded." Neville paused reflectively. "I hate the thought of sending her into the wilds to live rough when she seems to want to live in society."

"Did you not hear? I suppose you would not have. Cosette only told me just this morning. An excellent solution has been found." Something about Miss Bennet's smile was reminiscent of Elizabeth's.

"Pray tell me she is not to be a companion to some poor girl." Georgiana bit her knuckle, mostly to stop herself from further comment along those lines. Miss Bennet might be open to the notion that Bede was indeed difficult, but there was no point in risking whatever dragon was now listening in on their conversation would run with the notion.

Neville leaned low across the table. "Or a governess over children."

"Oh, heavens no! Did I tell you what happened when she met Mrs. Sharp and her zaltys, Mercy and Truth? Such a to-do! Bede began quoting six different books on nursery management and tried ever so hard to tell Mrs. Sharp her business! Mercy and Truth, who are by far the gentlest, most tolerant dragons I have ever met, forced her out and locked the door behind her. It is a wonder that they did not bite her!"

"Bite her?" Neville jumped back and glanced toward the door as though she were afraid of a dangerous dragon bursting forth. "They are poisonous?"

"You know their poison will only stun, not kill, correct? The nursery zaltys bit my mother—not that it was not well earned, mind you—and she recovered nicely. It is worth noting that she is not permitted at Pemberley any longer, though. In any case, Mercy and Truth take their responsibilities quite seriously. I am sure they were quite ready to resort to fangs if Bede had not left of her own accord."

"So, she is not to stay at Pemberley?" Georgiana asked.

"Absolutely not. I think Lizzy contemplated that for a day or so, but when Bede began her usual quoting and questioning, April pecked Bede's ears and chased her from Lizzy's office. Bede then tried to talk to Pemberley in the cellar. As Fern, the maid's puck, tells it, Bede criticized Lizzy to Pemberley and got her ears soundly boxed and her snout singed, to boot."

"What a sight that must have been." Georgiana giggled behind her hands.

"Bede was rather firmly put in her place. No one wants that encounter repeated. So, this morning, very early, Bede was sent off through the dragon tunnels directly to the Blue Order office in London. Mind you, they sent a guard drake with her to ensure that she does not get distracted along the way."

"The Blue Order offices? Whatever for?"

"As Cosette understands it, Bede has an encyclopedic memory for everything she has read or heard. A skill which makes her invaluable as a research assistant. She is going to serve my father, the Historian, in the great Blue Order library."

"Your father? And she will not drive him to distraction?" The tension between Elizabeth and her father was hardly a secret, but was that not too cruel?

"Have you met my father?" Miss Bennet laughed long and hard. She laughed a great deal. "No, in many ways, he is just as difficult as Bede is. Lizzy is convinced that they will suit each other well. Not necessarily as Friends, to be sure—Papa is not exactly the Friend-ly sort, although his secretary, Drew, is making a good effort—but she should be able to work with him in a meaningful way and contribute to Blue Order society."

"Without ever having to engage in the activities of polite society?" Neville's eyes grew wide. Was it astonishment at the possibility anyone might be able to work with Bede?

"My father hates the 'activities of polite society', as you aptly call them, and only attends when there is absolutely no other choice. He will actively discourage Bede from wasting her time in those trivialities."

"And we will all be better for it." Elizabeth?

Georgiana jumped as April zipped past her face and into a vase of honeysuckle.

"Do come in Lizzy. We were just talking about the excellent situation you arranged for Bede."

Elizabeth's expression turned a mite sheepish. "She is undoubtedly unique among all the dragons I have met. It is just a happy accident that I should know a warm-blood cut from the same cloth."

"Shall I pour you some tea or coffee?" Miss Bennet asked.

"No, thank you. I hate to interrupt your breakfast, but I need to discuss something with my sisters. Would you excuse us, Miss Withington?"

"Of course, you need not worry about me." Neville's answer was exactly what politeness required, but the curiosity rolled off her in almost-palpable waves.

Georgiana rose. Miss Bennet did not hide her puzzlement well, clearly biting her tongue as they followed Elizabeth not to her office, but to Fitzwilliam's.

The office had changed little since it had been Father's. So long ago now. The massive oak desk seemed as much a part of the room as the windows or fireplace, integral to its very nature. Neat and orderly, just as Father had kept it, smelling of books and leather, Fitzwilliam's shaving oil, and a hint of Elizabeth's perfume. Though warm in its own way, the warmth gave deference to the serious and important issues discussed there.

A group of five leather upholstered chairs had been drawn together near the screened fireplace—Mama had embroidered the riot of flowers on that screen. It was nice to see her touch in this most manly of rooms.

Richard and Fitzwilliam sat in the chairs nearest the fireplace. They must have just returned from—where had he been the last month? At some point, they had left Bantry Park, but she had not learned their destination.

Their expressions were difficult to read, although neither wore that grim look of determined disappointment she had seen just before being handed into Mrs. Fieldings' care. Good, good; perhaps now she could breathe again, if only just a little.

"You are looking well," Richard stood to greet them. "None the worse for wear after your ordeal, then?"

Georgiana dropped in a tiny curtsey. "Returning to Pemberley has done much to set things right."

Fitzwilliam stood with a small bow from his shoulders. Entirely more formal than he had to be, but it was not in his nature to do any less. "It is good to have you back home once again. Pray sit down, there are matters we must discuss."

"So Lizzy mysteriously told us. I can hardly wait to learn what sort of intrigues await us." Miss Bennet all but bounced to the chair next to Richard.

What an odd look they exchanged. A look that warranted further questions—in a more private setting, of course.

"Where to begin?" Elizabeth sighed as she sat beside Fitzwilliam.

"Has there been news of Mrs. Fieldings and the school?" Georgiana barely forced herself into a chair.

"That is as good a place to begin as any." Richard blew out a long breath through puffed cheeks. "Yes, there has been."

"Bad news or good?"

"On the whole, I think you would consider it good. Lady Astrid has exonerated Mrs. Fieldings of any culpability in Bede's tribulations, with the single exception of failing to supervise Quicksilver and Coxcomb closely enough. That they could have assaulted Bede under her care is problematic, but not sufficient to close the school. Gale and the other dragon staff are being held equally culpable for not screening dragon students adequately. A final decision has yet to be made regarding what changes will be necessary going forward, but there will be a going forward." Richard nodded slowly.

"Oh, that is splendid news! May I share that with Neville? It was awful to think she had been connected to anything terrible."

"I most heartily agree. And yes, you may share that piece of news." Fitzwilliam traded glances with Richard. "The dairy farmer and his wife, who drew your suspicions, have been detained for questioning by the Order. It looks like their lease may be terminated. If that is the case, the Order themselves will vet future tenants carefully. Quicksilver and Coxcomb have been dismissed from the school."

"What will the Order do with them?" Georgiana clenched her fists to stop them from trembling.

"That is a rather more complicated matter. Since their actions were from one dragon to another, the rules of warm-blooded society do not apply in this case." Elizabeth rubbed her palms together. "My father and Drew have spent many hours researching precedent, visiting parts of the library that have not been accessed in decades. You do not want to hear all the details, but it does not seem the Accords have much to say about bodily crimes perpetrated by minor dragons against other minor dragons. Very clear standards are used between major dragons, but minor dragons traditionally have been left to the jurisdiction of the major dragon in whose territory they live."

"What dragon would have authority in this case?" Miss Bennet looked far more interested than Georgiana would have expected her to be.

"That is the difficulty, I am afraid," Richard said. "There is no clear dragon to appeal to here. The school is not actually in any major dragon's territory. That land once belonged to a dragon, who has since disappeared—and no, we do not know the details on that, although I think Bede will be set to research the matter. Coxcomb and Quicksilver answer to different major dragons, and Bede, yet another. None of whom seem interested in dealing with the matter, probably out of concern for interfering with another dragon's territory."

"To make things more complicated, different dragons tolerate aggression between minor dragons differently. I already know one of the major dragons involved sees nothing wrong with their actions, considering the circumstances. So, it seems unlikely there will be any repercussions against Quicksilver and Coxcomb." Elizabeth's face suggested she did not agree. "Lady Astrid, though, will see that neither of them will receive a character letter from the Order. Though that will not ensure they are never engaged in staff positions, it will be a start."

"But was not their connection to the poachers, the snapdragons, enough for the Order to act?" Georgiana asked.

Fitzwilliam frowned and shook his head. "They made an agreement with Nob for Bede to be removed from their 'territory.' Apparently, they did not have direct knowledge of the poachers, so they cannot be held accountable for that."

"But surely, they would have known. I cannot imagine them so ignorant! The dragons I knew were far more perceptive than that."

"Coxcomb claims she was told that Bede had upset a local major dragon and was being brought to face that dragon's judgement. That dragon has denied any connections, but as Nob has inexplicably escaped and not been found, we can neither confirm nor disprove those claims," Fitzwilliam said. "However, the matter of the poachers brings us to the question of what must be done now."

"Not the least of which is insisting that the Order address the protection of minor dragons." Elizabeth clenched her fist and frowned.

"We have decided," Fitzwilliam glanced at Elizabeth, "that she and little Anne will go to London to begin that work and stay at least until the baby is born. Richard and I, and now Sir Horace, must focus on what is going on in Derbyshire, and I cannot do that while worrying about my family's safety."

"That family includes both of you, Lydia, Georgiana," Elizabeth said. "You may join me in London, if you wish. I expect to be caught up in much Order business, though, and cannot promise to be particularly entertaining, at least until Cotillion season is once again upon us."

"There is another option." Such a strange look in Richard's eyes. "It is asking a great deal, I know. But if you wish, you both can come to Netherford with me to help with our investigations. There will be a considerable amount of information to manage, of the kind that you helped with in London."

How polite of him, not to mention how little help she had actually been.

"I most decidedly want to help again." Miss Bennet bounced in her seat. "I mean no disrespect to you, Lizzy, but to be stuck among the papers and books at the Order, I would surely run mad."

"I expected that would be your preference. But surely you realize we cannot send you to Netherford alone. It would simply not be proper. If Georgiana wishes to visit her cousin and guardian, you may go as her particular friend, but otherwise, you must come with me."

Miss Bennet turned hopeful eyes to Georgiana.

This was a chance to redeem herself, if only in her own eyes, to do what she should have done before.

Everything about it sounded difficult and frightening, and maybe even dangerous. Did she dare? Could she even manage what Richard expected, or would she make an utter fool of herself again? What would Pax say?

And to be in constant company with the loud, lively, exuberant Miss Bennet? What would that be like?

She had learned how to deal with the personalities at Mrs. Fieldings'. It was uncomfortable at times, but tolerable. Maybe that would not be so bad.

"Do you think I might be of use to your efforts?" Georgiana dared not meet any of the eyes trained on her. "I did little in London and have no genuine experience to bring to bear."

"You were clever, resourceful, and brave when you went to Bede's aid." Elizabeth said.

Had she really just said that?

Elizabeth's eyes were so earnest and her posture so unguarded. She meant it.

"If you will have me, Richard, then yes, I will go to Netherford with you."

Don't miss a dragon update! Visit me at http://RandomBits ofFascination.com *for the latest updates and a place to subscribe to my newsletter.*

Acknowledgments

So many people have helped me along the journey taking this from an idea to a reality.

Debbie, Diana, Linda, Maureen, Patricia, and Ruth thank you so much for cold reading and being honest!

Friends of the Blue Order, your unflagging encouragement and imagination has been inspirational.

My dear friend Cathy, my biggest cheerleader, you have kept me from chickening out more than once!

Thank you!

Other Books by Maria Grace

Darcy Family Christmas Series
Darcy & Elizabeth: Christmas 1811
The Darcy's First Christmas
From Admiration to Love
Unexpected Gifts

Given Good Principles Series:
Darcy's Decision
The Future Mrs. Darcy
All the Appearance of Goodness
Twelfth Night at Longbourn

Fine Eyes and Pert Opinions
Remember the Past
The Darcy Brothers

Regency Life (Nonfiction) Series:
A Jane Austen Christmas: Regency Christmas

Traditions

Courtship and Marriage in Jane Austen's World
How Jane Austen Kept her Cool: An A to Z History of Georgian Ice Cream

Behind the Scene Anthologies (with Austen Variations):
Pride and Prejudice: Behind the Scenes
Persuasion: Behind the Scenes

Non-fiction Anthologies

Castles, Customs, and Kings Vol. 1

Castles, Customs, and Kings Vol. 2

Putting the Science in Fiction

Available in e-book, audiobook and paperback

About the Author

Six-time BRAG Medallion Honoree, #1 Best-selling Historical Fantasy author Maria Grace has her PhD in Educational Psychology and is a 16-year veteran of the university classroom where she taught courses in human growth and development, learning, test development and counseling. None of which have anything to do with her undergraduate studies in economics/sociology/managerial studies/behavior sciences. She pretends to be a mild-mannered writer/cat-lady, but most of her vacations require helmets and waivers or historical costumes, usually not at the same time.

She writes Gaslamp fantasy, historical romance and non-fiction to help justify her research addiction and the occasional dinosaur picture book to satisfy her grandchildren.

Check out her website RandomBitsofFasctination.com

Contact her at: author.MariaGrace@gmail.com

Made in United States
Troutdale, OR
06/19/2023

10664048R10190